inside him

inside him
new gay erotica

joël b. tan

CARROLL & GRAF PUBLISHERS
NEW YORK

INSIDE HIM
New Gay Erotica

Carroll & Graf Publishers
An Imprint of Avalon Publishing Group, Inc.
245 West 17th Street, 11th Floor
New York, NY 10011

AVALON
publishing group incorporated

Copyright © 2006 by Joël B. Tan. "Pasadena" copyright Philip Huang 2006. "Prince/Whore" copyright Darieck Scott 2006. "Dosed" copyright Tony Valenzuela 2006. "Street Hunter" copyright Wade Brown 2006. "The Abortionist's Lover" copyright Rigoberto González 2006. "Hislandia" copyright Louis Anthes 2006. "Coming Home" copyright Dale Chase. "The Best Sex Between Them" copyright Andy Quan 2006. "Start in Life" copyright Lou Dellaguzzo 2006. "Green Mountain Boys" copyright Jay Lygon 2006. "Knots" copyright Philip Clark 2006. "King of the Mat" copyright Davem Verne 2006. "Bonding" copyright Thomas Fuchs 2006. "Here You Go, Nancy" copyright David Christensen 2006. "Manila Suites" copyright R. Zamora Linmark 2006.

First Carroll & Graf edition 2006

All rights reserved. No part of this book may be reproduced in whole or in part without written permission from the publisher, except by reviewers who may quote brief excerpts in connection with a review in a newspaper, magazine, or electronic publication; nor may any part of this book be reproduced, stored in a retrieval system, or transmitted in any form or by any means electronic, mechanical, photocopying, recording, or other, without written permission from the publisher.

Library of Congress Cataloging-in-Publication Data is available.

ISBN-13: 978-0-78671-722-4
ISBN-10: 0-78671-722-X

Printed in the United States of America
Interior design by Maria E. Torres
Distributed by Publishers Group West

Contents

Preface • 1
Joël B. Tan

Pasadena
Philip Huang • 3

Prince/Whore
Darieck Scott • 9

Dosed
Tony Valenzuela • 31

Street Hunter
Christopher Pierce • 43

The Abortionist's Lover
Rigoberto González • 53

Hislandia
Louis Anthes • 65

Coming Home
Dale Chase • 81

The Best Sex Between Them
Andy Quan • 93

A Start in Life
Lou Dellaguzzo • 101

Green Mountain Boys
Jay Lygon • 117

Knots
Philip Clark • 129

King of the Mat
Davem Verne • 143

Bonding
Thomas Fuchs • 159

Here You Go, Nancy
David Christensen • 175

Manila Suites
R. Zamora Linmark • 187

Contributors • 211
About the Editor • 217

Preface

Joël B. Tan

HOW TO MEASURE ... EROTICA

If every story's already been told, what makes *Inside Him* new?

The newness of the erotica in this anthology is centered on stories collected around the world that innovate classic gay erotic forms and motifs to another level —anxious boy sex, hardened ex-con bottoms, Dungeons and Dragons–style pillage and plunders, wrestler lycra, Eagle Scout naughty, drug-induced romps, Manila hustling, car accidents, sadistic karate masters, exhausted dungeon daddy, and middle-aged romance. Oh yes. These yarns here are new. And turgid. And hot.

There wouldn't be an *Inside Him* had my lover refused to read countless submissions from around the world aloud to me. In bed. Naked. There are the obvious indicators—hence being naked in bed to measure for wood. Then there's the writing. Was the storytelling unique? Compelling voice? Innovative form? Having edited two previous anthologies and living amidst Gay San Francisco's diverse gay scene, sometimes I feel like I've seen, heard, and read it all. But this isn't the case with this collection. Nothing thrills me more than masterful sexual storytelling, and moreover, sex is about lifetime learning (and practice). I learned a lot reading these stories! For example, did you know that sex writers afforded their main character's penis three extra inches based on their own hang? Philip Clark illuminates this industry secret in his story, "Knots."

Does this same formula apply to sex editors?

Do readers also add on extra inches?

Buy or lift this book, find a partner, get naked, jump in bed, read aloud, and measure away.

Maraming Salamat, many thanks to Blanche and my beloved Quatorze.

Joël B. Tan

Pasadena

Philip Huang

I'm doing a number on the husband's nipples when the wife pokes her head in waving a burrito.

She says, "I'm really sorry to bother you, Harold, but I just need to let Glen know that I'm going over to my mother's with Bethie, and I'm leaving this burrito in the fridge in case we don't get back before dinner."

I don't usually allow interruptions, but I turn down the voltage on Glen's nipples so he can hear what his wife is saying.

She says, "If you need salsa I think there's half a jar left in the fridge."

Glen looks at me for permission to speak. I remove his mouthguard. He says, "Thank you, sir," and asks his wife if the burrito is chicken or carne asada.

"Chicken," the wife says.

Glen considers, then says, "OK."

He opens his mouth wide so I can put the mouthguard back in.

* * *

I'm starting slow with the nipples today. Two of my electrodes burned out otherwise I'd be doing both nipples plus the testicles at the same time. For the voltage, I'm using a car battery that I carried down to the basement in a milkcrate. Usually I don't use my own battery, but when I got to the house earlier Glen told me that his battery was running low and maybe I should use mine instead.

It takes a lot of sessions to drain a car battery. I'm thinking that Glen used someone else besides me when I went up to Toronto last week; maybe he had some buddies over, too, and they all took turns draining the juice.

I don't like the idea that Glen's having sessions with someone else without me knowing about it.

* * *

I've also brought down my usual gallon jug of water. I made Glen down half of it with a tablespoon of Celtic sea salt before I started working him over so he would be properly hydrated to take the voltage.

Electrolytes in the sea salt make sure the water gets in every cell, instead of going straight to the bladder.

That's it, boy, that's it. Wet as a snail. No use frying a dry twig.

* * *

After I fry his balls, I get his ankles in the stirrups so I can have a clear view of his cock and ass. It's like clearing the counter after you chop the vegetables, before you start preparing the roast. You want a good wide space to work in.

I lube up the dildo and plunge it down his ass. Hell, it falls right in, like a penny down a well. Sure enough, someone worked him over not two days ago. I start working the thin length of wire into his dickhole. Unfortunately he's gone limp. It's much harder to get the wire in if he's limp.

I let him sniff my palm until he gets hard enough, and then the wire slips right in his fat little prick, no problem.

I hook everything up to the battery.

* * *

I'm old school. I insist on using real juice, not the dinky lady-finger electrodes that they've started selling in sex shops. If you're fine with those dinky little deals, you're better off not calling me for my services.

* * *

The wife comes in holding the baby. She says, "I'm so sorry, Harold. I just need to ask Glen where the car keys are."

I take out the mouthguard and give Glen permission to speak.

"The Lexus?" he asks her.

"No," the wife says, "the Camry."

"I think they're over there, in my pants pocket," Glen says.

"Harold," the wife says to me, "I'm just going to scamper in and get the keys, if that's OK?"

I nod.

While she's looking through Glen's pants, I'm staring at the baby. It's right up against my face. It grabs the strap on my gas mask and tries to put it in its mouth.

On her way out of the room the wife says, "Oh, I almost forgot. Harold, I don't know if you had lunch before you came over. Feel free to have anything in the fridge after you're done. I just got some nice apricots from the farmer's market this morning. Just help yourself."

* * *

I don't usually have this much trouble hanging Glen. I can usually get his ankles strapped to the rafter on the first or second try, but today I can't get one or two knots in before he falls down again. It takes me on the fifth try before he's hanging still as a bat in the basement.

Either he's gotten fat or I'm getting old.

* * *

Glen's upside down and I'm in the sling, sticking my toes in his mouth, when the wife pokes her head in the door again.

"Harold," she says. "I'm really sorry to bother you about this but your car's blocking the driveway. I'd wait until you're done but my mother's nurse can't come in today and I've got to give her her shots before three. It's just one of those days I guess. And I'd move your car myself but you drive stick. I'd really do a number on your gears."

I sigh.

I leave Glen hanging, and follow her and the baby up the stairs.

* * *

The guy next door is washing his car.

"Well look who it is!" he says, waving at me.

I never remember his name. It's Steve or Bob or something.

I call him Bald Eagle, because he's bald as one and has a nose big as a beak.

He walks around the hedge holding his sponge.

"That a new gas mask?" he asks, getting up close.

He's dripping water on my leather kilt.

"Can I have a look at it?" he wants to know.

I take it off and hand it to him.

"Sheesh," he says, weighing it in his hand. "This ain't some amateur mask, is it? This is standard military issue, am I right?"

He puts it on and practices breathing inside it.

I'm going to have to clean it before I can put it on again.

He claps an arm around my shoulder and yells to an old woman on her lawn across the street.

"Mrs. Tomollilo! This is the guy, this is the Harold that Glen's always bragging about!"

So now the old lady's got her cane, coming across the street to have a better look at me.

Bald Eagle says to me, "I've got your card still. Soon as I get my basement set up I'm going to give you a call. You keep me in mind. Soon as I get things set up I'm getting a session with you."

I nod.

The guy's been feeding me that line for the past two years.

Mrs. Tomollilo's cupping my jaws in her hands, squinting at my face. "I thought you were that young fella I saw at the Jeffersons' the other day."

Bald Eagle gives her a tense look.

So I'm right. There's some young hotshot working my turf.

* * *

When I get back down to the basement, Glen's untied himself from the rafter and he's wearing his lamb outfit.

That's strictly prohibited, a client untying himself without my permission.

* * *

Things are getting lax all the time.

Last week, in Toronto, a client tried to suck my thumb while I was choking him. And another client, a guy I've been working over for years, asked me if I'd consider letting him masturbate with shoe polish while I pressed his eyeballs, when under no circumstances—and I mean *under no circumstances*—do I let a client touch his own genitals during a session.

That's rule number one with me.

He should've known better.

I'm telling you. This whole world is getting lax. People like me are scarce, people who believe in standards, who believe we'd all be much happier if we knew, very clearly, what's allowable and what is off limits. We wouldn't be in this mess with the Middle East and the rain forests and the street gangs if people accepted a little more discipline.

I raise the shepherd's crook over my head and tell Glen to assume the position.

You have to start somewhere.

Prince/Whore

Darieck Scott

To look upon the face of the Empress is to lose oneself, as a small boat is lost borne upon the vast shoreless seas, to become immersed, like mystics in the ecstatic contemplation of the deepest mysteries, in the Great Unfathomable that is the god. Arius clutched the sprigs of magenta delphinium and milky orchids in his right hand as he knelt before the high altar in the temple dedicated to his ancestors and his gods and offered his empty left palm to the Empress of the Seven Golden Cities in the East, the master of half the known world. To Arius she seemed to be a vision, a wraith, her willowy beauty clothed in an immaculate white bustier and white silk leggings that clung to her round hips and long legs, a white cape draped over her left shoulder and arm, leaving her right bare, her dark skin radiant like a glistening star shining over hills and valleys of virgin snow. She bent, stooping as though from the heavens, and a hush fell over the temple, the flames of the candles ebbed until they were mere flickers, tiny darts of light reflected on the marble walls and floors, as if hundreds of eyes long closed in sleep had suddenly opened in the stone to witness the moment of his Ascension. She kissed him on his cheek, and the scent of her seemed to envelop him; she placed a ring upon his finger; she said, in a voice that reached high to the temple's dome,

"Arius Romanos Paleologis Poitrain. You are one of Us. Welcome home."

A cheer burst through the sound of his blood beating in his ears. The Empress lifted him to his feet with a gentle grip and made him turn, so that she could present him, newborn, to the gathered throng. Arius saw his mother the Divina (as the Reigning Queens of Magis were called in honor of their ancestor the goddess) and his father the Divina's Consort, both beaming up at him from the lower steps; they were in flowing robes of purple, and the sheer cloth was like a soft mist of rain falling around their bodies, darkly silhouetted. They seemed shadows, almost, cast by the radiance within him. He saw his eight brothers watching him, tall and dark-eyed and muscled in their resplendent cropped-sleeved suits of supple black silk, bearing the star-and-moon insignia of House Poitrain on their chests. Regal, motionless, they were like the statues of the heroes and gods that lined the road to the temple. The expressions of their faces were various: pride in the eyes of his eldest brother, Lucius Raza, who had himself been crowned three years ago as High Prince of the City and heir to the Emperor of the West, and whom the ignorant northerners feared as the Dark Lord; an envious set of the jaw in Delios and Astara, who had not yet been crowned; alternating waves of excitement and boredom in the expressions of Nikhilos, Kirinos, and Asrafel; a smirk on the face of his favorite brother, Severis; a look of detached contempt on the face of Decius.

The cheers of the throng seemed to swell, and Arius felt a wave of expectation flowing toward him. It was as if the hundreds crowded on the floor below the high altar and pushing forward to see from the alcoves were all madly in love with him, as if they needed and lusted for him, and it was exhilarating and terrifying. What would they demand of him, now that he was a crowned prince of the House of Poitrain in the great city of Magis, center of the Western world? Arius was now a high lord of a tribe of lords: He was one of the other-human Ifah, a people destined by sacred prophecy to rule every corner of the earth, descended from the first Foremothers, called the Iron-Boned, the Motherless and Fatherless, the feared conquerors who long ago crossed the Middle Sea to lay claim to the West as they had the South and East, a folk cursed by their enemies and worshipped by their subjects: He was a born master in a world of deliciously beautiful slaves. As a member of House Poitrain he claimed a goddess as his great-great-great-grandmother, and traced his ancestry even to the founder of the line of only-human kings who had been his people's most accursed enemy, Helios the First. Crowned now as ruling prince, he would take his place as Supreme Justice of the Court of Magisters. He would be called upon to govern conquered lands, to cast spells of surpassing power, to bring the ecstasies and freedoms of the Dark-Moon god Ashva to the north, when the War at last was won. But as the Empress touched him again on his shoulder, reminding him to lift his arm and show the crowds his ring of ebony banded with glinting gold—for he, too, was now a Dark Lord—Arius thought only of what he might no longer be able to do. How, as a prince of Poitrain, would he be able to pursue his pleasures? What would his family and his people think of him if they discovered that their new prince's greatest happiness was to be manhandled and fucked, abused and pissed on, like a common whore?

In the latter years of the long war against the Truegodders, thousands of troops were quartered in the city by the harbor, where the barracks lie and whores ply their trade: lanky mercenaries out of the Far North, with their short beards and shaven heads; the notorious Rogue legions, dark, zealous recruits from the rural lands across the sea pledged to fanatic loyalty to the god Ashva and to the High Prince; and the seasoned, jaded soldiers sent by the Empress from the Seven Golden Cities in the East. It was among such men, in the alleys and bunk beds of the Soldiers' Quarter, that Arius enjoyed all the joy the Nine Gods grant to men's lives.

Usually under the light of the Witches' Moon, when Ashva's celestial orb appears as a black, bottomless well dimly rimmed by a crown of white flame, and the stars burn brightest, like warning beacons in the heavens, on that wondrous dark night of festival and debauch, Arius—after much preparation involving potions and chants, and teas of brewed herbs cultivated in the hothouse gardens of Napri—steals away from the great palace of the High Prince, cautioning his trusted guards to keep silent on pain of torture and death. In the dusky streets of Magis, lit by the flickering dance of torch-flames and the shimmer of oil-lamps and the sea-green waves of witch-fire, crowded with families and youths making their promenade after the day's heat is done and seeking amusement, Arius Poitrain, prince of the City, walks as something other than a Poitrain.

Sometimes he is Vita, tender virgin refugee from Miros. Vita was inspired by a nameless and insolent captive contessa from a lesser Sevoyan house, whom Arius as a little boy had the pleasure of watching his brother Severis strip, whip, and fuck before a gathered crowd in one of the outer courtyards of the palace, as punishment for her having called Severis an Ifah animal. The exercise left an indelible impression on little Arius: The image of his brother, stripped down to his leather jock and obscenely thick black belt, the tendons of his torso clenching and releasing as he put the strap to her again and again, the sound of the strange quiver in Severis's voice as he demanded that she scream out his name. When Severis had heard his name in tones high enough and full enough of pain and terror, he hissed, "Now, bitch, I'm going to teach you a lesson." He yanked his dark cock, leaking come in a steady stream from its wide slit, from the prison of the jock. The shaft jutted like a young boy's muscular arm. "You're wide enough. I'll ram it in hard, and you'll take it though it splits you in half. The tears will be running out of your eyes while I stroke it to you, while I fuck it in you. And when I'm done, my rebellious, insulting little slave, I'll wash my cock in your throat and let your tears run down over my balls to clean them. Your ass will be as loose as your mouth, and as long as you live, even if you return to the north and marry some soft, fat northern sot, you'll never forget the feeling of me going in and out of you, filling you, bursting you. The thought of my cock, the memory of the smell of my sweat, the sting of my hand on your ass and your nipples, will drive you mad. And before you die, you'll come back here, begging for me to use you again." Then Severis had arched back, wiggled his hips for the crowd's delight, did a few fake pumps where the tip of his monstrosity just nipped the girl's skin and laughed as she cried out as if her nails had been ripped from her fingers—and then, faster and harder than Arius could have dreamed, Severis battered through her sphincter and started fucking her. Her every twist and cry seemed to treble the ferocity of Severis's assault, and after a time Arius could only see Severis's body as the blur of its frenzied motion and the dark post of his tunneling cock.

And then, suddenly, Arius was overcome. His body was no longer his own. It was as if some playful god had tossed him into the open air and commanded him to fly. Tides of sensation, of discomfort inflating his skin and sinew to the point of bursting, of pleasure that made him wriggle, dancing on a floor of fire, surged over and through him. With a cry that—he was later told—made the whole crowd stop in their mad drive to satisfaction (for a brief and soon forgotten moment)—young Arius passed into the netherlands of unconsciousness on the balcony where he had been secretly watching.

Hours later, after his father the Divina's Consort had chastised him—"The punishment of slaves is a duty," he'd said gravely, "and is never to be abused for pleasure"—and after his mother the Divina, the Goddess's Own, had examined and soothed him—"Everything can be a pleasure," she whispered to him as she rubbed his stomach and let her fingers play around his groin, "and nothing, especially pain and degradation, should be without the most profound pleasure"—Arius learned that his mind had touched his brother's and the slave girl's at the same time, and that, in the moment that his brother's orgasm and the girl's paroxysm had peaked, his second navel had opened for the first time. His mother was proud of him, his father in awe: Only the most royal of Ifah heritage, sons and daughters of the line descended of the gods, were born with the second navel or the snake in their bellies, and fewer were born to the line every generation. His great-grandmother had a snake in her belly, and so never took a husband or gave birth to a child from a man's seed. Thus the line ran true in House Poitrain, but Arius's brothers (though copiously and somewhat frighteningly genitally endowed otherwise) bore as evidence of the descended divine only a circular white birthmark like a tattoo burned into the mahogany skin of their lower torsos where the strange, inhuman orifice would have been that, according to legend, could bear a child.

To commemorate the moment of his navel's opening, Arius's mother gave to him as a gift the shapely but somewhat ragged slip of a gown worn by the insolent slave girl (as part of her punishment, she was made to go naked thereafter). It had been artfully torn during her beating. Arius kept the dress for years, preserving it as if it were a family heirloom. Often he draped it over his pillow, and he would dream of beatings and plundered orifices in his slumber and wake to find it baptized with draughts of his come. One Witches' Moon night, when the lights of the palace had been doused, he sat watching from his window the glow of the Lower City below the seven hills of the nobles' district. A brilliant blue flash—the folk of the Lower City love fireworks—spilled its illumination upon the slave girl's dress that lay among the heap of his tousled bed sheets, and, as if possessed by the Moon-God Ashva himself, Arius impulsively decided to don the dress. Dashing below to the bed-slaves' quarters, he took perfumes and powders and unguents and polishes from their dressing-tables while they watched him and said nothing lest his guard, grim Litus the Far Norther, strike them dead on the spot. And from the table of an older bed-slave, a lovely crone whom his mother sometimes liked to use (for Ashva knows what purposes), Arius pilfered an exquisitely crafted blonde wig. Thus Vita, a pious Truegod girl come to preach the Word to southern heathens but actually in need of being taught the real truth—that she's a slut who needs to get buttfucked and have a wet cock slap across her lips and pushed up against her larynx every time she cries out the name of her silly god—was born. And oh! The *trouble* dear Vita had got into . . .

But Vita became only the first, and indeed the least durable, of Arius's many guises. On the wild nights of the Witches' Moon he still puts on a spell-mask—a little glamour that, say, lightens the dark earth-gold of his eyes and adds a tint of red to his skin, or narrows and lengthens his nose, sharpens his cheekbones—and he scents himself with musky oils, then walks through the courtyards on the lower slopes of the Upper City, past the late-evening markets of the Great Agora to the Sun-God's Gate to the Lower City: There, in a tight pair of silken vermilion briefs, he saunters down the cobblestoned lanes fronted by brothels, gambling houses, and bath houses, offering those who gawk at him a saucy smile. A black collar with a little chain of silver and jade links dangling from it adorns his neck. On these nights he is Mithris from Macumbe, sold into slavery by his impoverished uncle and shipped across the sea in a stinking hold, manhandled by pirates, and now a boy-whore forced to give what he earns to a dreadful master until he can afford to pay for his freedom. This story, this guise, brings him many an adventure. Something about his defenselessness, which he conveys with a pitiable look, and the hesitant naiveté of his manner dangerously arouses the rough soldiers, who are themselves mere instruments, toys in the hands of their lords. And, like the wolves they are, the soldiers have a penchant for hunting in packs.

Of the many times Arius has had the pleasure of being abused by a congeries of trained killers, none was as magnificent, as gloriously free and joyously degrading as his encounter with the Seventh

Rogues, a troop of zealots initiated in the harsh training of the War Hall in Jindis across the sea, men whose hard, sinewy bodies were living weapons, honed and trained to give pain and gain pleasure from the giving.

It was the month when the Witches' Moon lasts two nights full. The Seventh Rogues had been in Magis for six weeks, and Arius's brother the High Prince had not yet seen fit to deploy them in the field. So very far from home, the men of the Seventh, mostly peasants from wild country, must have felt obscurely threatened, even in the home city of the prince to whose service they were pledged. They must have ached for the clarity and release of battle. So when one of their number, drunk on Miroan beer he had never tasted in the barren plains of his native province, and temporarily sated after having given a little boy-whore from Macumbe six good hot loads of Rogue come up his soft little ass, tossed the whimpering body of the teasing little slut into the middle of the floor where his fellow Rogues were gathered smoking from the hookah and polishing swords and playing cards, all hell broke loose. The Rogue, a tall, svelte, broad-shouldered beauty with thick lips and rough tousled hair as black as a panther's pelt, almost felt sorry for the Macumban slave-thing—almost. But really—how dare the little man! Smile at a Rogue in a dark bar and smack your pretty wet lips, then saunter off into the streets at night without so much as offering to take the Rogue's cock in your little hand and jack him off till the come erupts over your arm and then fall on all fours to wipe him clean with your tongue: Why, it was like begging to be raped! The whole world knows what a Rogue is, what a Rogue does. It was the boy's own fault, he had it coming.

The Rogues in the barracks, all thirty-six of them, used Arius as if practicing the tortures they had been trained to use in the chastisement of the rebel Truegodders. They took rough hold of his arms and legs and spread them painfully wide, as wide as his limbs would stretch. They spit on him, called him a waste of manhood, and then they each stripped and sat on his face. They slapped him hard enough to make his skull ache if he didn't work his tongue into their assholes with sufficient fervor. They twisted or sank their teeth into his nipples if he did not moan with enough delight when his nose was pressed into their cracks and he was offered the privilege of licking a Rogue Soldier's ass-hairs. After watching a few get their asses lacquered, the others couldn't hold back. Arius—or Mithris, rather—saw as if in a moment of revelation an array of dongs and prongs, long and thick and hooded and cut and hairy and smooth and dripping with come all around him, like swords pointed at a traitor in the execution circle. It was true, what the gossips and bed-slaves said, though Arius did not know how it could be true: Rogues of Jindis had the biggest cocks of all. To a man they were longer and fatter than any he had ever seen, the middle roots alone of their shafts wider than three men's fingers together. The Rogues, dangling their mighty cocks before him in teasing and menacing fashion, anointed him with dribbles of pre-come and little squirts of nervous piss, then lifted their slave-toy up in their arms, tossed him high like circus acrobats bauble one another, and then they suspended him in midair, a score of them with their hands and musky muscular arms holding him at every point of his body off the floor, their hard cock-flesh bobbing beside him, rubbing against him, copious pits of crotch hair like burlap or suede throbbing impatiently against his soft skin that reeked of their brothers' come. The laughing Rogues held him, and circled him, moving around and down his body, using the bits of him they could use as they moved along, jeering and cheering and hooting as they watched their brothers mouth-fucking and ass-fucking him, offering breathless, expletive-laced commentary upon the thickness of one another's dicks and wagering whether such-and-such's cock would be long enough to rupture the whore's intestines. Arius-Mithris saw them kissing one another as they fucked him, saw them seize one another's face in their hands and kiss each other feverishly, fervidly.

A tall man—but they were all tall, this one just seemed taller than the rest, and his color, as Ashva's Moon bathed him in its light, was a gorgeous caramel brown that Arius only glimpsed before another dick slammed across his nose en route to his puffed, bruised lips and sore throat, but he happily thanked the gods every day after that it was a color he had been permitted to behold—this tall man, with the body of a thrice-exalted divinity, pierced Arius's boy-whore asshole with the full length of his arm, and made a sound of deepest satisfaction as he did so, somewhere between an ecstatic worshipper's moan and a serpentine hiss, while Arius screamed and his body erupted in convulsions because of the pressure. This tallest man took a slower time than the others forcing his monstrously thick cock into the slut's wide-open ass. (It was not wide enough.) And though what seemed to happen was not possible, Arius knew—unless—unless, Arius *had* heard of herbs that the ancients in the lands of Theria across the sea were said to possess, that could alter the internal cavities of the body—it was not possible, but the tall man's dick seemed to fill every part of Arius's buttocks, not just his rectum; it seemed to reach and touch and tickle each step along the ladder of Arius's spine. Even above all the shouting and cursing, Arius heard the man speak to him as he shoved cock to him, slow excruciating slither out to the tip, murderous deep lunge in with such force the tall man's thighs bounced back from the taut flesh of the boy's ass. The tall man said, "Fuck you, you little Macumban shit-slave." (Then he lunged in and wiggled in the depths while Mithris cried out for mercy.) "This is what you want, huh?" (The slow pull out.) "You wanna be *fucked!*" (Lunge.) The soldier screamed as he came, and then he said, "You're so lucky, bitch. Every little Macumban shit-fuck slut wants what you're getting." Then he spat in Arius's face.

At any given moment, Arius felt as many as five or six dicks fucking his armpits and thrusting against his protruding nipples. And there was rarely a moment when a salty cock wasn't forcing his mouth into its widest oval, banging against his tonsils and spilling hot thickness down his esophagus. If there wasn't a dick in his mouth it was because some innovative thinker preferred to have his hairy ass tongue-cleaned again, or needed the rank hair under his arms sniffed, or just wanted the pleasure of spitting onto Arius's outstretched tongue or slapping Arius's sore cheeks with cock until the slut winced. Some, after dicking his throat, liked to force a kiss on him, thrust their tongues in, and suck harshly. "No wonder whores like my dick," one beautiful one with his thick hair plaited in rows on his head said after tasting him. A couple of others wanted to sample what their brothers' dicks had left on Arius's tongue. Their faces were twisted, their eyes alight and demonic as they hungrily shoved their mouths against his.

The kissing happened toward the end; it was always toward the end, in these things. There was nothing new that the Rogues did, nothing every soldier did not think to do when he discovered he had a slave who thrilled to being dominated and mastered and yet cried and fought and was terrified, too—the combination of profound worship and abject fear in a sexual partner made men wonderfully, lovingly cruel, Arius had found. But the Rogues did all they did with more furor, more frank, savage delight than any Arius has had the pleasure to sample before or since.

They had him go and fetch food for them, and beer—this was perhaps a couple of hours later, after the first frenzy had ebbed—and they dressed him in clothes too big for him, boots his feet slid around in, leather trousers that reached all the way up to the top of his stomach. (And oh, how the heat of those trousers over his body felt, the belt-rim chafing his nipples, the smell of that unwashed leather that had been worn by one of his beloved soldiers—he remembers it still, and masturbates, just to the memory, fastened like the recollection of a first kiss's taste in his mind.) They laughed when they pushed him out in the street, made jokes about how cute he looked, cautioned him to make wise purchases with the coin in his hand or else. A cute olive-colored one with a smooth chest and dimpled shoulders stood at the barracks door and waved his half-hard prick at Arius as he moved off. "This is waiting for you, punk," he called to Mithris, seeming to know that to wave the wonderful thing at him would only make Mithris the slave-boy do whatever he could to hurry back.

During his trek to the market, poor Mithris was jeered and groped by trios and duos of drunk soldiers who passed him in the streets. One malicious hook-nosed fellow went so far as to clamp Mithris's nipple between thumb and forefinger while jamming his other hand into Mithris the slave-boy's mouth, and would have put him to still rougher and more thorough uses if Arius had not had the sense to make Mithris mumble, "I belong to the Seventh."

After several such close escapes, Arius/Mithris arrived breathlessly at the barracks' door, hauling a sled piled with beers and kebabs behind him. When he was allowed inside—they made him plead first, and shout to the rooftops how much he liked to be pissed on and manhandled by the men of the Seventh Rogues, the only real men in all the world—the soldiers stripped their clothes off him contemptuously, as if in punishment for his having stolen them. While most scrambled for the beer, one pungently aromatic fellow with ridged forearms like young tree trunks took the slave-bitch over his bare knees and playfully spanked him (playfully, but it hurt, and deliciously so) for dishonoring the Rogue uniform. This one had a long, lean brown body and a curtain of blue-black hair that hung over a quarter of his bright-eyed, perpetually amused face. His accent, Arius was sure, made him a native of Stralia, a province where the Jindesi had once exiled their criminals, hundreds of years ago. He called Arius by the name he'd assumed—"Mithris, you sweet little girl, you," he said, as he gave Arius's sore ass one loud smack after another. Then he pushed Arius off his knees, commanded him to lovingly swab his tongue in between each of his knobby, rank toes, and then pissed a thin, warm stream on Arius's chest, that slightly ironic and beatific expression on his face all the while.

Toes cleaned and piss drained, the Stralian flipped Arius over with one large hand, and—politely demanding that Arius kiss the tip of his dick and clean the slit of any excess drool—threw up the boy's legs and fucked him so hard and so painfully and at such a queer angle that Arius's anus—already traumatized many times over, so much so that it had gone into a kind of local shock and had ceased to feel like a part of the rest of his body—split and profusely bled, despite the many herbal and magical precautionary treatments Arius had employed. The Stralian was very proud of the way he had forced Mithris the slave-boy-scum-slave-twat, who had heretofore been so durable, taking everything they threw at him without complaint, to squeal in a completely new way. "Look, I made him bleed," the Stralian announced while straddling Mithris's face so that his ass was stuffed into Mithris's mouth and his balls draped over the slave's eyes; he moved back and forth, letting Mithris get a good long whiff and a good deep taste of butt, then posed for a long soak of his hirsute nuts, then arched a bit to saw the tip of his cock along Mithris's sweet, thick lips. The four or five fellows who stood by watching, draining beers and lazily pulling on their long cocks and heavy balls, leaned down for a better look, and to oblige them the Stralian encircled Arius's legs in one of his arms and pulled them upward so that Arius was almost standing on his head—but for the fact that the Stralian kept the slave-bitch's mouth full of testicles. He jammed a finger into the wound and waved it around, shaking off drops of blood. "See?" Two of his friends mumbled, "Cool," and the others, with startling synchronicity, moaned and fired off a new round of frothy ejaculate, so delighted were they by the evidence of their brother's mastery. (The Stralian would make a magnificent slave-master one day, Arius thought. He ought to be given an estate with hundreds of Truegodders to slake his lusts, as a reward when the Wars are done. Arius wished he could be one of the virgin Truegodder girls the Stralian popped—the Stralian would especially like young girls, he thought—perhaps a Trugodder senator's daughter, that would be nice, or even the young wife of Jor Arbust, the new Lord of Navar. Arius would love to see the Stralian's monster cock splitting the ass of the firebrand Truegodder Senator Prow's daughter and then the Senator's sons and the Senator himself, with that pleasant but-we're-only-playing-here smile on his face as he lowered each one onto the obscene width and hardness of it and cupped his ear to catch the full timbre of the first screams. Arius had made a mental note while willing the wound to heal quickly; and several days later, in his recommendations to the War Council, he said that he had been inspecting the troops, and singled out the Stralian as one to assign to lead the show-rapes on the frescoed floor of the Holy Mother's Basilica after the city's surrender.)

Then Arius was ordered to open beer bottles for some of them, sometimes with his teeth, once or twice by popping the lids with the lips of his anus (this was of course rather bloody, and didn't help the wound the Stralian had dealt him heal any faster—not that the Rogues minded blood, it aroused them). Then he was politely asked by way of a kick to pour for them, and then pushed till he sank onto his hands and knees so that they could rest their heavy legs and calves and large feet on his back. Of course throughout it all they kept pissing on him, too, and in him—in his mouth, up his ass. From hard cocks and shriveled (but still bigger than most men's hard) dicks and half-hards and spongy prongs Mithris lay on the latrine floor and let the rain fall upon him: his face—they liked to give him a good long arc of piss across the forehead down to the mouth and across his neck—his stomach, his groin soaked repeatedly, and some aimed to shoot a hard stream at his balls to see if it might hurt (it did). Some wanted him to hold their big, soft, leaking cocks over the chamber pot—and then drink from the pot. Others whipped it out, gave him a smack with its brawny, ass-smelling length across the face in the universal sign for "open your fucking mouth you whore," and filled up his stomach directly. A few of these liked to grab hold of his ears and manipulate his head up and down in order to shake out the last drips. Some put his face to their asses when they farted—he liked that, just the sheer boyish play of it—but none of them made him eat their shit, and for that he loved them all the more, because the one thing he had no taste for was scat. (Though for them, he would have done it.)

There was more fucking after that—more orderly this time, lazier. One or two, no more than three, would hoist him onto the mattress of their bunks and treat him as they one day hoped to treat their household Truegodder slaves: facedown, butt up; or facedown, flat on your stomach, thick fingers choking your mouth, or hands over your lips and nose or smashing your head down into the sheets from behind—hard, clean, fierce dickings a happy slave-whore gets just for being a slave-whore when the master wants an itch scratched. For fucks like that a Rogue likes the feel of a boy-ass gripping like a pussy would grip but tighter, so you give it to them; you glory in the warmth of their cocks pushing painfully into you or slipping fast into your gaping hole, you learn to love the queer writhing discomfort of it ballooning your innards, pressing against your bladder; you swoon for the scent and scrape of their heavy, hairy, musky bodies pressed against you, crushing you down so it's hard to breathe and you can barely get the gasps out that make it easier to take the violence of their thrusts, the swinging slap of their balls as they fall against your perineum or slide, as if made to fit a groove, in your crack.

The tallest man had Arius again. He took the Macumban slave aside from the others—there were hoots and catcalls as he dragged the boy by his wrists out of the common room with the bunks into the chamber where warriors of Ashva the Dark Moon Slayer-God enter battle-meditation. A few followed to watch (their long dicks swinging, balls bouncing against the muscle of their hairy thighs, one with a hard-on rising straight up beyond his navel). The tallest man bent Arius over the bench where the warrior entering battle-meditation kneels, and beat him with a leather strap—branding his tender flesh with heavy strokes that sounded wet and angry as they lashed him and he cried out for mercy. The beating seemed to go on interminably—the pale hairy one with the hard-on (no doubt one of the northerner converts adopted into the Jindesi fold; they were a fierce lot, and had to be, to be accepted by the dread Ifah Rogues—Arius wished he had paid more attention to him earlier, he did not remember what this one had done to him before) provided the only distraction as he lifted Arius's head by the hair, shoved his hairy-knuckled fist against Arius's teeth to make him open up, and dropped the slave-bitch's mouth down on his thick cock. The smell of it was different from the other men's—not salty or musky but like the smell of wet flesh, or meat hung in the market to sell. It thrilled Arius with the excitement of the new, and he was glad to get a chance to savor what he had missed in the wonderful frenzy of before. The northerner pressed down hard, moaning in the loudest and most obstreperous way when he heard choking sounds ("yeah, yeah, choke on my dick, choke on this motherfucka"), and fucked that huge dick of his upward into Arius's throat with a quick, heedless savagery that made Arius fear he'd never be able to speak or eat again, the damage it must have done to his mouth. This latest face-fucking was over very quickly. Unlike the tallest man expertly laying the strap to him, the northerner had no finesse, only brutish drive and strength; he rammed, he groaned, he came. There was an admirable and arousing efficiency about it (thinking of it now, Arius smiles, and feels his already hard cock twitch; he must get more of these converts from the North to fuck him; freed from the useless strictures of their so-called True God who despises the true glory of the male animal, they are like real beasts, like rutting elks).

The tallest man, meanwhile, varied the speed and heft of his assault, angling the strap here and there and then back, quickly, to a spot still tender. Arius could not see, but felt he could hear, the tallest man's dick smack up against his stomach and down against his thigh as his arm rose and fell. *How marvelous these men will be in the field,* he thought. *What lessons they will be able to teach the Truegodder rebels with the skills they possess!*

When the northerner had gone, and the others, too, the tallest man, now alone with his slave, ceased to beat him. He turned Arius over, gruffly, and pushed him down to the floor. "My balls," he said, his voice almost strangled with desire. Arius made love to the man's nuts, big and round and covered in a wiry beard. The taste and smell, of sweat and the faint stink of urine mixed with the wafting odor of a man's ass, the salty tang of bronzed skin unlike any other in the world, was exquisite, more pleasing than any spice he'd tasted in the finest kitchens of the continent. The tallest man's hands played in his hair, sometimes gently, and sometimes, when the pleasure of the whore's mouth on the skin of his balls was greater, he gripped Arius more urgently. They were locked together, the tall warrior standing, the Macumban slave born to serve the cocks of his superiors where he belonged on his knees. In the sphere created around his head by the smell of the man's crotch—it was a sort of halo, Arius decided—Arius drifted into eternity. He was no longer in the world, no longer of the world, he was spirit rampant, spirit run wild, and yet purely, purely flesh, completely an animal. It was a sacred moment, a brush with the divine.

The tallest man made very little sound—just a sigh, small, but joyous with relief—when he let fly long, pulsing lassos of come: one, two, three, four, five bursts—and a sixth spurt a few beats later that made his great body twist almost completely round. Arius came, too, for perhaps the fifteenth time of that glorious night. As at all the other times, he had not even touched himself (and it was better for him that he didn't, for a boy-whore cannot touch his own dick unless the men who buy him permit). He would have sunk to the floor, spent, but the tallest man lifted him from his feet and hugged his dangling body to his broad chest, pressing Arius's sore, swollen lips into the cleft of his massive chest. Arius could not see, but again, he thought he could hear, or feel, a smile on the angry warrior's handsome, strong-jawed face. Then Arius felt a tickling. The tallest man was poking his finger in a spot hidden near the top of the trim tangle of Arius's pubic hair.

Arius gasped in horror, and for the first time that night tried violently to pull away, but of course he could not. The tallest man's finger pushed, gently but insistently—and like a trap door, Arius's second navel, his greatest secret, sprung open and with a surge of pent-up greed and ardor sucked the tallest man's finger down into its mysterious, other-human warmth.

The sheer pleasure of the penetration—more profound than any other erotic sensation, more thrilling than nipple caresses or slobbery kissing or a hole clasped around his dick or a dick tunneling into his ass and savagely bucking against his prostate—made Arius come again, and loudly cry out. But at the same time he was mortified. His second navel had rarely opened before against his will, and he never used it when playing Mithris, for fear that his identity might be discovered. Would the tallest man now call the others in to see that they had fucked and mastered one soon to be a named prince of the blood?

But if the tallest man was surprised, or if he knew, he said nothing, showed nothing. He merely pulled his finger free from Arius's secret hole and lifted the slender youth higher, grasping him by the hips now. As Arius rose up into the air in the man's grip, he saw that the man was indeed smiling—and then he lapped the little miraculous hole like a kitten laps a bowl of milk set before her by the master who has just taken her from her mother: gingerly, even shyly, though with mounting hunger. Arius wriggled in excruciating pleasure.

Then the tallest man set Arius down on the floor, and motioned him over to the wall, where there was a wooden bench that ran the length of the room, and two wide basin bowls, and a smoldering fire in a pit piled with coals. There were urns filled with water aligned on the other wall, and the tallest man took one of these, thrust it next to the smoldering fire, waited, then, heedless of the heat of the urn in his hands, poured the water into the basin. With a gesture he had Arius kneel, and when Arius bent his head, he felt warm water cascade down his neck, over his back and chest, saturating his shaven crotch and the crack of his ass. Again and again the tallest man did this, saying nothing, until Arius, wet, baptized by his master, was clean.

Arius remembered nothing else. The drugs he'd taken, the spells he'd chanted to make his body supple and strong and hardy to endure the kinds of nights he craved when he braved the Military Quarter, could never have been proof against the punishment and pleasure to which his royal person was subjected. He was not a warrior like his brothers, but a magister, and his endurance, though greater than human, had limits. He fell into a sleep of oblivion, without dreams, without feeling. He did not know what else was done to him; he hoped it was as evil and as wonderful as what happened earlier.

His darkness, deep, silent, was broken at last by the sound of a rough snore, and gray light sifting into the black shadows of the common room where the soldiers slept. He was in the lowermost of one of the triple bunks, lying on his side entangled in a bundle of sweat-sticky hard male bodies. They were a trio, so alike in smell and feel that if he could see all their faces it would not have surprised him that they were of the same family. One, a black-bearded heavy-muscled fellow, was snoring into Arius's face, his tongue lolling forward a bit from his open mouth. One of his arms was around Arius's neck. Another was behind him, a half-hard morning dick pressed into the small of Arius's back, his chest against the back of Arius's head; he was farther up on the mattress, and his large hand lay over Arius's chest, the tips of his longest fingers touching Arius's painfully dilated left nipple. The last of them was lowest on the mattress, curled up like a babe with Arius's legs arranged in a scissor around his slim torso, his hands buried in Arius's butt-crack and his head resting between the large thighs of his brother.

Arius, weary, beaten, inhaled the smell of them. The bearded one in front of his face awakened for a moment, watched the boy through dark eyes. He reached down where his brother's hand was, moved it aside, and shoved all of his fingers into Arius's loose ass. Arius gasped, and the man's tongue—thick and damp and aggressive like the rest of him—slipped into Arius's open mouth. They kissed, long and lingeringly. "Mmm. The smell of my men is on you," the man whispered into Arius's mouth. (Arius, lost in the kiss, later wondered if this one might be the Rogues' Lord Captain.)

Then the man fell back into sleep, his hand lodged in Arius's battered rectum.

When Mithris the Macumban slave-bitch awoke again, sun was streaming over him, and he was lying just beyond the gates of the Military Quarter. A couple of military police, tall and strong in their red leather armor, sneered at him from their post at the gates. He smiled crookedly at them. He couldn't resist blowing them a kiss. They spat. "Cheap slut," the nastier and more masterful of the two growled (his hand tugged his groin as he spoke). "I hope you liked eating all the come that's leaking out of you."

Cheap! Arius thought ruefully. In fact, he recalled, the Seventh Rogues hadn't paid him. And there *were*, he saw, dried come stains on his bare chest, and a few fresh globs of soldiers' seed running down his legs. Had the military police boys had their way with a comatose whore, or did his beloved Seventh dump a few morning loads on him before casting his filthy body out in the street?

He looked at himself. His briefs were gone—so much for those!—but with a quick press of his fingers across his features he determined that his spell-mask was still intact. He couldn't remember: Spell-masks could be dislodged by loss of concentration, and it was a risk to use them as Arius did. Surely in the ecstasy to which the Seventh Rogues had driven him his mask had slipped? Had some kind soul amongst them with a tender concern for the modesty and public majesty of a prince of the House of Poitrain spoken a few words in the ancient Dumasa in his ear placing the mask on him again exactly as he'd worn it? He thought of the tallest man, and the Stralian, and the northerner, and the thick-dick waving its warning and beckoning in the doorway, and he hoped that his mask had slipped, and that they had replaced it. He liked the idea of sharing secrets with such men, he liked the idea of being in their power, and he hoped that if they replaced the mask, they had altered it slightly, perhaps given it a tiny scar, so that each time he repeated the spell he would bear the mark of their mastery of him.

Mithris the slave-bitch, Arius Romanos of Poitrain the Ruling House of Magis and Descendant of Gods, strode through the gates—for whores, like nobles, were given free passage without challenge. He took note of the nasty military police guard's features (tall, golden skin, dark hair cut close to his skull, hazel eyes, unshaven chin, narrow waist, big thighs, and big bulge) and the name and crest emblazoned on the uniform (Ciro, of House Napoli)—and, already plotting a new adventure involving transgressions that would insure an interrogation at the gates, made his way back along the gently sloping cobblestone street toward the Upper City's seven sun-splashed hills and golden mansions and high views of the jewel-blue bay, whistling happily as he went.

Dosed

Tony Valenzuela

I'm sitting at my desk. The midday heat of this blistering summer makes the skin of my thighs, ass, and back stick to the faux leather chair. I'm logged on, staring at my laptop. In the courtyard below, two neighbors are speaking disparagingly about a third and it surprises me that the tenants of my building even care to know one another. The ceiling fan wiggles like a hula dancer, relieving me negligibly from the day's suffocating humidity.

Lingering online in the LA men for men's rooms, I wait for a dominant top to pursue me. That is my rule: to be sought after, not to be the one combing through personal profiles or introducing myself to prospective hookups with the abridged language of the instant message: "sup," "hot," "pnp?" After all, this isn't a Sadie Hawkins Dance; total bottoms shouldn't have to ask. We should be baited, searched for, and prowled after with wayward confidence.

My profile:

Name: not important, 31, 5'10", musc, hairy chest, br/br, hot sub 4 dom
   Location: WeHo
   Gender: male

Hobbies & Interests: anonymous, role play, blindfolds, bb. U B fit,
nice face, big dk, uninhibited

The link to my picture shows me from the waist up sitting back, hands behind my head, looking at the camera self-satisfied. The additional picture I send out, if the top suits me, is an ass shot, my hole a purple starfish.

SexyGreek4now asks, —*what are you into?*

If he can't figure it out from my profile, it won't work. I ignore him. The next guy, *Nicenfun,* sends a picture in a suit and tie, as if what I'm into is uptown and dapper. His name says it all.

—not my type, I write back.

Vgl8x7lkn4azz, —*you a good sub boy?*

He sends a headless picture. He's slouching in a chair squeezing his hulking bronze erection at the base like a video-game joystick, pushing his balls down so that they press through his sack like ripe avocadoes. He's in a wife beater but it's pulled up above his pecs to show off a smooth, square chest and flat, hard stomach; on his shoulder, a black-and-red fire-spewing dragon. I ask for a face picture. He says he's discreet but guarantees that he's handsome. Tells me it won't matter anyway, because I'll be blindfolded. I give him my address.

If I'm going to be blindfolded, then I want to get twisted, gnarly high on Tina where I don't care about tomorrow and yesterday and time is reduced to an acute yen for body parts. In the bathroom I pull out a 3ml needle-less plastic syringe from the medicine cabinet. Outside the small window above my shower, I hear the guttural shouts of Russian kids playing in the apartments next door. Their roughhousing reminds me of Moscow. I was a closeted teenage exchange student and witnessed soldiers holding hands in a startling display of intimacy around the onion domes of Red Square; foreign proprieties of male physical contact. Young men sitting in each other's laps on stone banisters outside GUM Department Store—images of erotic innocence I masturbated to in the cold, tiled shower of my Intourist Hotel room.

With a pen cap, I scoop out half the baggie of Tina and pour it into the syringe, pressing my thumb at the injection opening to prevent it from leaking. Shards of crystal collect at the tip like a little mound of broken glass. I carefully fill the syringe with water leaving a quarter-inch space empty at the top. I push the plunger back in, securing the gasket at the base of the tube, then turn the syringe upside down tapping it like an alleyway junkie to allow the meth to float down into the water. Tina begins to melt like artificial sweetener in iced tea.

I lie down on my bed, throw my legs up in the air spread wide, dab lube into my ass, and push the length of the syringe into my hole, injecting the bionic liquid with a determined press of the plunger. I lie there, hugging my legs from beneath the knees, waiting for the delirious rush. The Tina takes effect almost immediately with a blustery surge of elation and desire. *What is this yearning for?* I've asked myself a million times. *The insatiable hunger to be penetrated by other men?*

On crystal, all that remains of me is my body with its moist orifices, ravenous as summer tornadoes. I am, otherwise, held in glorious suspension from the nuisance of the day's worries. I am erased of complicated history, like high-school textbooks in the South. There is only lust here now, an empire of prurience whose frontier plots against the horizon: orgasm is defeat, is desire's drowning. On crystal, sex is my sole ambition.

Still on my back, I watch the ceiling disappear, then notice the pictures on the wall break up into nanoparticles: the popcorn ceiling runs in place like a conveyer belt gone mad.

An hour passes. *Vgl8x7lkn4azz* hasn't shown. I check back online.

He's not there, either. I decide my carpet needs a quick vacuum. I tidy up, concentrating on the bedroom and bathroom: disinfecting around the toilet and tub, vigorously wiping down the sink and mirror, making my bed and putting away clean laundry, my mind still on cock that hasn't yet arrived. It's a quarter past three. I regret not getting the prick's phone number. Now, I'll have to start all over.

GlendaleHot writes, —*Looking for sweet faced pussy boy.*

In his pic he's naked and raking leaves, presumably in his back yard. He's wearing construction boots and looking down at the lawn seemingly unaware of the camera. I wonder who took the photo. He looks like a big man (his profile says 6'2"), muscular calves and triceps and a great big ass gleaming like white marble. Naturalists are a turn-on. I ask for another picture and he sends me a standard close-up cock shot. His dick Heil-Hitlers from his crotch.

He asks, —*you poz boy?*

Yes.

You do what I tell you?

Yes.

You partying, bitch?

Yes.

Sweet.

He arrives in under a half-hour. It's surprising how clean-cut and handsome he is. His online picture is grainy, slightly muting the features of his face. In person he is wholesome with milky white skin and, in a striking contrast, his hair is the color of tar. He is dressed in a tank top, powder-blue corduroy shorts, and the construction boots. He sinks into my couch, introduces himself as Pete, and asks if I have drugs to share. I offer him crystal and/or G. He opts for the G, and I decide to join him in order to smooth down my sandpaper high. I pour two glasses of Lemon-Lime Gatorade then grab the G from the fridge where I keep it in an old jelly jar that my mother sent me. I pour about a tablespoon in each glass and hand him one.

"I can do more than that," he says. "I'm a lot bigger than you."

I want to tell him I've already shot a quarter gram of crystal up my ass and that I'd be lucky to feel the G, but I don't say anything. He takes the jar from my hand and pours another spoonful in his glass.

"You into blindfolds?" I ask. Pete is leaning against the stove, sipping his concoction. He nods, cracks a sly, knowing smile, then gulps down the rest of his drink.

Pete complains about my sweltering apartment, so I turn on the AC in my bedroom. The loud drone of the wall unit spinning its cooling motors fills the room. I stand at the foot of the bed and Pete places the blindfold over my eyes, tenderly. I got the blindfold flying first class on Delta from LA to Barcelona last summer. The flight was an upgrade with miles. The blindfold came in a complimentary travel case.

My world goes dark. Pete pushes my shoulders down so that I fall to my knees. "So you like to be a little whore, don't you? You little cocksucker. You gonna do what I tell you, right pussy boy?"

"Yes, fucker," I answer. He slaps the right side of my head with a solid open-handed blow as if to test me: how far will I let him go? A sensation like needles lingers at my temple. In the dark, my senses are acute to sound and touch. I hear car horns honking simultaneously down on Santa Monica. The cool air in the room shimmers along my body like silk pajamas. Pete orders me to put my arms behind my back. I hear the glide of his shirt over his torso as he pulls it off, the scuff of boots being kicked off, the slight sweaty whiff of socks. I think of his bare feet and start to get hard. He unzips his shorts slowly in front of my face. I imagine his powder-blue cords and think of junior high.

Blind and on my knees, I draw a mental diagram of the bedroom: to my immediate left, the bed covered in pale yellow linens; two steps behind Pete, a maroon-and-beige striped couch; to my right, a natural wood dresser with a spread of friends and family photographs and a small Sony television; three steps behind me, a sliding-door closet. He attempts to tie my wrists together with, I think, a sock. He has trouble tying the knot and eventually gives up. He stomps about and my downstairs neighbor, the shy, taciturn USC undergrad who drives a Cabriolet, comes to mind. The closet door rumbles open. After a short pause, he slams it shut and is back at my wrists, this time fastening them together with what is unmistakably, a silk tie. The loose ends of the cool, sleek fabric brush against my bare ass.

"Oh yeaahhh! Feels gooooood!" he purrs. He moves around to my front, the floor creaks loudly, and the dresser crashes up against the wall knocking over some of my photographs. "Sorry," he whispers. Breaking the scene to apologize strikes me as amateurish.

He regains control of the moment by grabbing a handful of my hair. He spits out a litany of titillating insults: *cocksucker, bitch boy, whore*. He smacks my face with his hard dick, playing carrot-on-a-stick with his cock. He commands me to suck. He slips only the head in my mouth then quickly pulls it away. The acrid musk of sweat and the sense of his hard-on hovers over my nose and lips. He probably hasn't showered since yesterday. This makes me want to swallow the man all the more. Having only seen the online picture, I imagine the impressive length of it jutting out like a mast. I want to hang my fucking sail on it. I try to follow the gravitational pull of his dick, mouth open and tongue out. "Aaaah, aaah," but he yanks me by the hair and holds me still.

"Move over," he orders, pushing me aside so he can sit on the bed. On my knees I adjust my position by baby-walking in between his legs. "Blow me, cocksucker."

Pete fucks my mouth, thrusting my head back and forth. "Deeper, you little cunt. Right, uh-huh. All the way, pussy boy!" I am a black hole feasting on the stars. Dicks are always bigger when you haven't actually looked at them before sucking. Blindness for some reason increases girth in one's mouth. In the darkened glory-hole hallways of sex clubs, even the smaller ones don't seem so small. I take him all the way to the back of my throat without gagging. It's an awesome feeling to suck a big one without a gag reflex, no impediment between his dick and my tonsils; I press my mouth down on the base of his shaft, his pubic hair giving me a mustache. His balls, a double chin.

After a few minutes of this, he slurs: "Suuuck, yooouuu biiiiii-itchhh boyyyyyy." He loosens his grip on my brown curls; soon, his palm is flat and resting on my head like I'm a "good boy." A heavy bouncing on the bed and Pete's dick slips out of my mouth. I kneel there for a few seconds in silence.

"Pete?"

I attempt to move my hands but they're tied too tightly. I press my face against the mattress and slide the blindfold off using my head. Pete has fallen backward on the bed. I yank my hands forcefully to free myself of the tie and stand up. His eyes are shut in pink fleshy slits. I crawl up next to him and shake him by the shoulders. No response. He's out cold, limbs limp and lifeless. His mouth slightly open in a pucker that makes him look a little retarded. His dick is hard as granite. This I find interesting. I grab it and squeeze for a few seconds to see if it'll go soft. It doesn't.

Maybe I should be panicked but instead I study Pete's naked body—hard, ruddy nipples, coiled belly button, his soft, hairy legs dangling off the bed at the knees. His thick calves and thighs are spread listlessly on the mattress; his ass cheeks spill out from underneath him like small moons. He might just need to sleep it off but he also may have overdosed and could be dead soon if I don't act—G being the circle-and-slash drug if there ever was one.

I stare at his plum-colored cock lying lopsided on his belly, pointing northeast toward the Valley like a compass arrow leading me across the high desert, past the Plains states then to Newfoundland and beyond. I fight against the urge to climb on top of it as I contemplate the line between sloppy excess and a dire situation. What if he's bluffing, playing the passed-out dude as a cue for me to sit on his dick? How can I tell? If I call an ambulance, cops will show and I will definitely be arrested for being high, having drugs in my apartment, and probably for felony use of the date-rape drug. If I don't call an ambulance, he may die and I'll still likely go to jail. I grab hold of his dick once again and place my ear down on his stomach to see if the pale, smooth landscape of his chest is rising.

I sign back online. In one of the M4M rooms I announce:

Would someone please IM me with instructions on how to care for a person passed out on G and, in particular, how to make sure he's ok.

Gay men are remarkable resources. *Beefyuncut* responds.

Is he breathing?

I think so

Well make sure and put him on his side, not his stomach or back

Ok. Then what?

Make sure he's breathing regularly. Watch him for at least 15 minutes to make sure he doesn't turn blue

And if he does?

Call an ambulance

Thanks a lot

Sure . . . is he hot?

Back in my room, I hook my hands underneath his armpits to pull him all the way up to the headboard. How is it that I can bench-press my own weight and yet dragging a 190-pound man feels exponentially more difficult? Once his feet are over the edge, I push his shoulder up to get him on his side. His upper body lifts but his legs lay flat on the bed like a pair of wet logs so I start over by crossing his right leg over his left. His erection is turning eggplant-purple and the head of his penis has mushroomed into a Portobello crown. I consider soaking it in olive oil. Can a hard-on grow to dangerous proportions? Priapus was ruined by his formidable phallus, after all.

At his side, I slide my hands palms down underneath his back and heave forward. He turns all the way over landing on his stomach but he quickly slides off the left side of the bed in a walloping thump.

"Fuck!" I yell. I hear a bang at the front door. I freeze and look around, dumbstruck. I'm not answering it.

Pete has landed on his back. He lets out a distressed moan, then shakes his head from side to side as if having a nightmare. My heart is machine-gunning out of my chest, but I'm relieved he didn't land wrong and break an arm. I examine him carefully for further damage. Nothing is twisted, nothing bleeding. His cock is now magenta, but he doesn't appear to be turning blue. Again, there's the banging at my door.

"Fuck!" I run to look through the peephole. It's a man with a shaved head. His muscular arms are crossed, a reptilian tail winds out his short sleeve toward his elbow. It's *Vgl8x7lkn4azz*. I open the door in the nude.

"Sorry I'm late. Woof," he says.

I stop to consider how late. Two hours maybe?

"You have to help me," I say pulling him into the living room and closing the door. I race back to my room and he follows.

"Jesus!" he cries looking down at Pete's body.

"Help me lift him on the bed. He passed out on G, and I don't know what to do with him. I don't know if I should call an ambulance or if he's going to sleep it off or what!"

Vgl8x7lkn4azz grabs his arms, I take hold of his legs, and we hoist him to the center of the bed. "We need to put him on his side," he tells me, and I'm astonished that with all my drug experimentation I'd never before heard of this lifesaving position. We manage to rest him on his side by crossing one leg over the other, propping his back with two pillows, and placing his arms one above his head and the other at a perpendicular angle. We stand back and survey our accomplishment. Pete is now a department-store mannequin just out of the crate.

"His cock looks like it's gonna explode," he tells me. "Suck on it to see if he comes."

"Seriously?" I ask.

"Yeah, bitch. Do it. He's fine. He's just sleeping."

Although I often disregard conventional morality, I have to wonder about the ethics of this. Would having sex with him in this state be technically considered rape? What if he wakes up? *Vgl8x7lkn4azz* starts to shed his clothes. He's short and swarthy—Puerto Rican maybe? He has another tattoo, a ring of fire circling his belly button that wasn't in the picture.

"What's your name, anyway?" I ask staring at the thick bush of pubes. His dick is fat and dark, like it's been in the sun a while.

"Charles," he answers. Charles is the last name in the world he looks like. "But people call me Cheech."

Pete's chest heaves in and out more deeply. He looks downright peaceful lying on the bed.

"How long can someone stay passed out on G?"

"Few hours I guess," he says grabbing onto Pete's dick like a meaty handlebar. "You partying?"

"I was."

Cheech asks me what drugs I have, and I give him the Tina. He snorts a few lines on the bathroom sink counter with a rolled-up dollar bill.

"Okay, now," he says, "you're going to do everything I tell you to. Right, bitch?"

I'm getting tired of being addressed as "bitch" but I decide I'll go along for a while since I'm horny all over again at the thought of molesting Pete. Cheech lays him over onto his back and says we'll watch his breathing.

"Make out with him," Cheech barks.

I climb onto the bed and straddle Pete, bending my knees on either side of his waist. I lean in close to his face. His long, curly lashes are like the blades of a Christmas sleigh. His rugged nose, a cow's skull head in the desert. He's breathing out of his mouth, his lips a cartoonish open pucker. Now, if I make out with him, it'll cut off his oxygen. Cheech is standing at the side of the bed and strokes a gob of lube across the length of his hardening dick. As I stare into Pete's face, I remember the only time I ever passed out on G. This online trick, a burly hairstylist with nipple rings. I recall making out, fucking, sucking, then, next thing I know, I'm waking up. The hairstylist, still at my side, tells me I was out for an hour. I didn't believe him until now.

"I said make out with him," Cheech bellows.

I press my lips to Pete's and stick my tongue in his mouth.

"That's right, whore. Do it to the dead guy."

I wish he wouldn't have said that. Pete starts to cough and moves his head to one side, continuing to breathe through his mouth more loudly until his breath turns into a wheezing snore. Ignoring Cheech, I crawl down to Pete's dick instead. What I really want is to sit on it. If I'm going to go through with this, I want his cock in my ass. I start by putting the head in my mouth. Pete's penis is now as hard and dark as aged salami. How else to describe a cock but as a sausage? That we call men pigs becomes monumentally clear in that moment. We are pigs and therefore, pork products.

Cheech watches me blow Pete like I'm the Superbowl and he's had too many beers. "That's right, fucker. Take it all the way down. Go, motherfucker!" I keep glancing up to see if Pete is reacting. Occasionally he turns his head from one side to the other, and at one point he moves his arm up to his chest.

"Now ride his dick. Make the corpse blow his load up your hole."

I get up on my feet and squat over Pete's distressed boner. My thighs flex into sinewy bands of muscle. Cheech reaches underneath me and positions Pete's dick to my hole. I lower down slowly and feel the overblown head dock at my anus. I lower myself further and the shaft enters me cleanly. There is no other pleasure that approximates the bliss of getting fucked. If it feels better than this in a real pussy then women are the blessed gender.

Cheech is watching from behind, repeating, "Fuck yeah. *Fuck yeah.*"

I rise and fall on his dick. His head is turned to one side, and he is lost in twilight. I grind against his cock, making sure it kisses my prostate.

Pete suddenly opens his eyes and grabs onto my waist. He digs his fingers painfully into my hip bones. His eyes are red and hysterical. Sweat gathers above his brow. He pants like a tired dog then shoves me off his cock and jets into the bathroom. I hear the toilet lid slam up, followed by Pete violently heaving and retching as if he's exorcising demons.

Cheech is now frantically zipping up his shorts and scrambling for his sandals on the floor. He finds his flip-flops at the foot of the bed, slides them onto his feet, doesn't bother to put on his shirt, and dashes out the bedroom leaving me behind to hear the slam of the front door. I get up and peek into the bathroom where Pete is holding onto the seat with both hands, his head buried inside the bowl. Ah, this is why you don't keep them on their backs! They might choke on their own vomit.

I bring him a tall glass of cold water from the kitchen and set it on the bathroom counter, then pet his head gently for a few strokes to let him know I'm here. From the toilet bowl comes a weary childlike "thank you."

I go back to my room and sit at the edge of the bed as Pete finishes spitting into the toilet between gulps of water. I hear him stand up followed by gargling. He turns on the shower, and I hear the Russian kids outside laughing again. I lie on my back waiting for Pete to come out, thinking what I might tell him if he asks.

Street Hunter

Christopher Pierce

MEET ME OUT BACK FOR HEAD, the scrawled writing on the inside of the restroom stall said. *Fuck,* Garrett thought, this'll be easy. His victims were now announcing themselves to him, he hardly had to hunt at all. The sorry specimen that had written this message in the childish hand would most likely be his last catch of the day.

Garrett finished pissing into the dirty toilet bowl and shook his sizable cock to free the last drops of urine before tucking the organ back into his camouflage pants. He hit the flush lever with his booted foot and the noise of draining water and groaning pipes seemed very loud in the tiny restroom. Something touched his boot, and he looked down. His lip curled with disgust as he saw a grimy tennis shoe sticking under the wall of the stall. Obviously the guy using the urinal next to the stall wanted to know if Garrett was available for some action.

The hunter pulled his boot away and slammed open the door of the stall. He strode out and glared at the obviously drugged-out young man cowering in front of the urinal.

"Fuck off, scum," Garrett said, "or I'll smash your head through that wall." Without waiting for a response, Garrett headed for the door. Since the restroom was located at the back of the adult bookstore, he had to walk the entire length of the establishment to get to the front door. As he walked among the racks and shelves, he ignored the attempts at eye contact the other customers tried to establish with him.

Garrett knew he was hot, with his sleeveless T-shirt, bulging bicep muscles, and military buzz-cut hair. He exuded unself-conscious sexuality. His physical presence, which made him so attractive to gay men, had also made him arrogant. He felt disdain for the guys who tried to connect with him, considering them wretched souls who weren't even worthy of a few moments of his attention.

They were weak.

But he was strong.

He took what he wanted, when he wanted it. And what Garrett wanted right then was one more catch to finish off the day's hunting. And he had a feeling he'd find it behind this very store.

He walked out of the store's entrance and headed to the rear of the building. Reflections of headlights from cars driving by fell across him as he walked. It was very late, but this part of the city never slept. It was cruising time, Garrett's favorite time of the day or night. As he walked, he pulled a small amber bottle and a grimy hand-towel out of his pocket. When he saw that no one was looking, he dumped some of the contents of the bottle into the towel, then stuffed them both back in his pocket.

Behind the bookstore it was dark, with trees from the public park next door blocking out most of the moonlight. But there was enough to see the overflowing garbage Dumpster and the nervous, twitching man who was haunting its shadow.

This is appropriate, Garrett thought. *Trash by the trash bin. And trash is free—anyone can take what they want from it. Just like I'm going to do right now.*

The young man made a little noise of excited surprise when he looked up and saw Garrett standing there. His eyes went wide as he took in the sight of the stud that had accepted the invitation he'd written on the bathroom wall. Garrett cocked his head slightly, evaluating his prey. The guy was slender, almost gaunt, wearing dirty cargo pants and a torn T-shirt. His hair was messy, but he had what might have been called a pretty face, before a few years of booze and drugs had taken their toll. He was probably about twenty-five, and was wearing new athletic tennis shoes that he'd most likely stolen from his last trick.

He made a "come here" gesture with his hands, and Garrett obliged, stepping out of the fragile moonlight into the shadows next to the Dumpster. The guy started to sink down on his knees, but the hunter stopped him.

"Get your back against the wall, cocksucker," Garrett growled, and the guy obeyed, scooting back on his haunches. Garrett stepped forward, trapping his prey between the rear of the building and his own bulky body. "What's your name?"

"M-Mark," the guy stuttered. Garrett unbuckled his belt and let his camo pants open by themselves from the pressure of the hard cock within. Like a bad porn flick, the erect rod jutted out like a prong, and Mark practically licked his lips with anticipation.

"Open your fucking mouth, Mark," the hunter said. Mark did what he was told, and was rewarded as Garrett forced his big cock between the young man's lips. Mark choked on the size of it, but Garrett didn't give a shit, and started pumping his hips, face-fucking his prey until the young man was hacking up bile.

"Yeah, you're a good little cocksucker, a good little cock-whore, aren't you?" Garrett rumbled as Mark did his best to service the huge organ that had been stuffed into his mouth. It never took long for Garrett to get off, even when he was enjoying himself and wanted it to last longer. "Good little cock-whore, that's what you are, Mark..." he said, "and now you're gonna eat my cream."

Garrett's powerful body flexed as his orgasm shuddered through him. He kept a firm grip on Mark's head so the young man couldn't pull away, and his prey swallowed greedily as the hunter's sperm shot down his throat in three massive spurts. Only when the last drop had been squeezed out did Garrett let go of Mark, and the young man gasped for air.

"Mmmmmm," the hunter said, "that felt good, cocksucker. You made me feel nice. And now we're gonna see how much money you're worth."

Mark looked so surprised by this statement that he didn't notice Garrett pulling something from his pocket.

"What are you talk—" was as far as he got before the hunter smashed his hand against Mark's face, pinning his head to the wall and covering his nose and mouth with the chloroform-soaked towel.

Mark tried to dislodge the towel from his face, but Garrett was much stronger than him and easily kept it in place over his victim's nose and mouth. The young man punched his fists against the hunter's muscular chest and abdomen, but he might as well have been pounding on a brick wall for all the good it did him. Mark tried to call out for help, but the noise was muffled by the towel and went unheard.

Not that anyone would come to his rescue anyway.

Mark's struggles became less insistent, and slowly ceased altogether as the chemical fumes did their job. His body sagged against the wall as he lost consciousness.

Without wasting any time, Garrett stuffed the rag back into the pocket of his camo pants and grabbed Mark under his armpits. Lifting the smaller man up off the ground easily, the hunter ducked down and hefted his prey's body over one shoulder. Standing up, Garrett adjusted the weight of his burden on his shoulder and secured him in place with one arm around his legs. Mark dangled over Garrett's back, his arms swinging as the bigger man started walking.

The hunter walked out of the alley, back around to the sidewalk near the front of the store. He carried his prey easily, as if the young man weighed no more than a bag of laundry.

A few late-night cruisers walked by, but Garrett ignored them, twisting his face into a silent snarl. He had his last catch of the day, he was done hunting for tonight. Mark would be out from the chloroform for a while, so he didn't have to worry about him regaining consciousness. Not that he would be able to free himself if he did—Garrett could just issue a good solid punch to Mark's face, and he'd be out like a light again.

But he hoped he wouldn't have to do that. Undamaged merchandise was worth more money. If the dealer had to give medical attention to a catch, the hunter's fee was lowered. And Garrett needed money. He had rent and utility bills hanging over him that needed to get paid.

As he carried his catch down the street, the hunter ignored the curious stares of people in passing cars. He guessed it was sort of unusual to see a man carrying another man over his shoulder, at least outside of a wrestling match or a battlefield, but he didn't care. No one had ever called the police on him, and he hoped that would remain the case; for all anyone in this part of town could guess, Mark was drunk and being carried home.

Turning down a side street, Garrett brought his prey to his parked truck. It was an older model, dented in a few places, but with a lot of character. Sort of like Garrett himself. There was a canopy over the bed to enclose whatever cargo he was carrying. Keeping Mark slung over his shoulder, the hunter used his other hand to reach into his pocket and pull out a set of keys. After looking around to make sure he was alone on the dark street, he unlocked the canopy and pulled his truck's tailgate down.

It was dark inside the canopy, but there was enough light from the moon and nearby street lamps to see what was inside.

Two big duffel bags, military-style and stuffed to capacity, lay on the floor of the pick-up bed. Each bag was big enough to hold a man inside, and that in fact was exactly what they both contained—one man in each. Hunter's prey, to be exact. One of the bags stirred at the noise and squirmed.

"Wh . . . happening . . . help . . ." a muffled voice came from the squirming bag. Without losing his grip on Mark, Garrett reached into the bed and gave the bag a punch in the general area of the stomach.

"Shut the fuck up!" the hunter snarled, and the man inside the bag yelped with pain and stopped moving. The hunter lowered his burden down onto the tailgate of the truck. Mark didn't move. Garrett opened a side panel just inside the canopy and pulled out a few coils of rope and some long strips of black cloth. He sat Mark down on the tailgate, then grabbed his wrists and tied them together with one of the ropes, pulling the knots tight. Then he did the same with the young man's ankles, anchoring them together with rope. One of the black cloths was wound around Mark's head then, covering his eyes and getting tied behind his head. Last but not least, the hunter shoved one of the cloths into Mark's mouth and then secured it in place with the last cloth, tying it around his head to hold the gag in.

Garrett checked over his work and was pleased. It wasn't high-tech or complicated bondage, but it was good enough for him. This guy wasn't going anywhere. After checking again that no one was watching, Garrett reached into the pick-up bed and grabbed a third duffel bag, this one empty. The hunter maneuvered Mark into the bag headfirst, stuffing him in until his entire body was contained inside the canvas sack. Then he closed the bag and pulled the drawstrings tight before tying them securely.

The hunter pushed his bagged prey into the pick-up bed with his other catches and closed the tailgate and canopy door securely.

When he was satisfied, Garrett got back into his truck and started up the engine. He found himself wiping his forehead with a dirty towel from the passenger seat. He was tired. Three catches in one night was a lot of work.

He was still horny, though, his big cock flopping around inside his camo pants ready for more action. He just might have to make use of one of his catches before he brought them to their new home. But he'd need to get to a more deserted spot for that. Garrett checked his watch and was happy to see that there was still time to get some fucking done before the dealer closed for the night.

He drove around until he found another dark alley, this one between two closed office buildings. The hunter parked his truck among the shadows and got out. Going around to the rear of his vehicle, he opened the canopy and climbed in, closing it behind him.

Hmmm. Three catches. Which one should he fuck? He'd already shot a load into Mark, so he figured he'd use one of the others. Which of the other two would be hottest to fuck? Garrett decided on David, the guy he'd caught before Mark.

David had been hustling on the boulevard, giving his skinny twenty-year-old body to anyone with a few bucks to share. It'd been easy to bag David—Garrett had simply pulled his truck over to the side of the road and got out, walking over to the young man. The hustler barely had time to introduce himself and ask the big man what he wanted, before he was punched in the face and knocked out cold.

After a quick look around to make sure no one was nearby, the hunter had tossed him over one shoulder and carried him to the back of his truck. He'd tied David's hands and legs together and duct-taped his mouth shut, then stuffed him into one of the empty duffel bags in the back.

Now the hunter pulled the bag containing the hustler closer and untied the sack's drawstrings. He opened the bag, grabbed his prey's feet, and yanked his legs out to the waist. Garrett untied David's feet and removed his shoes, then pulled a switchblade out of his pocket. Extending the blade, he cut the young man's pants off and tossed them aside. Where David was going, he didn't need pants. Or any clothes.

Garrett hiked David's legs up onto his shoulders and undid his own belt. The hunter pulled his camo pants down far enough to allow his hard dick to pop out. Spitting into his hand for lubrication, the big man saw that his second catch of the night (David) was still knocked out woozy from the punch he'd dealt him earlier. He figured he'd cold-cock the guy again if he woke up.

A few strokes with his sticky hand and Garrett's cock was ready for fucking. The hunter pulled the unconscious hustler's body closer and pierced him, leaving his torso, arms, and head still in the bag. Burying his cock deep into David, the hunter fucked his catch hard, grunting like an animal. Within a few minutes he was ready to come again. Gritting his teeth and closing his eyes, the hunter blew his seed into the young man.

When he was done shooting, Garrett stuffed his cock back into his pants, then retied David's legs together and shoved him the rest of the way into the duffel bag and cinched it shut.

He had to get some sleep before he got up tomorrow. After jumping out of the canopy and locking it closed, Garret got back in the cab of his truck and started it up again. The hunter drove the rest of the way to his destination, an empty-looking office building in the city's grubby downtown.

He pulled the truck up to the loading dock at the back of the building and after making sure no one was watching, turned off the ignition and got out. Garrett opened the canopy and grabbed the duffel bag that contained his first catch of the night. He briefly considered taking two bags at once, then decided against it— didn't want to hurt his back. Leaning over, he hoisted the first duffel up and over his right shoulder. Locking the canopy once again, the hunter carried his catch to an unmarked door next to the loading dock. He knocked, then turned to face the domed camera on the wall to the left of the door.

After the person on the other end of the camera had gotten a look at him, within seconds the door was electronically unlocked with a loud click.

Garrett carried his prey into the building, and the door closed behind him. He hefted the duffel bag on his shoulder and walked down the short corridor the door had opened onto. At the end of the hallway another door buzzed open to admit him. The room he walked into was small and dimly lit, with a long counter and black curtains behind it. The man standing behind the counter looked as though he had once been hot, but now looked gaunt and tired.

"Hey, Jarvis," the hunter said as he carried the duffel bag over to the counter.

"Garrett," Jarvis said with a nod, "whatcha got for me?"

"Three catches tonight," Garrett said as he swung the bag down off his shoulder onto the counter.

"Let's take a look," Jarvis said, untying the bag's drawstrings. He opened the top of the sack and revealed the head of the hunter's first catch of the night. Together, Garrett and Jarvis pulled the young man out of the duffel bag and laid him on the counter.

He had short blond hair. His eyes were closed, and his chest expanded and contracted with deep breaths of unconscious sleep. His wrists and ankles were bound in the same way that Mark's were. Jarvis looked down at the captured young man, evaluating. The hunter was impatient, he wanted to know how much his catch was worth, but he knew better than to interrupt Jarvis. The dealer would give his appraisal when he was ready to.

The man behind the counter took the young man's chin in his hand and turned his head from side to side, getting a good look at his face, then checking his teeth. He lifted the catch's T-shirt to examine his flat, hard belly. He unbuttoned his jeans and pulled the young man's cock out, hefting it in his hand, checking it for size and weight. Then he looked up at Garrett.

"Not bad," he said, "you got more?"

"Yeah. Two more."

"Bring 'em in."

After the hunter had carried his other two catches into the room and Jarvis had taken his time evaluating them, the dealer looked up.

"I'll give you five hundred each," he said.

"Fifteen hundred for three catches?" said Garrett in disbelief. "I remember when you used to give me fifteen hundred for each catch, and I was giving you a break!"

"Tough shit. Fifteen hundred."

"Come on, Jarvis," the hunter said. "We go way back. Don't tell me demand is low, man, I follow the industry, demand's never been higher!"

"Take it or leave it."

"You're an asshole. I'll take it," Garrett said.

Jarvis pulled the cash out of a safe under the counter and handed it to the hunter.

"Give me my fucking bags back," Garrett said, and took them out of the dealer's hand. Tossing the empty sacks over his shoulder, the hunter left the building, swearing under his breath. How was a hunter supposed to earn a living if this was all he could make? He wondered. He could try to find another dealer, or he could shoot for more than three catches a night.

He was too tired to think about it now. The hunter threw the duffel bags in the back of his truck, got into the cab, and headed home, into the night.

The Abortionist's Lover

Rigoberto González

for M

When he slips under the covers at night, my lover's hands are cold as the bathroom mirror. His hands don't match mine in either size or color. They are white and small—harmless-looking things. Their compactness keeps his profession a secret. I will let him touch me, I will let him feel me, and I will let him pinch and prod me, to remind him that his fingertips are not desensitized, though they are completely sanitized. The warm points of his desire, I will show him, have not scrubbed off.

"Fourteen procedures today," he announces as he walks into the bedroom. The lights have been dimmed in anticipation. I am already naked. I hear him remove his clothes, tap one of the computer keys to wake it up, though he knows he shouldn't do this—check his email on a Thursday afternoon. The screen projects its blue glow against the wall. A creature of routine, he expects the following program this day of every week: sex at 6:15, dinner by 7:15, bedtime at 10:00.

"Procedures," he calls them, and it makes me want to scoff. But it's this skill that has insured him a job at the Bronx hospital, and that pays the mortgage for his penthouse in the Meatpacking District.

I am facing the tight square of the window, picturing the traffic on Fourteenth street. I have seen Stuart naked so many times I can recall his body through memory. His arms are thin, and his nipples are red as blood against the pale skin. He is circumcised, and the first thing he does is reach over to pull my foreskin back, stimulating my erection.

Even after a year of this ceremony I have not learned to stop thinking, when he begins to fuck me, about what he does at work—perform "procedures" on poor women, Puerto Rican, Dominican, Haitian, Black. Any one of them could be my sister, Dalia, back in Mexico. Except that here these "procedures" are legal. All of them done cautiously, hygenically, by my Jewish doctor from a wealthy family in Chicago.

Lowering himself behind me, he fits his chin into the curve of my neck and runs his tongue along my skin. The tickling forces my thighs to press his knuckle deeper into my crotch. I reach back, weave the long, silky strands of his blond hair into my fingers, and invite him into me. When he pumps the lube bottle on the nightstand, I'm temporarily shaken out of the moment. The spurting sound is clinical and obscene. But then he enters me so smoothly, my body locks into place with his so perfectly, that I dismiss those thoughts of "procedures" and women and tiny fetuses that have met their end at my lover's hands. The more he thrusts, the more I forgive him. Maybe I will come before him, maybe he will come before me. This is the only part that goes unplanned. The bed squeaks, picking up the pace to catch up with our quick succession of moans. I ejaculate first this time, and my semen oozes out between his fingers.

I reach over for the box of tissues.

"Gracias, papito," he whispers into my ear.

I follow him into the bathroom. The light is too bright and hurts my eyes. As he stands over the toilet to pee, I turn the shower knobs. On one side of the tub, the shampoos for his type of hair; on the other side, for mine. Stuart wraps his arms around me. I can feel the wet tip of his penis. In a minute I will wash it for him with the soft sponge.

He will scrub between my ass cheeks with the loofah. We will lather each other's heads and dry each other off with matching towels. And in between we will kiss. Because we are the same height, all of these reciprocal activities give the semblance of equality. But we are far from it.

"I had this patient today," Stuart tells me as I stir the pot of lentil soup over the stove. He slices the bread loaf. We're in our robes. "Big fat cow. I mean, the only way I could tell she was pregnant was after studying the sonogram. I was expecting to see a tumor in there. Or maybe a huge mass of fecal matter. But instead I found a baby."

"Would you mind terribly if we changed the subject?" I say.

"Oh, pobre papito," Stuart says in that gringo accent that annoys me. "Have I offended thee?"

"We're about to eat," I say. "I don't want those images in my head."

"I'm a doctor," he says. "I speak doctor speak. You want polite babble, go back to those lazy artists you were hanging out with in the tacky railroad apartments of Williamsburg."

"*Big fat cow* is doctor speak?" I say. "Hmm . . . sophisticated. I'll have to grab the medical dictionary to look that up."

Without warning, I feel the hot sting of his hand across my face. It's the surprise of his first act of violence that knocks me down, not the force. Stuart drops beside me immediately.

"Oh, baby," he says, kissing me on the warm cheek. "See what you made me do?"

I'm stunned into paralysis. He rolls me over on my stomach and lifts the robe up over my ass. He continues to coo apologies and to kiss the back of my neck as he penetrates me on the floor. The adrenaline has excited him, and though I'm not prepared to receive him, I let him exhaust himself on top of me.

On Fridays I have my own routine. Stuart is on call for 24 hours at the hospital. He will not be back until Saturday morning, when he will drop dead until early afternoon. I clean up the mess he leaves in the kitchen after fixing his lunch, dinner, and midnight snack to go. There are small errands to run before I head to work: drop off the laundry, pick up the dry cleaning, check Barney's Co-Op for any sales. All of these activities are good for me; they eat up the morning hours until Jaysen rings the buzzer at noon.

The elevator at the end of the hallway hasn't closed yet by the time I'm unzipping Jaysen's pants. He stands at the doorway passively, letting me stretch open his fly to reach in for his cock. It's a beautiful cock, long and thick at the base, the shaft narrows down to the head, which points out and narrows like the tip of an arrow. I take it flaccid into my mouth and swirl it around with my tongue. Stuart never lets me take his penis if it's not erect. It's an insecurity I've only seen in white guys.

"I guess you're hungry," Jaysen says. The tone in his voice alarms me; he sounds disinterested. I look up at him, pull away from his cock, which is now semi-erect.

"Something wrong?" I ask. He doesn't answer.

I've been dreading this moment. It's the part in the affair where the married man finally succumbs to regret or guilt or shame or a combination of all three. It's the part where he thinks he should turn himself around and make right by his woman, breaking off the illicit meetings with his whore, cleansing himself, or so he believes, of the dirty kisses, when all he's really doing is ending one chapter to move on to the next—another fool who will start a romance from scratch, long before it wears thin with monotony.

"I see," I say. It's the serious breakup because he didn't even let me finish the blowjob.

"I'm sorry, papi," Jaysen says. "It's just that things are getting bad at home."

"Of course they're bad," I say. "Why else would you come over to let me suck your dick?"

"Look, I don't want problems, okay? I get enough of that shit at home," Jaysen says. He zips his pants and throws himself on the couch.

"I'm in the mood for a drink," I say. "How about you?"

"I'll take whiskey," Jaysen says.

"That serious, huh?" I say. I pour him a double shot of Maker's Mark and hand it to him. I step back into the kitchen to mix a martini.

"What happened to your face, anyway?" he asks.

I'm startled by the revelation. All morning I was running around the streets of Chelsea and not one look to betray the visible traces of rage on me.

"I fell," I say.

"Don't bullshit me," Jaysen says. "He kicked your ass, didn't he? Was it because of me?"

"Don't flatter yourself, hon," I say, walking to the living room slowly, to keep from spilling my drink. I take a sip. "It's none of your business anyway."

"All right, all right," he says. We drink the rest of our cocktails in silence. Meanwhile, the world of car horns and fire-truck sirens continues outside without us.

"Would you like another?" I ask him, reaching over for his glass.

"I'm good," he says.

"I know you're good," I say. "What I want to know is if you're horny."

"I take it you are?" he asks.

"Well," I say. "Since this is good-bye and the probability of us crossing paths again is remote, what with you being a working-class bloke and me the penthouse dweller. Unless your next trick also goes to my gym and feels like flapping his lips at the exercise bikes about his new stud, I'll never hear from you again."

I snuggle up next to Jaysen and place my hand on his crotch. "So what do you say? I've had a shitty week myself, and I'm about to be left behind by the best piece of ass in both Upper and Lower Manhattan. I've got to have something juicy to tell the girls the next time we gather for a quick lunchtime shop and bite at Bloomingdale's."

"You sure do have a way with words, Lorenzo," he says. "Now will you shut the fuck up and suck my dick?"

At its full glory, Jaysen's cock is nine inches. I've developed an internal measuring stick, and I can tell a guy's size by how far it slides in and what part inside my throat it touches. But the best part of sex with Jaysen is not the cocksuck, but the fuck itself. He's got a smooth, round ass with a small tuft of prickly ass hairs that tickles the shaft on my dick. He's a great bottom, Jaysen. As he's squeezing me between his ass cheeks one last time, a sadness overcomes me that this is the final screw. I'd like to commemorate it somehow, maybe by giving him a pair of Stuart's cufflinks, but Jaysen's not the type to wear them, and I'm not the type to reward my lay with small tacky gifts that show him the size of my appreciation.

I lie back on the couch with my pants around my knees as Jaysen walks into the bathroom to clean up. The water runs in the sink. The clouds are gathering behind the skyline, and I make a mental note to take my umbrella to work. In a minute I will dress in my retailer's black, I will walk two blocks to the 6 and step out into the platform leading to the lower level of Bloomie's. But before all this I will walk out to the terrace and talk myself out of jumping.

Beneath me is Fourteenth Street. There is always foot traffic, day and night. No matter what hour I choose to fling myself over the guardrail, chances are somebody will be around to bear witness to the tragedy. Once Stuart and I dropped maraschino cherries on pedestrians and never once hit our targets. A mathematician or a physicist might have. The only time we come out here anymore is to breathe in the cool autumn air. Even a penthouse can be oppressive as any shoebox apartment after a while. My mother has a saying: *Jaula, aunque sea de oro, no deja de ser prisión.* I always thought it was a Mexican woman thing, this perspective of marriage and society as prison. But my mother is still serving her time. My sister, on the other hand, got out the hard way.

The setting: Morelia, Mochaoán, mid-1990s. The players: my beloved sister, Dalia, and a husband who cheated on her with other men. The conflict: a shitty marriage. The plot: my sister punishing her husband by terminating her first pregnancy. The twist: a botched abortion. The closing scene: unwritten. Dalia is still in a coma, and her husband, my mother warns me, is still out looking for me.

"And what's he going to do if he finds me? Kiss me to death?" I told my mother over the phone the last time she called.

"He says going to shoot you," my mother said, her voice so soft and sullen, as if she believed his threats. And then she adds, her voice shaky: "Please promise me you won't come back."

As I look over the edge of the building I call out Dalia's name to the wind. If I were standing next to her at the hospital, she still wouldn't hear me, no matter what those doctors say. My mother, who has faith in things invisible like God and the subconscious, visits my sister every week and speaks to her, tells her that I miss her, and that I'm sorry. The last part is not true. I am not sorry I told her about her husband, who from the days they were dating had his eye on me. At first I thought it was all in my head, wishful thinking and silly adolescent fantasy—what had gotten me through many nights of compulsive masturbation. And then one night he was in my room, my dream materialized.

"Shh . . . " he said to me, though it was quite unnecessary. I knew it would be a secret between us—that and the warm hand crawling under the covers, my erection already waiting for his grip. I came almost immediately upon contact, and it embarrassed me. But when he bent down to kiss me on the lips, the first kiss I'd ever received from a man, I knew that he understood, and that he would give me another chance to do better.

I thought these exchanges would end when he married Dalia, but he expected them to continue. And when I put a stop to them myself, he started to hate me because he was forced to seek his pleasure elsewhere.

"Are you sure about this, Dalia?" I heard my mother say over afternoon tea.

"Positive," Dalia said. "You know a wife senses these things."

I pictured my mother nodding her head in agreement, having been through the same bullshit with my father, though she never left him. But neither did he affront her with the additional shame of being a faggot like the son she helped move out to the north, worlds away from her husband's line of sight.

Fourteenth Street and Ninth Avenue is my favorite intersection, connecting Chelsea with the Meatpacking District with the Village. When I finally pour out into the bustle of the streets, I'm simply another anonymous body in motion. The only people I make eye contact with are those I'd like to fuck. And there are plenty of beautiful men to choose from.

As I make my way on the north side of Fourteenth, I'm grateful for having decided on Manhattan as my hiding place from the troubles at home. This is the city where people come to disappear from the old identities and to reappear as the new ones. I arrived a scared teenager on a student visa with a fetish for the English language and American things. I'm now a twenty-seven-year-old college dropout, but fit and versatile. This goddamn island is my oyster.

"Lorenzo!"

I turn my head to check who has called. No one steps forward to claim responsibility for shouting out my name. I keep walking. Maybe it was simply the wind carrying back a response from Dalia from so far away.

The best perk about working as a retailer at Bloomie's is that I'm just as desirable as the merchandise. That's how I met Stuart. And Robbie before him. And Ahmed before that. And on Fridays after work, the other queens and I head out to the O.W. or to the Townhouse, to drink and flirt and poke fun at the dumb tourists whose eyes go wide as clocks when they find out that Bloomingdale's is actually affordable. But I'm not feeling it tonight. After a first round of cocktails, my energy begins to wane.

"Girl, I got a hot number tonight," Kenny says. He works in women's jewelry. I'm stuck down in the basement, dusting off the designer labels and putting up with the bitchy queens who have saved all season for a Kenneth Cole outfit to go with the shoes from Century-21.

"Well, call right now," Martin dares him, pulling out his cell phone. He's the youngest of the group and circulates among the perfume counters.

"Are you kidding me? And kill the play I'm getting from that dude in the trucker hat?"

Martin and I turn at the same time to face a drunk patron nodding off at the end of the bar. We burst out laughing.

"You know what, girls?" I say. "I think I'm calling it a night."

"You're kidding, right? The party's just getting good," Kenny says.

"I'm sorry," I say. "Man trouble."

"Say no more, sweetheart," Martin says. "Go home, get your beauty sleep, and Prozac your headaches away."

"I'll try," I say. I kiss them both on the cheek and walk out.

A few blocks up I will arrive at the Hot and Crusty, hostile with Upper East Side sociopaths and intoxicated businessmen, and most surely, fending them off with his disarming looks, I will find Shiraz.

"Cup of coffee, two sugars and cream, please," I tell him. I check my watch. Quitting time for him is midnight, in an hour.

"How are you, my friend?" he says. "Haven't seen you around here lately."

"I'm doing fine," I say. "Busy. But I'm free tonight." I wink.

I sit with my elbows on the crumb-filled table for the next hour. The line of customers grows and shortens quickly at fifteen-minute intervals. To pass the time I pretend I'm reading a book from Stuart's shelf. But what I'm really doing is going over what's about to transpire after midnight.

Shiraz and I walk down from Second Avenue to Central Park and grab the first dark spot we can find. All the way there we chitchat about harmless things like work and the weather and the rising price of a subway ride. But as soon as we are out of view he tackles me with a bear hug, knocking the wind out of my body. I don't have time to breathe again before Shiraz pins me to the ground, his right arm wrapped around my neck. He's adept with one-hand maneuvering. I've seen him work his skill over sandwich preparations. Somehow he has unbuttoned our pants and pulled them down at the same time. He guides his cock inside me. My lower back feels the hairy bristles of his stomach.

"You little slut," he spits into my ear. "This is what you came for, isn't it?"

I squirm beneath him, wanting to tell him to ease up, just a little, but he has cut off my breathing. I open my mouth and nothing comes out, except the hollow sound of strained air escaping. I'm wondering how long after I pass out will I come to. It would be embarrassing to wake up in the daylight like this, my pants around my knees telling the whole sordid story. Or what if I never come to and meet up with my sister in that nebulous limbo where those stuck between the living and the dead must gather? How would I explain what took me there?

"So you *are* the promiscuous little faggot my husband told me about," she will say. And how could I deny it?

But when I black out there is no such encounter or dream. When I wake up, it is only about an hour later. Shiraz has run away, scared shitless that he fucked me to death. I pull myself together, brush the leaves off my shirt, and stumble to the nearest bench for a rest. A cruiser on his way to the rambles mistakes my pose for a solicitation and grabs his crotch while he walks by. I ignore him.

I suppose that a soul search is appropriate at a moment like this, but I don't care for one. I know exactly what I'm doing anyway—punishing Stuart for being cruel, and Jaysen for leaving, and Dalia for marrying that prick, and Shiraz for—for being so goddamn irresistible in that little white hat. Contrast it against the bread, and he's completely edible. Ha, ha.

When I wipe a tear off my face I'm stunned. Have I been crying all this time? It is almost 2:30 in the morning. In five hours Stuart will be home, expecting to sleep peacefully, and to wake up rested for an evening on the town, maybe a movie at the Angelika, maybe a browse through The Strand, maybe a stroll along the pier, where he will apologize profusely for the fifth or sixth time for having raised his hand at me. He will hand me a pair of cufflinks. And I will take that hand and kiss every knuckle, rub it against my cheek to assure him that it is meant to be in service to the women who might otherwise hurt themselves without the attentiveness of a doctor like him. I have heard the stories, and I have known instances of women who turn to unhealthy and unsanitary alternatives, in places where procedures like the ones he performs are not available. He is not a bad man, my lover. And I will forgive him as surely as I know he will forgive me for taking that leap from the penthouse terrace. But he will have his peace of mind because it's not really me who jumped, but that person who I became when I set foot in New York City, that terrible glutton, seduced by all the hungers accessible to him in a horn of plenty.

And I will return to my origin, a chair next to my unconscious sister, where I will hold her hand and ask for forgiveness, for having conjured up the most stupid fantasy of all—that when she left her husband, she would also understand why I would take her place beside him, so jealous I became of all his other lovers, I thought that this would solve all of our problems. Who would have imagined that she was carrying life inside her belly? Who would have imagined that by plucking out the fruit she would also fell the tree? And if her husband comes knocking on the door, a weapon hot and heavy in his fist, I will welcome the fury because from the beginning I have been making sure that the bullet is meant for me. Oh, my parade of sorrow-eyed lovers, designing my death is like writing poetry.

Hislandia

Louis Anthes

The Middle: Unsung Bombay Words
Like a slow faucet leak, it overflowed, flooding the whole flat. Fortunately for me, I kept cool and dry, shielded by a white envelope sealed months before its contents were at last exposed during the Indian monsoon. And when the deluge happened, nothing felt wet, nothing felt dry. Everyone, including the Thief, felt the truth.

But where to start: the beginning or the end? I like to fiddle around the middle, which is a kind of a muddle, I admit. And somewhere in that muddled middle is the envelope, which is not just a metaphor for a secret but a real physical white #10 paper envelope. The envelope was the Secret, handed to the Thief at the beginning until he could no longer resist the desire to open it—this happened at the end. But I'm jumping behind and ahead of myself.

"You look like you want to."
"What?"
"You know."
"Know what?"
"You keep staring at it."
"At what?"
"You know."

"Know what?"

We're talking about the Secret—the white paper thing, the envelope sealed begging to be opened and resting on top of a jumbled-up pile of our bags and baggy clothes.

"You kidding?"

"I don't know what you're talking about."

The one asking questions was me, the envelope-maker, and the one most comfortable unanswering the questions, was Him, the Thief, who I was hopelessly entangled with until the envelope was opened. Now, we're no more, although the loving won't go.

I want to give away the end so badly, to tell the Secret, because the end was happening days before I arrived at an American-style coffee shop in Bandra, a mixed-class Bombay suburb. I referred to him as the Thief because it feels good calling him that now that the Secret is out. Sorry for the verb-tense-change issues there. My past is bleeding into my present. That's what happens when you break up. You revisit the past, and your grammar suffers.

Our final exchanges, jumbles of unclear statements and questions seeking clarity only to be complicated by more unclear statements. The slow faucet leak effect: conversation that drips, drips, drips—accumulating into messy nonsense. That's probably why the Thief got into the habit of rolling a joint to plug the leak of questions and unanswers spilling all over the bedroom floor toward the end. All the while I would keep plumbing with more precise questions to get him to answer me, as if all he was was an answer to my questions: "Can you tell me you haven't thought about opening it? Can you tell me that you haven't even touched it, or . . ."

"Mary, give it a break!"

"Give *me* a break. I saw you checking the envelope out. How'd it end up on top of that pile of clothes anyway?"

Long pause.

"Maybe it fell out?"

"Fell out? Fell out and up on to the clothes?"

"Dude, chill! Can you roll this for me?" I refused to roll his joint. So, his busy fingers focused before him, the Thief knelt down, smiled condescendingly, as if he actually knew I was thinking, "I've caught you." He's a mind reader, he is. A chubby-cuddly, forty-year-old, mind-reading thief, who, when he starts to drip all over the room with his question-avoidance skills, smiles condescendingly, beneath his thick chartreuse, plastic-frame glasses and above his graying, braided black beard.

I wish he didn't smell so good: natural peppermint soap mixed with grass, mixed with a little mansweat, mixed with me. Do you know what it's like to be with someone whose odor pulls you closer and closer until you recognize your own scent is already there? It makes you think, or at least it makes me think, things like, *Why can't we just drop the words and caress, savor, stare, inhale each other up, down, and all over, like we used to?*

It's probably mostly my fault since I was the one who'd sealed those words inside the envelope before leaving for India. How appropriate our affair should end with more words (these ones here), except of course, I write these out in the open, albeit for myself. Maybe one day, I'll sing and pluck my guitar well enough to share the feelings of my words. But at this moment, I write and wonder if someone else is receiving.

Unsung words are lonely.

The Beginning: Twitch and Bone
The Thief was born Darryl John Johnson. After second or third grade, he insisted on DJ, which killed the "John Johnson" fiasco his parents conceived. Lucky for him, his name change also decided his career, which is not something most eight- or nine-year-olds do: deciding what they want to be and then actually becoming it. I shouldn't give DJ too much credit, though. Luck was important. Of course, he's talented enough to make his living on the turntables, but luck was important. It's also how we met.

We? Oh, yes. I left out the Me in We. Isn't that curious when you forget yourself, but then suddenly, out of the blue, you remember yourself, as if you've become a space-ghost in someone else's star trekking? Being painfully in love, then separating, sometimes feels like becoming a space-ghost, because the living part of you remains in some other world, Hislandia, and you realize the other part of you doesn't quite matter in the way you used to.

A year ago, I thought I was a pretty happy dude living in San Francisco, running around and around and around and around, in size thirty-two leather pants and various flannel shirts. Basically, I was Numb. Numb was working a nine-to-five, calling himself by his given name, Alex Shelley, and hopping from bar to bar, and bed to bed, tricking with the tempting and the tacky, while trying to ease his way out of a long-distance, West Hollywood–Castro connection, as if something like that needs easing out of, that's how ready Numb was to beam off planet Earth the day before he met the Thief.

Then, my luck changed at a friend's party where DJ was DJ-ing. I glimpsed, for the first time, planet Hislandia, shrouded in Ginsbergian clouds, howling above oceans and continents of free love, pot, music, aglitter in the light of the constellation Nirvana and the Sixties nebula. In Hislandia, you wear day clothes in bed, eat vegetarian in bed, watch a lot of TV in bed, get stoned or trip in bed, laugh at horoscopes and double entendres in bed (probably piss and shit in bed if it was cool), and when you're done doing all that, you cuddle and make out in bed, until making out becomes a little 69, which can become, well . . .

After meeting up a few times, we got into the groove of making love while watching *The Simpsons* with me lying behind him, beside him, holding his barreled chest with one arm. We spooned, laughing at Harry Shearer's jokes, pitching a few of our own along the way as we shared a bowl. After the show, he'd zap off the TV and put on a CD mix, beginning with Roy Ayers or the like, and I'd yank off his T-shirt, stamped with some sort of one-word teaser like "Endurance" or "Explore," as he closed his eyes, our flesh moving in writhing undulation. My tongue tip danced over his tattooed torso, my lips teasing out the music trapped inside his gut, until he freed his song, low elephant ummmms and lusty gasps into the atmosphere. His vibrating bass voice, cascading bolts of subcutaneous, subatomic volts, shocking my nervous system, triggering twitches at first and then, finally, a bone straining the stitches of my size thirty-two leather pants. Jill Scott took over, and DJ hummed along, diddling my fly with his right hand, popping each button in four-four time, warming my instrument with his right hand now freed from its cold case. His left mitt massaged my pecs, then he'd pinch one nipple, twisting gently, then harder, exacting from deep inside, animal groans. Molded by his skillful fingering, I'd crescendo to guttural grunts, rising, then falling, my lust vocals the twitter scat to Miles Davis's *Sketches of Spain*, then John Coltrane's *Blue Train*.

He yanked my two hard heads with his two soft hands to pull me into him and him into me, too. Intuitively, our tongues tied, pink ribbons flapping in the currents of air passing between our lungs, and we tried gazing beyond the eye-to-eye to the Third Eye. The music dissipated inside my ears, unheard. His hands dropped and did a little dance to free his joystick, before we fell down sideways. His crotch odor drifted over and loosened lips. I breathed it in and breathed again, until he ordered, "Suck it." And he flipped me, smacking my ass. It's 2005, then it's 2000, it's 1990, 1980, 1979-and-a-half. "Go on, suck it." I slithered my piehole around Darryl John Johnson's Johnson, until I gagged as he slapped and slapped, disciplining the twitch of my crack. I started again and again as he, the rhythm master, gagged me, slapped me, gag, slap, gag, slap letting me breathe and go slow, gag, slap, pushing his pierced tongue along my glans. Nibble. Gag. Slap. Nibble. Bite. Gag. Slap.

"Not yet," he ordered, pulling away. "Lick my balls." He twisted onto his back, and pulled my thigh across his neck, until I was straddling my commander. My mouth slurped his hefty sac, my ass opened, diving back on his face—slurp, dive, slurp, slap, dive, dive again, gag, slap. He slipped the tip of his braided black beard inside his mouth, tickling my balls bouncing off his chin with his beatnik face fur. I laughed, tempted to chomp my molars down, but I grinned instead, gurgling, giggling. Slap. Slap. Slap. SMACK!

I stopped smiling.

"Get on your feet."

Flexing my meaty calves, I assumed the position, and he dripped slippery spit in his palm, rubbed some on my head, and with a different palm, he spit until the rubbing became his jerking us, in sync, at first nice and slow, and at last, he let go launching us to hyperdrive as our warp engines flowed, and all the while, my mouth roamed and roamed and roamed, until he exploded all over my neck. And I fired a long-ass multiload, over the giant gold Om medallion resting between both his collar bones.

On any particular day, we might have been cumming to Sonic Youth's *Goo* or Al Green's *Al Green Explores Your Mind*. But, I slowly ceased to notice. Over time, my field of perception gravitated toward Hislandia. I surrendered my twitch and bone to his stoner zone, abandoning my quest for an ideal "open relationship" I had sought for many years. Thereafter, everything my man did, everything he said, went to my heart and to my head, more and more, deeper and deeper, until I was always there, and I never wanted to come back down to Earth and its musical poets. I had discovered my own.

True or false: India is in Hislandia. If you said, "false," it's because you've never been connected to DJ. But because we were connected, which feels like truth, I'm told, I believed India is or was or had to be in Hislandia. Here's why:

My San Francisco friends started asking me, "What's the deal with you going to India, is it . . . ?" And I would stare at them incredulously, until they persisted, "Why there?" Even I recognized at the time that I could have hardly replied, "'Cause it's in Hislandia," though I did feel I should have adequately satisfied their curiosity. Instead, I usually offered a marathon explanation like, "Well, I'm dying to go somewhere other than New York or Europe, and India, well, because my sister's there. I mean, we were thinkin' of doin' some sort of cross-country *Zen and the Art of Motorcycle Maintenance thing* but then DJ and I, we talked about it, and we changed it to India."

"Ooo, Alex loves DJ . . . " they would mock me, laughing.

"C'mon! I'm doing this for myself, too. I finally got that car-accident-settlement check in, so why not travel? Sure, I want to do this with DJ. I could do this by myself but I wanted to share it. With him. And when I asked him if he was interested, he thought about it. Like I said, when we talked about taking some sort of trip, we started planning a cross-country trip, maybe making money with his DJ-ing at first, but we decided on India."

"Why not the road trip?" they used to ask.

"Buying a bike would've just eaten into the settlement check. Anyway, I called my sister, got DJ a plane ticket, changed mine, and now we're going over there."

Skeptically they'd ask, "And do what?"

"Nothing or everything. No plan. We're just going to hang out, and whatever happens, happens."

"Whatever happens, happens?"

"Well, we might go and try to get him to do some DJ-ing over there. But, who knows. Anyway, there's pretty much no agenda. I figure that if we can do this and pull it off, then we can do anything. He thinks so, too."

"And what're you gonna do when you get back?"

"Maybe we won't come back."

If it weren't for my buddy Gary, I would have left it all there, and DJ and I would've done the trip and whatever happened, would have happened, but I didn't, because Gary swaggered over and said to me in his low voice, "Alex, I love you, and I don't want to see you hurt. Can I offer some advice?"

"Shoot," I said cheerfully.

"Listen, I don't know DJ all that well, and frankly, you two haven't been going out that long. What, it's been four months? So, maybe you might think about ways of taking care of yourself, of Alex, before you leave, right?"

And maybe I should've been offended, maybe I should have made a case for adventure and lorded my love for DJ over my friend, but I kept silent, listening.

"Give yourself a little insurance policy, because you're quitting your job, right?"

"Yep."

"And breaking your lease?"

"Yep."

"Well, see that's it. All I have to say is, don't show up on my doorstep penniless, hungry, and homeless. Now wait. Before you react to what I'm sayin', hear me out. I hope it works out and you two find what you're looking for. Do you plan to stay in India?"

"Could happen."

"Well, if it doesn't, you need to have a plan. Do you even know his motives for going?"

And before I was able to speak, I realized I'd taken DJ at his word all along about wanting to go as lovebirds on a musical adventure, and giving everything our best shot. I didn't realize that I had taken him at his word because I lived in Hislandia, and in Hislandia you don't really reserve judgment, because, well, that would mean returning to Earth, And frankly, who really wants to live there?

"Well . . ."

"You want some advice?"

"Well . . ."

"Okay, listen. Search your heart, and try and see into the future. You're paying for the entire trip, right? Make a prediction of the worst thing that could happen, and reduce it to one sentence, write it down, seal it in an envelope and give it to him before you two leave but tell him not to open it and if he ever opens it, you two are over and he's on his own, then save as much of the rest of your money as possible. Are you taking the same plane over?"

"What're you talking about? I ain't crazy, just 'cause I think love is love. And I do." Making a little Aimee Mann reference felt right, right then.

Ignoring me, he asked, "Are you taking the same plane over?"

"They're one day apart. I leave first. Did you hear me, though?"

"You are paying for this whole trip for the both of you. In case something happens, then at least he knows you knew all along and that you weren't just being chumped. And this way, you give yourself an out to leave him in good conscience."

In good conscience? The last thing I was thinking about was conscience. I was in love. "And if he never opens it?" I asked, because why would he do that?

"If he never opens it, burn it when you both get back. And tell him you want to marry him in Maui. Or not."

I laughed but actually felt more afraid than humored. "And if he asks what it was that I burned?"

"Tell him it was—the past."

That night at a Castro bar, I thought it all over by myself and decided that whether I gave a sealed envelope to DJ or not, I would at least try and drum up a list of possible worst-case predictions on a cocktail napkin:

- "You're cheating on me."
- "You're taking too many chances with our safety."
- "You've abandoned me."

And I stopped there because I recognized my predictions revealed a pattern of me playing the victim, and I wondered, *What if my worst-case prediction isn't my being hurt, but me being ugly and hurting DJ?* So I wrote down on the other side of the same napkin:

- "I'm seeing someone better for me."
- "You're boring."
- "I need to focus on myself."

And I stopped there, because I recognized that regardless of who was playing the victim, they were all still "someone-done-did-someone-wrong" sentences. It dawned on me that whatever prediction I sealed in the envelope would likely lead to my paranoia or my temptation. For example, I thought, let's say we start arguing a lot, and I grow angrier and angrier, then I might go looking for evidence to prove "you are cheating on me," just as an example, mind you, to justify my feelings. And the envelope could then serve as an escape. The same would be true, I figured, if I wrote down, "I am seeing someone else": again, I thought, if we start arguing, then I might start seeing someone else to give myself an out, and, then, the envelope becomes true. I crumpled up the napkin and tossed it in a nearby trashcan.

I wondered, maybe, Gary's envelope idea wasn't meant to hide a specific "secret prediction" that might actually be a self-fulfilling prophecy in disguise. Instead, I decided the envelope represented secrecy itself. And then I saw that, if he reached the point where he actually opened it, instead of throwing it away, he would have reached the point where he was willing to do something I asked him not to do, which would have told me that he was unambiguously disconnecting. And I saw the wisdom of my friend's advice: the envelope wasn't an effect; it was a cause. Whatever else happened, opening the envelope was in and of itself the worst-case scenario.

So, I wrote my prediction down on a small piece of paper, locked it inside the envelope with blood-red wax, and stamped a seal with the letter "T." At the airport, I gave it to DJ just before I boarded my plane.

"Baby, I want you to hold on to this for me." I took out the sealed envelope and handed it to him, but he didn't accept it.

Chuckling, he asked, "What is it?"

"I want you to take it. Keep it. Don't open it."

"Wait, what? Why not?"

"Don't open it. Just keep it. If you open it, you open a can of worms."

"Dude, what is this, some sort of game? I don't play games."

I took DJ by the hands, stared straight into his eyes, and said, "Listen, this is important to me. You and I are looking into the future with our eyes wide open, taking some big risks. I need you to do this. Take it, keep it, and don't open it. Can you hold on to it for me? Please."

He met my gaze, communicating that he was concerned, vulnerable. He forced a reluctant smile and said, "Yes."

"And always remember that I love you," I affirmed, putting into his hands all of my hope. He then carefully folded and stuffed the envelope into his back pocket.

He sighed, then returned with, "I love you, too." As we embraced each other, I felt a little twitch and bone in my pants and wanted so badly to believe that the next time I would see him wouldn't just be halfway around the planet, but in Hislandia, maybe forevermore.

"DJ, I'll see you in a couple of days, baby."

"Two days." He smiled. "Have a safe journey. Love you." And we parted.

Forty-eight hours later he landed at the Bombay International Airport, and I greeted him with a deep kiss, causing a minor public scandal. Bearded fathers in kurtas scowled at us, and mothers and daughters held their children tightly to their stunning saris. I proudly took DJ's bags and lagged behind him while he walked ahead chatting with my sister. I spied the envelope, still sealed, peeking above the top of his back pocket of the tripped-out hippie pants he'd been wearing the day I left San Francisco.

The End: The End

Commitment. It's not a word easy for fags. But, for a lot of San Francisco's fags, *commitment* is a political word. And in Bombay, *fag* is a political word, too—fagotry is illegal there, Section 377 of the India Penal Code. Lots of parties and festivals, but no gay bars, no gay clubs and so queer love, committed or not, is mainly underground, like drugs and prostitution in most countries. Sure, there are Bombay activists, there are couples, but the family is the primary social arrangement mandated and supported by state, cultures, religions—which explains one of the obvious differences between Bollywood and Hollywood. Of course, you can overstate the differences between the two countries, but you can overstate the similarities equally. Romanticizing anti-colonialism only blinds you to the fact that Amitabh Bachchan and Asha Bhosle are as invisible in San Francisco as Ellen Degeneres and RuPaul are in Bombay even if there are people living in both cities who know all four stars. I'm just not one to romanticize politics. When it comes to romance, I skip over politics and head right for love. When it comes to politics, I get political.

But, what does "commitment" mean, even in San Francisco? For example, does it mean, oh, let's say, just randomly, exploring drugs and prostitution and avoiding "connection," which is what commitment ultimately is, if nothing else, right—communication, on one level or another, spoken or unspoken, poetic or therapeutic—connection? Sure, none of those things are inconsistent: drugs, prostitution, and commitment. They are only if you feel they are. And toward the end, my head was swirling with the anxiety that those things were becoming inconsistent in Hislandia.

The night before the end, it was a Tuesday, just as the first monsoon rains started outside, we were playing question-asker and question-dodger during what must have been our seventy-first drippy conversation. You know, the one like:

"You used to say you wanted to."

"What?"

"You know."

"Know what?"

"You know."

Long pause.

"Good night, DJ."

Except this time, it wasn't about The Secret that was resting on a pile of his own clothes, now separated from mine by about fifteen feet. This time, our leaky exchange was about opening the relationship we had agreed was indefinitely monogamous. I couldn't sleep. So, I took a long hot shower wishing I could rinse away my paranoid suspicions that his "Explore" shirt was no longer meant for me but for college-age Bombay dudes and chicks, groupies he had befriended that were in some sort of pseudo-underground witchy world of grass, hash, acid, X and bisexual, illegal Indian sex, and he was a DJ, more and more *their* DJ, and I was, well, I wasn't. And now, in his eyes, I was old, jealous, while all I wanted to do was dance the Hislandian dance. Connect to the man I loved.

After I finished my bath, I dried off, hating drippy words, my words, his words, any words, so much so I wanted to be plugged up, unable to use them. I woke DJ, pleading with him to stop me from wanting to talk to him and begging him to restrain my flesh and bones with whatever was available, so I could sleep, so he could sleep.

He pulled me to the bed with a reluctant, but ultimately willing, "Fine." He first tightly bound my ankles with a leather belt. Then, he secured my hands with another belt. Next, he took out two hankies, orange and white—the white one he used to blindfold my eyes. Finally, he stuffed a clean tube sock into my mouth, far enough in to keep me from using my tongue to push it out, and he secured my silence with the orange hanky, wrapped around my head.

"There. Sleep."

My anxiety abated, and I fell asleep after a while, for a few hours, until I awoke with DJs hands, reaching underneath my waist, pulling my shorts down. I felt his fingertip probe my pucker, as strands of warm spittle sprinkled down. A pause, and then my ears recognized a high-pitched squishing of some nearby tube. Another pause, and then he lifted my feet, dipping into my crack and teasing me with his slippery prick (I think it was sheathed), as I moaned into my cotton gag. It felt like what I wanted at that moment, some sort of release, from words, from the faucet leak, from boring, passionless uncommitment, when he decided to enter, quickly, deeply, slapping my cheeks once or twice, clearing his throat to the beat of his fucking. And that's what it was—he fucked me like I was his property. Fucked me for less than a minute, until he found release, too, without a grunt or a peep. It was the one and only time we fucked. Apparently, we had stopped making love before then, but I never got the notice. Anyway, he withdrew, disappeared for a few seconds, to clean up I imagined, and returned to free me.

Untied, I sat up, stretching my jaw, staring at my loose arms and legs, and he handed me what I thought was the envelope that I had given him before we left San Francisco. He walked away. I noticed it was opened.

My first feeling was that of victory. I'd submitted to submission, become his property, proving to him that I could transcend drippy words but that he was too selfish to recognize my selflessness. My humiliation had humiliated him, and he ran away. After the flooding of all those questions and unanswers, I suddenly felt warm and dry, confident he had caused the worst-case scenario. He now saw who he was: the Thief, who had stolen our trip for himself, who had stolen my heart and then fucked the temple that protected it, who had stolen our love to love his newfound fan base.

Then, I looked inside the real physical white #10 paper envelope, but I found it empty.

"DJ?" I yelled into the other room. "DJ?!"

"What?"

"What did you do with what was in the envelope?"

"Nothing."

"Nothing?"

"Nothing!"

Confused, I inspected the envelope more closely by reclosing it and saw a waxy "I" where the embossed "T" was supposed to be. It wasn't the same one he took from me in San Francisco. Or was it? Did I just falsely remember it as a "T" or did I mistake an "I" for a "T"? I let it go.

Later that day, I took off to the coffee shop and started to write down the muddled middle of this story, that appears at the beginning of this telling—the part with all my talk of DJ being the Thief and so on. I got back from my coffee trip, happy I'd found my own, selfish words again. But, he'd disappeared for the day, and so I took a break from writing to clean the bedroom. As I returned his belts, hankies, and sock to his pile, I happened upon the envelope with the "T."

I removed it and split the wax seal. I removed the paper, unfolded it, and read to myself the prediction I'd made months before: "No trust."

Some say I have returned to life in San Francisco, back on Earth, but I keep thinking I never even went to India because the whole time, I thought I was in Hislandia, where, it turns out, I may have never been. And now I don't know where I was or am at all, except somewhere beyond this end.

Coming Home

Dale Chase

Bellman has no home, and I sometimes envy him that. A journalist, he moves from country to country, living in hotels, writing in cafes, often amid the bloody events he covers. As a result I seldom see him but am always on the lookout for his byline.

If you put us side by side, we are the ultimate contrast, but I think, as with any match of opposites, that may be what makes it work. Both of us possess inquiring minds: me the stay-put version, quiet, academic, him the action figure who, if not at the center of things, is surely close by. I wonder if he ever envies me.

When he arrives, it's in a rush, which I like as it tears away the trappings of my life, substitutes his. For the few days he is in town, I exist around world events and deadlines, caught up in a pace that is foreign and therefore wonderful. The sex is equally frenzied.

He has been away five months this time—New York, Israel, Iraq. He calls me from the plane and I meet him at the airport. He is forty-six now, gray, handsome, brisk. He sweeps up to me and says, "Let's fuck." I laugh out loud.

In the car he keeps a hand on my thigh and does not talk. This is his most remarkable quality, the ability to quell himself in anticipation. He exudes sexual energy, and I know the first round will be frantic, one of those clothes-strewn, living-room-floor fucks that rip open my life. I navigate afternoon traffic with a hard-on.

We are soul mates. Both of us know this, but it remains unsaid because of the lives we have chosen to lead. At my Berkeley cottage he drops his bags—I'm always amazed how lightly he travels—falls to his knees, fishes out my dick, and starts to suck. Anticipation works against me; I shoot into his throat.

When he has swallowed my spunk, he releases me but stays down there playing with my spent cock. It makes me wonder what he does on the road. In homage to the journalistic stereotype, I allow that he fucks everything in sight.

He pulls down my khakis, gets in at my balls, then starts sucking them. He rubs his face into my crotch, and I hear his long inhale. Finally he relents but only to turn me, get at my backside where he pulls open my butt cheeks and starts licking my rim. I'm pulling on my dick. How could I not?

His tongue goes in, and I let out a cry. This is his thing; I won't lick ass for anyone. It makes him crazy, and I know he's in the stretch now. Sure enough, he rises, rips away every stitch while I do likewise. He retrieves condom and lube, and while I undress, he prepares himself. I get onto the floor, and he mounts me from behind, uttering a long moan as he goes in. Home at last. I always think the same thing.

He is rough, urgent, and I love it. The most sex I have in his absence is an occasional interlude with a fellow professor, a fuck buddy if you will, but Mark is never rough. Nor urgent, come to think of it.

Bellman pounds at me, and I listen to the sound of us, my living room alive with that glorious fleshy slap. He grunts as his climax nears, and when it hits I hear a strangled sound, wonderfully primitive. I think about what he's giving me, what he's spurting up my chute, and I love him for it. He shudders and finally quiets.

He flattens me, cock still viable, and we lie together. I like this part, him against my back, that furry chest of his. He doesn't pull out until his cock softens.

At last it's over, and he rolls off. We lie side by side on the rug. "Welcome home," I say.

He doesn't reply. I listen as he regains his breath. Finally he says he needs to sleep. "I'm so done," he adds.

I put him into bed. It is 4:00 P.M. but that doesn't matter as he is lost between two realities. I kiss his cheek, shut the door.

In the living room I put his laptop on the desk where he will use it as soon as he can once again navigate. It's an enemy of sorts, fueling him, which I like, but also stealing him, which I dislike. I have an early dinner, read a while, get into bed at ten. It is Friday and I am grateful for the rare synchronization of my life. Usually I have to call in sick when Bellman appears.

He does not allow himself to be held unless he's engaged in sex. He is not a cuddler. I lie on my side with the lamp on, gazing at him naked, covers pushed back. His snore is steady; he is not a quiet sleeper. He's not a quiet anything.

Age has not diminished him. He is absent the thickening I continually fight, his body lean, hard. His chest I find delightful, tit nubs buried in the fur. I reach over, rub one, and he murmurs but does not wake. The little thing gets hard. So do I.

I want him to get at me again. I want to go to sleep in that just-fucked state where nothing matters but the person who has done you. I reach for his cock, which causes him to stir, offer a languid thrust. Will he take me in his sleep?

His eyes remain closed, his breathing steady, even as I stroke his dick. It fills quickly, and when it is up, I fetch a rubber and lube, dress it, grease it. I grease my hole, too. Then I crawl over him, squat and descend, thrilling as the thing goes up me. At this Bellman opens his eyes. "Is it still today?" he asks.

"Yes."

He nods, looking wonderfully sleepy. "Lie still," I say. "I'll do the work. I can't resist you."

"Yeah," he murmurs.

I sit on him and simply clench my muscle, savoring the fact that he's inside me. I've got the cock I want, the man I want. He issues a drowsy moan as I start to rise up, then descend, a workout for sedentary thighs but I want it slow, sensual, lengthy. Over and over I feel him go up me. My eyes are closed, my mouth open. I am lost to him.

Periodically I settle, slowly grind my bottom against him. The first time I do this he groans, smiles. A bit more and he laughs. "C'mon, fuck," he says, and I resume my squats.

My dick is hard, flopping gently as I go up and down, giving myself a fuck or taking one really, stealing it from a man who welcomes thievery. I don't relinquish Bellman's cock until he utters an "oh shit," grabs me at the waist, and thrusts. He bares his teeth as he unloads, then issues a series of moans, ever quieter as things fade. He immediately goes soft. I climb off, remove the condom, fetch a warm cloth, and wash him. His eyes are closed but he quietly keens with the attention.

As he remains in his sleep-wake state and as I am quite hard, I crawl up to him and poke my cock at his cheek. He turns his head, opens his mouth, and when I enter he begins to suck. I can't help but thrust, which he receives well. It becomes a pure mouth fuck and drives me over in seconds. He takes my come, and when I am spent he continues sucking like a baby at a tit. Fixed on the knob, he pulls at me until at last I fall from his mouth. He's asleep now. I cover him, lie at his side, my arm against his.

I awaken alone on Saturday morning, find Bellman naked in the kitchen, cell phone at his ear. He's made coffee, sips as he listens. A notepad is on the counter, and he writes hurriedly. He looks at me, smiles, and for one brilliant second I allow myself to imagine this is reality, that he shares my life and we are a couple risen to the day. A familiar ache begins. I head for the shower.

I'm shampooing when he joins me. My eyes are shut and it's all by feel. His hands join mine, and I relinquish the task, touched by his washing my hair. It is perhaps the most intimate thing he has ever done. He guides me under the spray to rinse, and once this is accomplished, he stops to lick one tit then the other. I discovered early on that Bellman is a tit man and he attends mine until they are hard and red. His cock is up, but there are priorities. His fingers play with my nipples, squeezing and pinching. I've soaped my dick and stroke it because I cannot let it alone when he does this. When he starts sucking one tit and fingering the other, I spray come onto him, crying out with the release.

My climax does not deter him. He continues at my tits, then takes the soap and washes the poor abused things. The soap then descends to my crotch where he washes my dick and balls. I turn and he spends time at my bottom, runs the bar up my crack, puts a soapy finger into me. "Ah hell, let's fuck," he says and he gets out to find a rubber.

Back in, sheathed, he bends me, goes in, and we fuck until the water turns cold. He is in no rush this time and so we get out, get onto the little rug where he has me on my back. I love this position, legs high. His expression is mellow compared to last night, the urgency gone. Pleasure now, the first fuck of the day.

He looks down at our connection, watches what he's doing to me. I see it register on his face, that visual wallow we all crave. Then his eyes rise to mine and I get a glimpse of that other connection, the painful one that breaks my heart over and over. It is longing in the purest form, agony for me because it gives him to me at the same time it takes him away, reminding me that no matter how it looks he will not remain. I clench my muscle—what else do I have?—and he issues a throaty chuckle. I want to reach for him, pet his fur, but the position doesn't allow it. And then he's coming and it's all asunder. He cries out with this one, carries on, all the "fuck yeah" shit everyone does. Then he goes quiet, pulls out, blows a long breath as if he's used up everything. He tosses the rubber and hops back into the shower.

"It's gonna be cold," I remind him.

"I don't care."

The shower is brief. He emerges shaking himself out like a dog, not toweling his hair. He's gorgeous like this. He drops the towel, doesn't dress, and says let's eat. I cook him breakfast while he's on the phone.

He turns the thing off while we eat and I listen to his adventures. I ask questions that bring answers sometimes horrific. He has seen the worst of man but it does not scare him. Rather, I think it energizes him and this is something on which I refuse to dwell. He also tells me silly hotel stories. We laugh amid the carnage.

"How long do you have?" I ask during a lull, hating the answer before I've even heard it.

"Monday."

"So we have the weekend."

For most couples this means a day trip or at least dinner and a movie. For us, the non-couple, it is the opposite. Even with two days we do not leave the house. Between long bouts of sex, Bellman acquaints himself with his surroundings, as if he's never been here before. I think it's his way of reminding himself lives like this do exist and that he is allowed inside. He fingers my books, standing naked at the wall of shelves, but he does not take down a volume. I know his books are in storage at his mother's house in Los Angeles. There is no way I could live like he does, without my personal library, and yet without them there is such freedom because books tend to ground a person. I know I will never move from this place. The task is beyond comprehension, and that is precisely why Bellman's hotel life has its appeal.

He always asks what I'm reading or rereading. "Trollope," I say.

He reads mostly non-fiction while he's on the road, devouring books on planes then leaving them behind, stuff on the political situation, social issues, the mess that is life on the larger scale.

"You should try it sometimes," I offer. "There is nothing like another era for escape."

"You have to go that far?"

"These days, yeah."

We differ politically, me a liberal, him a wounded conservative now reconsidering. We rarely discuss politics.

Saturday afternoon we are on the sofa playing with each other in an unhurried state. Lying splayed together, I fondle his balls while he puts a finger up my butt, prods gently. It's a kind of interlude, not foreplay, just play. We often do this, connecting the only way we know. Sex will be later. For now we just want to touch the good parts.

"How long are you planning to teach?" he asks out of nowhere.

Surprised, I have no immediate answer. I'm fifty and have never considered retiring. I like my life as it is. "No idea," I tell him.

"You don't think about moving on?"

"Do you?" I say, realizing the question isn't about me.

"I start thinking I've maybe seen too much, like a fighter who starts to worry about losing before he gets into the ring. Not a good sign."

"Too much what?"

His finger finds my prostate, and I wince. He withdraws, gathers lube, puts two fingers up me, and starts in again. I squirm, forget the conversation.

Time gets lost while Bellman is around. There is no need of it. He suffers jet lag, and I go along. We sleep when we want, which may or may not be at night. This day we fuck at dinner time, end up eating at ten. We've been naked all day. He has no compunction about nakedness, even in the kitchen. I make omelets and toast while he sits watching.

"I've been offered a job editing a travel magazine in San

Francisco," he says. I'm flipping an omelet, and I tear it; cheese runs into the skillet. "Shit," I say, attempting repairs with my spatula.

"What?" he asks.

"The omelet, it tore."

He laughs. "Then scramble it. Who cares anyway?"

"I care."

I continue with the meal, knowing I should reply to his statement, afraid to do so. What am I supposed to do, hope? When I'm seated across from him at the table, he asks if I heard him before.

"Yes," I say, buttering toast.

"And? What do you think?"

I look at him then, this man I adore, and try to hold it all in check because I'm not sure it can be rounded up again once it's been set loose. I work toward objectivity. "How would that be after all the adventure?" I ask.

"Adventure is not all it's cracked up to be. Gets old after the first twenty years."

"Has it been that long?"

"I got my first overseas assignment at twenty-six."

I have never asked him who he has loved. Surely a man cannot go twenty years untouched but I cannot bring myself to approach the subject. "So you've maybe had enough?"

"Maybe."

"You'd have a fixed address," I offer. He chuckles.

"You could get your books out of storage," I add.

He goes quiet at this, concentrates on the meal. "This is good," he says. "Lots of cheese."

He loves extra sharp cheddar, and he loves chocolate milk and iceberg lettuce. Tomatoes only if they are the reddest red. Raw potatoes. Beethoven. Old movies. I want to cry.

It is 3:00 A.M. when we crawl into bed. Lying side by side in the dark he asks, "You think I could do it, the nine-to-five routine?"

"Nothing has ever stood in your way," I tell him. "Why should routine? You know, it gets a lot of bad press but actually settling down can be pretty good, having a place to go to each day, a place to come home to." I want to add "a person to come home to" but am afraid to go that far. He sighs; we sleep.

I spend Sunday dreading Monday because I am certain it was all just talk. I'm after him early for sex, waking him by sucking his cock. I keep at him until he grabs at mine, and we suck one another until we let go seconds apart, then fall back asleep. The next is him crawling onto me hours later, hard cock poking at my butt. He's already sheathed and lubed. All that's left is to get in. No foreplay, no how-de-do, he pulls me open and shoves in. I'm lying flat and he's going at me with the old urgency. He's issuing little cries as if he's been ready for hours. His strokes are short and quick, the kind I've seen in primates at the zoo. Frantic, his voice rises, and he cries out, pumping furiously. It is not your typical climax. When he finishes, he pulls out, rushes to the bathroom, and slams the door. There are sounds. Is he throwing up?

He is pale when he returns. He slumps onto the bed, shoulders rounded as he sits with hands between his legs. "What is it?" I ask, realizing as soon as I speak that I may not want to know. Compassion running into the path of caution, damn it to hell. He shakes his head, gets up, brushes his hair, looks at himself in the mirror, then comes back to bed and lies down. I am up on one elbow and he takes my cock in hand, pulls on it, and sighs. It's not the answer, I want to tell him, but I allow him to roll me over so he can get his face down where it doesn't belong. As he parts me and licks, I wonder if he'll reach a conclusion before Monday or if he'll force himself back into a life that may not fit any longer. His tongue's in now and he's back there making all kinds of slurping sounds. No way he could fuck. He's working himself up to something else.

When he relents it is only to change from tongue to finger. He probes and prods, works me steadily, lies beside me but keeps the digit going. Time is lost to us.

When I become dry I tell him to add lube but he simply withdraws. Then it's just him and me. "It's okay," I say after a while. "You can be like the rest of us, you'll do just fine, and think of what you'll be bringing to the magazine. Topflight journalist who has seen the world, experienced life as few do. You'll always have that."

"How long have I been coming here?" he asks.

I quickly calculate. "Six and a half years. Since that talk you gave at the Herbst Theater. Remember, the panel on Vietnam? I felt like a groupie."

"How do you do it, me dropping into your life then dropping back out for months?"

"One time it was a year."

"God, really?"

"I wouldn't have missed a minute," I tell him. "You bring me a passion that is immense, an energy, a force, and a big dick."

He issues a short laugh. "A force," he muses. "What happens if I stop?"

"You're still you whether it's in some foreign country or at a desk in San Francisco. You stop sometimes when you're out there, don't you?"

"Not really."

It is later when we take up this conversation again. In the interim I suggest a bath and we lie together in the tub for hours, fucking first, me lying atop him with his cock up me, enjoying the floating sensation as he does it easily, gently. He plays with my tits the whole time and it is as he does this that I make the great leap, willing at last to be hurt beyond repair. "You know I've always loved you."

"Yes," he says, and as if to deflect the need to reciprocate, he begins to thrust in earnest and splashes out a good come. After that he works me until I care about nothing else, spurt gobs onto the water where they float around us like little islands.

He gets to his finish when he starts to pack that night. Still naked, he's already secured the laptop and has the suitcase half full. It lies open on the bed and I find him staring into it. I approach from behind, circle my arms around his chest, tweak a nipple. He chuckles. "You don't have to go," I say. "Stay with me. Stay."

He pushes back at me, rubs his butt against my dick and I know he'll fuck rather than decide and I can't let that happen. Time has returned.

I turn him to me but hold him at arm's length. "Decide," I say. "Make a decision. We'll fuck either way, but you can't go on like this, and neither can I. Six and a half years of not waiting, not allowing what I want most. So it's over if you leave. I've come too far this trip to go back to what it was. I want you here with me always. Let's be the couple you know we are. I love you, Larry. I love you."

He's breathing hard, like he's still fighting it, thrashing around inside.

"You wear yourself out when it's really so simple," I explain. "Tell me yes, you'll stay. Let yourself go. Let yourself feel for once."

Tears are in his eyes and I can hold off no longer. I take him into my arms and it is probably the first nonsexual embrace we've known. He shudders in my grasp. "I do love you," he finally manages and I can hear him holding back the crying but that's okay.

"You'll stay?" I ask.

"Yeah. I'm done with it all."

I hold him awhile longer then take him to bed where I lie on top kissing and humping until our cocks are up. When he rolls me off it is onto my side. He gets in behind, enters, and we lie doing it quietly.

The Best Sex Between Them

Andy Quan

They know that they shouldn't. But the things that we know don't always help us.

"Would this be all right?" Geoffrey looks at Max searchingly.

"It's up to you." Max looks neither happy nor sad.

"Why is it always up to me?"

They step towards each other, not without hesitation, and kiss.

Sex had never been great between Geoffrey and Max. Their physical attraction to each other had been, but it didn't seem to translate to the right chemistry. Geoffrey may have been in his forties but his body was boyish and thin with soft skin and barely a hair on his torso. For Max, it was a perfect combination of the sex appeal of wisdom and a fantasy of a young university student.

Max, on the other hand, was thick: solid neck and shoulders, a jutting chest covered with salt-and-pepper hair, and barrel-shaped thighs.

"You make my throat dry," Geoffrey told Max the first time they had sex. He was often given over to extravagant statements; he was an ad man who wanted to write novels.

The words didn't make sense to Max but the context did. Kissing was good. In fact, it was excellent: the shape of their mouths a perfect match; they would take turns naturally, licking the outside gums of the other, sucking on the other's tongue, nibbling the other's bottom lip. They lost themselves in that motion.

But the first weeks, unusually, Max couldn't come. He couldn't explain why, but he liked Geoffrey so much that it made him nervous. It short-circuited the simple order of being aroused, sexual play and a burst of semen from the tip of one's cock.

"You don't mind, do you?" asked Max, and Geoffrey admitted that if this is the way sex was going to be between them, that it might be a problem.

"I like some sort of equality. It's not just about me wanting you to come. It's that I think you'll be more satisfied if you've had an orgasm, too."

"But I don't mind."

Max was telling the truth but Geoffrey was unconvinced.

Geoffrey pulls up Max's rugby shirt and balances it up onto the shelf of Max's chest while he takes a great mouthful of the body that is revealed. He licks and softly bites Max's pectoral muscles, these broad, round shapes. If they were vessels, they would be made of metal, thick-walled, and unable to be easily lifted when filled with water. A great chest has always been an obsession of Geoffrey's. Will he ever again find one as beautiful as this: one you can grab onto, that makes you think of strength, and makes your cock stand out sharp as a salute? They stay like that for a time before Max reaches up and lifts off his shirt completely, then reaches down and eases Geoffrey out of his. It's already unbuttoned so Max eases Geoffrey's arms back, pushes gently at the fabric of the business shirt, and it wrinkles down onto the floor, Geoffrey's mouth never having lost contact with Max's chest.

The problem of orgasm (or lack of one) didn't last but instead changed into something else. It was Geoffrey this time, and at first he thought it was mental. It was the first time that his combination of antiretroviral therapy was failing, and though his doctor advised him not to overworry, he found it an impossible state, like failing to clear your mind when meditating because you are thinking the whole time about clearing your mind. So Geoffrey thought it was stress that was causing a pronounced lack of sexual drive. But after weeks, when the doctor assured him that the new medication regimen was working, he wondered if the dip in his libido could be due to his new meds.

He knew that Max was frustrated, and he knew that only months into a new relationship was not a good time to draw away from sex. But he couldn't seem to do anything about it. He and Max would masturbate together; they would kiss, too. But the level and intensity of lovemaking was underwhelming.

When they came back—desire, energy—the problems were resolved only for a time. It was like a singer who didn't have time to warm his vocal chords properly before a performance. He sings his way through stumblingly but the orchestra plays its final notes before he can find his way. They were never in sync.

"Have you talked about it?"

Geoffrey was seeing a counsellor. He'd never done it before but he'd worried about things not working with Max. He didn't want to quit therapy unless he knew he'd put in a good effort. He was too old to give up too easily and a relationship that had only lasted a year seemed trivial. Plus he couldn't be certain that the problem wasn't something deep-seated and invisible to him but an issue that came from him rather than being mutual.

"Well, what would you like him to do? Really. Is there some situation that you can describe, some way that you would like him to be when you're having sex?"

He liked this counsellor. He liked the questions, which poked and prodded and made him think and talk or come to sudden revelations like this one:

"I'd like him to take charge. I'd like him to throw me onto the bed and make love to me instead of me making love to him." Geoffrey thought about big, strong Max: the odd juxtaposition of his size, and his gentle disposition. Was he hoping for something that Max just couldn't give?

Max has closed his eyes. Geoffrey is still working on his chest. It's a long foreplay before they'll get to crotch level. Geoffrey treats it as a separate sexual act, as if sexual orientations were divided into a much wider spectrum than homo, hetero, and bi, and he's discovered that there are only certain men with chests he can make love to. It helps when they are broad (just like it helps, frankly, to have a large penis) and it also depends on the shape and size of the nipples. Small and flat doesn't really work; the mouth glides over them, there's nothing to bite, there's little to differentiate them from the surrounding skin. What works is jutting. What works is fleshy. Of course, Geoffrey has also met men who have the perfect chests for worship but aren't interesting in participating, being focused on other body parts, other motions, or being the active partner. With Max, Geoffrey's pretty much found nirvana. He can make patterns of his soft bite marks on Max's chest, the hairs of the chest brushing over Geoffrey's lips like a comb. He can suckle for long minutes the round coins of flesh with small fingertips pointing out of them, protrusions just large enough to nibble, to inhale. He licks and nips at them until the whole area of these parts of Max's chest has turned the pink of roses.

It's a blow job of a different type but has a similar effect on Max, a direct pleasure circuit between what is happening on the surface of his pectoral muscles and the tip of his penis, out of which pre-cum is forming, enough to coat its head but not enough to actually form a drop that falls onto the floor. If Max could ask for more, he'd ask to be bitten harder, a real clamp-down. But Geoffrey seems too afraid to do it. He backs off just when things are getting good. Still, Max's cock is hard with blood. He's responding to pleasure.

Geoffrey can feel this pleasure in the grip of his hand and is excited by it. The thought comes to him (which he loses, purposefully, moments later) that this may be the most magnificent chest that he's ever made love to and that he may never be able to do it again.

Sex was easy, Geoffrey told himself, though the truth was that it was plentiful, but not simple. Still, it could be found in saunas and sex clubs, in cruising grounds, in the locker rooms of swimming pools and gymnasiums. But someone to fall asleep with, someone to lie beside, and someone whose arms in which you can awake—how often do you find that? Geoffrey thinks that he's found quite a lot of sex in his forty-some years. But partners have been few. *Trade-offs,* he thinks. *Everything is a trade-off.* In this case, the items are sleeping together and having good sex. If he was challenged on this, he would have to back down. They did have sex. They sometimes had good sex. Sex and sleeping together were not opposite things. In fact, they were quite complementary. So, he would have been forced to clarify: in this relationship, what was important to him was waking up in Max's arms, the intimacy of shared sleep, falling asleep to his partner's breathing. Really hot fucking wasn't something that could be expected or demanded. Maybe, in the end, it wasn't even that important. At least that's what he told himself.

The pre-cum is flowing for both of them now, Max more than Geoffrey. They've rimmed each other, then Geoffrey has inserted one, then two fingers into Max and is now feeling the smooth walls of the rectum while his other hand plays with the hair on Max's belly.

They'll return to habits soon. For Geoffrey, it will be to lie on his back, with Max kneeling over him with his balls positioned over Geoffrey's mouth. Geoffrey will suck and lick and look up at Max's great form: the most beautiful view of a man, Geoffrey thinks. If he's not careful, Geoffrey will come right then, Max's hand reaching back to jerk him off. But he'll be able to restrain himself enough to slide his body and head down, one last suck on Max's balls, a lick of his arsehole. Then, he'll flip himself around and get up, push Max down onto his hands and knees and fuck him slowly while reaching around and massaging his belly, especially between his belly button and crotch, the way that Max likes and requested the first time they fucked.

They will feel delicious and comfortable that they know each other's bodies, customs, and fantasies so well.

It was Max who was frustrated with the sex. But it was Geoffrey who decided to end the relationship.

"Are you happy with this?" he'd asked angrily one morning. They'd snarked at each other for days.

"No, I'm not," replied Max.

"Then you'd better figure out what you want out of this."

But that was the problem. Max didn't know. He was in love with Geoffrey—frustrating, crazy-making, annoying Geoffrey—and that was enough. He didn't demand the future. He didn't want something out of it. The present was enough to deal with, with its imperfections and lopsidedness.

Though Geoffrey didn't exactly know what he wanted, either, he knew from the weight felt across his shoulders, that he didn't want this.

Geoffrey is an awkward bottom, sometimes finding it hard to relax, unable to be penetrated if a cock is too thick or too long. So he has always marveled at how open Max is, how relaxed and flexible his anus is. Not only that but his flexibility in general. Such a big man, but he can lift his knees up so they touch his shoulders and then even stretch his legs out nearly straight from there.

The condoms are out. A wrapper falls away easily. Lubricant is pumped onto a palm and then smeared onto latex, and onto skin. Geoffrey enters Max easily in one plain motion, simpler than speech, quicker than argument. The slight friction between their body parts creates heat like swallowing a mouthful of whiskey.

He fucks him for a while in Max's favourite position, kneeled over with Geoffrey's hand on his belly. But this time, they're really going to make it last, they'll fuck as long as they can, as hard as they can—in no particular order:

lying on bed from the side, one of Max's legs lifted and resting on Geoffrey's shoulder;

standing, Max's right hand balancing against the corner of a wardrobe for balance, Geoffrey behind him, his hands on each side of Max's shoulders, thrusting;

Geoffrey lying on his back, Max on top facing him, leaning down occasionally to kiss.

Like a concerto that returns to the theme of its opening bars, they return to their first tableau: the same action and postures. Max squeezes all of the muscles inside of him, like holding in laughter. He feels his sphincter and anus constrict around Geoffrey's cock. Geoffrey gasps and moans at the same time.

It's as good as it's ever been. Why couldn't sex have been as unencumbered when they were together? Geoffrey is free of a dozen worries and a dozen insecurities—among them: Do we always have to do it the same way? Do I always have to be the top? Am I enjoying this? Worst of all but perhaps hidden, even to Geoffrey himself: If it's good, really good, does it mean that we should be together forever?

Max feels the same liberty and joy. Gone is the worry of whether Geoffrey loves him as much as he loves Geoffrey. Of whether Max is attractive enough. Or whether he is truly the ideal lover that Geoffrey wanted. He's happy, so very much so, to fall into the motion of truly great sex; that Geoffrey is not holding back; that there is force in these thin but strong arms, grabbing him and making him into an object of pleasure.

They shouldn't really be doing this in any case, this forbidden act of sleeping with one's ex, of making the messy messier, of complicating *matters considerably and doing what all your friends say you shouldn't do. Breaking taboos can cause even more excitement. Not that they'll do it again—in different ways, they both know that. It makes this last time all the more sweeter.*

It was just a visit to pick up the last of his possessions, but Geoffrey senses that he won't return. He doesn't feel sad but there's an empty, unreplied feeling, like wandering into the entranceway of a run-down old home and calling out to see if anyone is there.

With some difficulty, he opens the front door to leave Max's apartment building. His hands are each carrying a few large plastic bags, and on top of this he's balancing a small box of miscellanea. He manages to put it all into his car then frets—*there he goes again*—turning circles in his mind:

Will what they did make it harder to be . . . friends? Is that what they'd be? Cordial ex-boyfriends? In contact?

Yes, he decides, it will make things more difficult. But—his heart beating fast and at an erratic pace—it was worth it. Well worth it.

Max doesn't think as much, or at least, he pretends not to. There are things that he's putting out of his mind already: the lead-up, the background story, the dialogue. It won't happen right away, but eventually he'll be left with just memories of the physical act and the windstorm of emotions that accompanied it. Now, he remembers Geoffrey's head, the dead weight of it, on his right side on top of where his chest and stomach meet, resting on his torso after this last sex, this best sex they've ever had. He knows that it's ridiculous but honestly it feels like there's still an indentation there, as if in a down pillow after a deep, motionless sleep. It will take time to fill in again, for his body to regain form.

A Start in Life

Lou Dellaguzzo

The chess board has a shiny surface. Pieces seem to float. Billy watches Hal and John play. The two men are locked in serious combat—although they hardly move, except to down their drinks and munch on burgers.

Wet blond hair clings to the boy's square head, curls around his prominent ears. He wears a baseball cap in reverse. When the twenty-year-old tries to right his horned rimmed glasses, they slide back down his slender, upturned nose.

"Pass the ketchup please?" Billy asks.

Both men scowl. Hal grabs the bottle and slides it over to Billy. "Anything else?" he asks, gesturing towards the other condiments lined along the restaurant window.

"No thanks," Billy whispers. "I'm good."

"Not if you keep interrupting," John kids, nudging the boy's leg with his massive calf.

Billy looks down at the chess board—on which nothing has happened in the last three minutes. Hal plays white. With a jittery hand, he moves a pawn to claim John's second bishop. The advance doesn't calm Hal. He shakes his leg like a motorized Lay-Z-Boy. Billy doesn't like sitting next to the edgy, short-tempered man. But he hasn't any choice. Across from him, John's muscular frame dominates a banquette meant for two. He has short blond hair and a broad, Slavic face turned pink by too much booze.

Tall and thin by contrast, Hal encroaches less. Billy likes how the man's black hair tumbles over a wide, pale brow, points to sharp features. Terse lips. Like some brooding film actor from the fifties.

"Got a problem?" Hal asks. His brown eyes squint.

"No," Billy answers.

"Then quit staring; it breaks my concentration."

"Sorry," Billy says, and plants his eyes on his food.

Man, what a creep, he thinks. *It's just a friggin' game.* As he munches on a french fry, he imagines swiping every piece off the chess board.

Hal rolls his shoulders. Tension pricks his neck like a thorn. He has four highly mobile pieces left on the board to protect his king and win the game. John's beleaguered monarch has but two remaining pawns. Hal keeps them on the defensive. The endgame looks good; his next move, decisive. He hopes. Usually Hal takes a nonchalant attitude when playing chess. But so much rides on this one game. His heavy debt to John, wiped clean.

If he can mate.

Should Hal lose, he'll have to work overtime the remaining summer. That means getting up early to help John's crew in the small mattress supply shop before making his deliveries. Hal's usual job. In addition to the nightly clean-up. If he wins, Hal won't mind that Billy will have to stay with him a while. Until the kid can get his bearings. At the last minute, John added Billy to the money bet. *Leave it to John. He'd have a hook in it somewhere*, Hal thinks without rancor. He likes his boss, owes John more than money.

Besides, the kid looks like he'll make a good, convenient lay, should things develop along those lines. No pressure. None needed.

Hal thinks boys like Billy want a daddy. Hal was such a boy himself. And John swears the kid's trustworthy: "Billy only lacks direction, like plenty guys his age."

Hal can sympathize. At thirty-eight, he's still trying to find his way. He enjoys a peripheral view of the lithe blond.

No. Hal won't mind sharing his bed with handsome Billy for a time.

When he got out of prison two years ago, no one else in his hometown would give Hal a chance. Only John. Two counts of armed robbery tend to scare off prospective employers—no matter how long ago the crimes occurred, how much time was served in payment. Eighteen years. That's more than enough.

Meanwhile Billy wishes he were back at John's place, all settled in. But making small talk, marching through the spacious house for a final check, John never really looked at Billy. Not eye to eye. It came as no surprise when the man said, "There's been a change of plans. Take your bags with you," as the two got ready to leave for the restaurant. "Don't you worry," John had assured, patting the young man's shoulder.

Sure; don't worry.

No explanation. No apology.

The boy didn't object. He never questioned why he couldn't stay with John as the man had offered—for the second time—only last week. (John was drunk on both occasions.) Billy got his bags ready, just as he did earlier that night, after his father kicked him out over a minor infraction contrived on the spot. The boy had placed his stockinged feet on the new sofa. He had to go.

Now Billy stares across the table at John and wonders why he believed the man. *You never asked me to spend the night even once*, he thinks. Not once in the year they'd been hooking up every week or so. Whenever Billy wanted a gentle bear to fuck him, offer reassurance about his hazy future.

"I think this game's over, buddy," Hal announces. He slides his white knight between his bishop and the black king, hemming in the doomed monarch.

"Son of a bitch." John laughs. His small blue eyes disappear in a wide smile; his breath's a boozy mist. "You got no respect for your boss, do you?"

Hal's win appears authentic, hard earned. But John had full control from the start, including the coin toss he faked to give Hal an opening advantage. John practically directed his opponent's moves. If Hal really knew chess, he'd recognize how unlikely it is to mate with a knight as he'd done.

Three grand in one game. John shakes his head in mock dismay and continues to work on his burger. He doesn't feel like a loser. Often he thought to forgive the remaining debt Hal incurred setting himself up with an apartment, some decent furniture. No one in the shop works as hard as Hal. And for less. Still, it's fortunate John withheld his debt forgiveness. Now he can get the kid off his hands without leaving Billy stranded. *You couldn't cope*, he thinks, smiling at the thin, clueless youth. *Hal will be good for you. Toughen you up.*

"It's a correspondence course," Billy says. Rain pelts the car. The steady, humming sound reminds him of his mom's old sewing machine.

Hal drives his station wagon like a timid senior citizen. Last week, he almost got a ticket. A motorcycle cop claimed he'd rolled past a blinking red light. Hal had to take a sobriety test. It was minor bullshit, but the encounter had spooked him. Hal has at least ten more years of probation to go. So long as he doesn't screw up.

"How can you learn commercial art through a correspondence course?" he asks.

"I get an assignment with instructions. And some finished examples. When I'm done, I mail it in. The teacher critiques my work—and sends me more stuff to do."

"Sounds pretty lame to me. A real gyp."

"It's already paid for," Billy mumbles. "And thanks a lot for your support." He's sorry he brought up the subject to make himself appear more substantial.

Before his mom died, he signed up for the course. Desperate, she supported the idea. Anything to get Billy out of his two-year withdrawal from the world after he graduated high school. After the car accident that summer. His three friends dead; Billy in the hospital for a month. He wasn't the driver. But he refuses to get behind the wheel again. And his license has lapsed.

Hal sounds much like Billy's dad did after he saw the canceled check for the correspondence course. The man harped about it for weeks. He called Billy an idiot to throw good money away on a scam. "You better shape up or ship out," his dad warned, tired of seeing Billy mope around the house, drifting through a stream of part-time jobs in downtown Jersey City, just for pocket money.

"You want to be an artist?" Hal says. "Take some courses at a community college. They're cheap *and* good. I took some in prison. Only remedial stuff—English and math. We had teachers come to *us*. Part of an extension program for inmates. Shit, man—you wouldn't catch me at home waiting for the mail to arrive if I could go to school. Wouldn't find me at home, *period*."

Billy doesn't say anything. But Hal senses a big change, as if Billy had opened his window, let in a blast of hot, wet air. Hal's intended effect. He wants Billy to understand he's not a guy to mess with. This way, Hal won't find anything missing from his place. He won't come home to see kids high, lying on the floor in a stupor—a problem he had with Jack before Hal kicked him out, slapped the kid around a little as a warning, in case Jack made a second set of keys. Hal won't change his locks over some hopped-up twink.

"And you should learn to drive," Hal says for the second time that night, buzzing from an overload of booze and nervous, not wanting further encounters with the law. Hal got annoyed when Billy said he never learned how. Billy always lies about it. He wants to avoid any mention of the accident. He never speaks about it.

The hallway in the three-family house, painted mahogany and badly lighted, has a narrow staircase. It spirals and creaks. "Keep it down," Hal orders, annoyed with Billy's heavy tread. "You'll wake up the nutcase downstairs from me."

"Okay," Billy says, his foot landing on a strident wooden plank. "Nutcase?"

"Shhhh," Hal hisses. Halfway up the flight, he realizes Billy doesn't follow. "What's the matter now?"

"Quit it," Billy says

Hal can't see the kid's face, but knows he's turning teary. "Quit what?"

"You know. Treating me like this. Like I'm shit. You gotta stop it. I'm afraid to breathe even. If you don't quit—I'm gonna leave." Billy hopes he doesn't have to make good his threat. Hal lives in a pretty tough neighborhood in Elizabeth, close to the Newark airport. *And where could I go?* Billy wonders. His soggy dungarees and T-shirt hold back his sweat, overheating him. He'd like to tear them off, throw them in Hal's face.

"Calm down. I'm tired, a little drunk," Hal says, by way of apology. With one large hand, he beckons Billy to follow, the way an impatient parent gestures to a straggling child. Not much conciliation there, but Billy grabs it. "That's better," he says, causing Hal to chuckle, appreciating the kid has his dignity to maintain. *Give the guy a break*, Hall tells himself. *He ain't Jack.*

"Why not?" Billy asks when Hal says he can't take a shower.

"It's too late; the shower pipes make noise—like little hammers tapping. The guy downstairs will go ballistic."

"I'm so hot." Billy can't wait to get out of his damp clothes—only to get wet again so he can cool off. All the windows in the kitchen and living room are open. "Could you turn on the air-conditioning?"

"Don't have it," Hal says. "This old place never was wired for it. Anyway, air-conditioning gives me the sniffles."

Billy shrugs. "Can I wash up some—brush my teeth?"

"Of course. Use the sink; it's quiet." Hal goes to the bathroom closet. "Here's a washrag and towel." His gaze lingers until Billy looks away. "Don't spill water all over the rug," Hal says, thinking of Jack, the mess he frequently made.

Like a sponge, the claustrophobic room swells with heat, sucking up breathable air. Billy forgoes his privacy, opens the creaky door wide. A small breeze visits. Heavy with moisture, it rolls into the room, a reluctant wave.

He stares at the basin mirror. Scrubbing too hard, he tries to project some future for the skinny kid he sees there. Worry glazes his round, gray eyes. An ashy color rings them. His curly blond hair has dried into a bird's nest around his pale, square face, along the graceful neck men like to kiss while on top of him, midway through their lovemaking—before their pace quickens, their gentleness ends. In the humid air, Billy's naked body glows white. His mind races with questions like: *What's gonna happen to me? What'll I do with my life now?* He feels so ill prepared for independence.

Since he can't project a future, Billy races back to his past, tries to *re*imagine it as he has done for two years. In daydreams. But he hasn't the energy to resurrect the dead again, provide all concerned a happy life, himself included. He can't even conjure the faces of his three friends—before the accident burned them away. No transient relief in make-believe. Not tonight.

"Where'd ya get those?" Hal points to an elaborate web of tiny violet starbursts that brand Billy's back. He got the scars after being thrown from the car, before it crumpled against an overpass support. Billy lay on a blanket of shattered bottles hurled from the overpass. The glass punctured his skin as bolts do leather, his blood diluted, carried off by a steady rain that pounded the roadside. Hidden under his thick, long hair, more starry embossments decorate his scalp.

Billy has one foot hovering over the basin. His naked back faces Hal. Cold water flows between his toes. They're slightly swollen—pink—from wearing wet shoes all night.

"Close the door, would ya?" he says, more like an order. "Please," he adds, deferential now—though he's losing patience with Hal's persistent rudeness. "I'm almost done."

"Sure, kid. I mean—Billy." For the first time, Hal uses his guest's name. Tired as he is, Billy notices. He looks again at Hal's reflection. The man's brown eyes—softer, less guarded than they've been all night—crease in an awkward grin. "No hurry," Hal says.

"I'll try not to be any trouble," Billy says, damned if he'll thank the man again for letting him stay. "Give me the house rules in the morning. I promise to live by them." He turns around, towels his foot dry before slipping it into a red shower sandal. His legs glisten with moisture. Wrapping the towel around his waist, Billy says, "I can cook." He wants Hal to know he has some practical talents to contribute. "And I'm good around the house. Can fix things like clogged drains, faulty electrical switches. My dad's a professional handyman. If you ever get an air-conditioner," Billy jokes, "I can fix that, too."

Hal's face reddens. "That ain't gonna happen," he says, exiting the small bathroom. *I'm gonna be walking on eggshells all the time*, Billy thinks. In his tired mind, eggshells turn into glass shards. Unlike his sponge bath, the image cools his body.

Mostly everything in the bedroom is blue. The walls, a pale azure; the bed clothes and curtains, teal plaid. In their cobalt frames, drawings of nude men and women hang from the walls. Even the night light beside the bed has a wan blue cast. Billy finds the monochromatic scheme claustrophobic. Institutional. He wonders if Hal's prison cell was painted an anemic blue as well. The air hangs heavily. And there's no window fan in sight. *This guy must have Freon for blood*, Billy thinks.

"Nice room," he says, getting into his oversized T-shirt and boxers. He's eager to lie down, hug his edge of the double bed, and sleep well past noon undisturbed.

But one look at Billy in his underwear gives Hal other ideas. "Thought you were hot," he says.

"Well, yeah," the boy answers, thinking: *What's his problem now?*

"It won't bother me if you—want to sleep naked."

"I always sleep this way," Billy lies.

"Up to you."

Sounds like the Chess Master is disappointed, Billy thinks, turning away to hide his smile. *That oughta even the score a little.*

But he watches Hal's progress in a dresser mirror, admires his host's muscular arms, the graceful chest—with its sprinkling of dark hair that clings to his flesh before turning bushy past the narrow waist. "I'm really tired," Billy says.

"Then we should hit the sack," Hal answers. "The bedroom doesn't get morning light, and the trees give good shade. We can sleep late, even with the curtains open. On Sundays, it stays quiet around here."

"Thought I smelled pine trees," Billy says, looking out the back window. "Wow, they're huge! So, it's green all year long for you, even in winter." Hal doesn't answer. From behind, Billy hears the rustle of sheets whipped away from each other in one swift move. An impatient sound? Billy can't tell. Walking backward until he reaches the bedside, he gets in without turning around.

"Goodnight," he says, as Hal tosses the top sheet on both of them, bringing the oatmeal smell of warm flesh across their faces.

"G'night," Hal mumbles. Gazing at Billy's back in the darkness, Hal puts his hand on the young man's arm. "Glad you're here," he says. "I meant to say that when we got home. But I—"

"Gee, thanks," Billy interrupts, pissed off that his host chooses this time—this place—to show some friendliness. "I'll try not to overstay my welcome," he says, matter-of-factly. Hal's hand doesn't move away.

"You just got here," he says, ignoring Billy's reserve. "Don't worry about it." His nearness to Billy, the young man's steady breathing, his graceful neck fringed with curls that smell of rain and oily sweat, make it difficult for Hal to turn away. He doesn't mean to come onto Billy. That's what he tells himself. Not this way— without a clear welcome signal. But the warm, yielding flesh he holds has an electrical charge. Hal can't pull away. He finds himself stroking Billy's arm, letting his fingers dip along the narrow waist and curved hip.

Billy remains still. He's angered by Hal's imposition—not wholly unexpected—yet roused, despite himself, by the recollection of Hal's naked body, the man's rough beauty and masculine ease.

So much time to make up for, Hal thinks, edging closer to Billy. The booze he drank earlier—on its dark, downward cycle—fuels memories of prison, always looming in the background, like storm clouds that spill with lightning. Memories buzz in his head like a sea of cicadas. They demand gratification, some primal human contact.

Eighteen years, Hal thinks, conforming his body to Billy's, seeing himself in the youth's lithe, strong body. Hal was only three years older than Billy when his felonies—his convictions—stole his youth. His arm curves around Billy's flat stomach. He grazes the boy's dick, which stretches higher in response, its swollen knob sprouting from the loose boxer shorts.

"Wanna fool around?" Hal asks.

If Billy felt completely free, he'd like to say yes. He likes the smell of Hal's gin-laced breath, the sharp musk rising from the man's armpit. But Billy doesn't feel free. More like obliged. He needs some clarification, even if it means looking for new living arrangements come morning. He has some money to get by. Money given to him by a few guys—much older, married guys—he sleeps with when necessary to supplement his sporadic work. But he wouldn't want to make a career out of it.

"Is this like, a requirement?" he asks. "You know, for my living here?" Billy's heart pounds from his harsh words, his vulnerable situation. Heat floods his skin in waves. They emerge from his skull. "I need to know if I can say *yes* or *no*. I'd like to," he admits. "Yeah, I would. Fool around. But not if I *have* to."

Hal backs off. "Of course not," he says, ashamed, his ego wounded. "I only thought you might need to feel wanted—like a lot of guys your age. I've been with dozens of you, in prison and out. You all just wanna be loved."

Gimme a break, Billy thinks. *You wanna fuck, man? Let's fuck.* "So, how do you want me?" he asks, as if he were dealing with one of his randy clients. "On my back, on my side—?"

"Side's fine," Hal says, assuming Billy doesn't want any foreplay. He's thrown by the sudden, impersonal demeanor. "Get undressed."

Billy slides out of bed to disrobe so he can watch Hal, make sure he's taking precautions. He doesn't see any.

"Where's the condom?" he asks, putting his glasses on.

There's a pause; it heats the air. "Don't use any," Hal says, too casual, his back to Billy.

"Why not?"

"Don't like 'em."

"So who does? That's not the point."

"It is if you can't keep stiff with one on—look, you wanna fool around or not?"

As an answer, Billy puts his underclothes back on.

"All right then," Hal says, throwing the lube, the thin white towel back into his bed-stand drawer.

"Fuckin' rude punk," Billy mumbles, unable to hold back.

"What'd you say?" Hal walks up to Billy.

"You heard me." Billy's scared but not willing to retract. "All night, you've been a *rude punk*. Treating me like a third wheel, as if you're Mister Big Fuckin' Wonderful for letting me stay with you. And now you wanna fuck me without a rubber. You're livin' in a dreamworld—*punk*." Billy can't control his harsh words. He can feel Hal's breath against his face, see the man's wide eyes. But not from anger—or the sparse light. Billy can tell. Hal's face has gone all soft. He looks younger, somehow cowed—yet excited, in a solemn way. This sudden change confuses Billy. And just when he thought he had the guy pegged.

"Fuck me," Hal says.

"What?"

"You think I'm a punk. Then fuck me."

Billy's not sure what's happening—whether Hal's words are a challenge. "I don't want to fight you," he says, confused, frightened. "You don't need to pick a quarrel. If you want me to leave—I'll leave."

He's got enough money to last about a month if he can find a cheap room. Maybe in Hoboken or Kearny. They're both easy commutes to Manhattan by train, where Billy can make more money—one way or another—while he completes his correspondence course. But he doesn't want to live alone. Alone with himself.

"I told you what I want." Hal's calloused hands plunge under Billy's T-shirt, travel across the smooth chest. "Nice," he says, peeling away the shirt, rubbing his thumbs against Billy's face. "Real nice." He covers Billy's mouth with his own.

The surprising development—the reversal of his assumptions—puts Billy in a passionate trance. He's drawn to the man's hard, generous body, waiting to be used. Used by Billy. For once, it's his turn to use someone else. He hasn't fucked a guy before—much less someone like Hal. Grabbing a handful of black hair, Billy forces the man's head back, biting gently on Hal's neck, while stroking his round, firm ass—smacking it a few times, the way some men have smacked Billy's.

"Punk," he whispers in Hal's ear, causing the man to breathe hard, yield to arms smaller than his own. "That's the magic word, right?" Billy asks, knowing the answer, gliding his tongue along Hal's large ear. It tastes like salty flour.

Riffling through his backpack, Billy grabs a condom. "Feels fine to me, punk," he says, rolling the thin shield over his bouncing dick. He climbs onto the bed, lets Hal lube him. Unsure suddenly, Billy squats on his haunches, his member jutting up toward the ceiling. "How do you wanna do this?"

Hal gets on his back, raises his legs. His calves widen when pressed against his thighs. "Yeah. That's what I want," Billy says, lifting Hal's legs over his sturdy shoulders, amazed at the feel—the look—of having this strong, large man lying passive in his arms, responding with pleasure to Billy's clumsy initial foray.

"I want your mouth, punk," Billy says. Hal stays put, his profile burrowed in a pillow. Billy makes a grab for Hal's jaw, loses his balance. Both men fall on their sides, still connected. Locked even tighter. Billy's tongue drills the other man's mouth in sync with his cock. He doesn't want to stop, would like to stay where all of him converges, where his mind grows round and hard, sharper than it's been since—But he can't. His body turns rigid. He feels like he's bursting apart, shattered like glass into a thousand shards.

"Come with me to the bathroom," Hal whispers as Billy rests, still inside the man, lingering sleepily, not wanting to pull out.

"Don't you want me to—"

"In the bathroom," Hal answers, cutting the boy short.

He grabs Billy by the waist and hoists him into the bathtub as if he were a doll. Straddling the cold enamel, Billy's feet rest on the narrow rim. Hal kneels before the young man as if praying, eyes closed—face rapt—his left hand working hard. It's happening too fast for Billy to think.

"Pee on me," Hal says, his voice choked with anticipation.

"Pee?"

"Come on, kid. Make it last long as you can."

Now I'm kid again, Billy thinks. He starts with a timid dribble.

"More. Faster," come the harsh pleas—the orders—from below.

Closing his eyes, Billy tries to relax. His muscles comply, allowing a steady stream of piss to shower his host. Under the spell of a prison memory, Hal opens his mouth, catches Billy's piss, then lets it spout out like a fountain. Meanwhile, Hal pumps his cock furiously, climaxing at last at Billy's feet.

"You okay?" Billy asks, after a long silence watching Hal hunched over himself.

"Shit," Hal says, turning his back to Billy, avoiding his gaze. "Now I'm gonna have to use the friggin' shower. Why didn't you remind me?"

"About what?" Billy asks.

"The pipes. They're gonna make a racket."

How's this my fault? Billy thinks. But he knows better than to argue. "I'm getting down now," is all he can say. His toes are stiff from the tub's curved rim. When he hits the floor, his feet ache.

It's cooler now that the rain has stopped. Billy can smell the soaked pine trees through the bedroom window. Hal slips into bed. Each man hugs his own side.

Good thing the clamorous pipes didn't provoke a complaint from Hal's neighbor. *Go figure*, he thinks.

The scene in the bathtub has left Hal feeling exposed, vulnerable to the young boy. He didn't mean to take his embarrassment out on Billy. It would be different if Hal weren't going to see the boy again—much less live with him a while, share the same bed. That's all Hal could think about afterward. Himself. Not how Billy must've felt getting reamed out for doing what he was asked. What he was *told*.

He wants to apologize, indirectly. But he can't figure out how to go about it, say the right words. *If Billy would speak*, Hal thinks. *Mumble goodnight. But why should he?*

"Sorry," Hal says, barely a whisper—could be the sound of his skin moving on the bedsheet. *Try again*, he thinks. "Sorry," said too loud this time.

Billy jumps; a small gasp rends the air. "It's okay," he whispers. Although it's not.

"I kinda got carried away."

Against his pillow, Billy can hear the old house hum. "I liked the first part a lot," he says. Which he did. "The second part was okay—until you started acting like a creep."

Time passes, filled with things unsaid. Sleep begins to overtake Billy; his eyelids fight to stay open. Before he knocks off, he'd like to know if he still has a place to stay.

Billy remembers how intensely Hal had played against John. *Seems years ago now*, Billy thinks. *You take a few breaths, and something new happens in your life. It changes. You're in a place you didn't know existed, with a guy you can't figure out—but might like to.* "Think you could teach me chess some time?" Billy asks.

The rough bedsheet rustles as Hal moves closer. He grabs Billy by the waist, draws him to the center. "It'll take time," he says, "to make you a good chess player."

"That's okay. I'm a patient guy," Billy says.

"We can start tomorrow, maybe."

"Yeah. Tomorrow."

Green Mountain Boys

Jay Lygon

We rode home from the county swimming pool in the back of Jimmy's truck. Matt sprawled in a corner, his wet bathing suit snug against his crotch. Rushing air picked up locks of his dark brown hair and curled them in a wild tangle. He chewed his gum and grinned at me, not saying a word. His pits were thick with hair, and between his brown nipples, he was getting furry. Since spring, when our big coats and bulky sweaters were put away, I caught myself noticing how he filled out over the winter.

When we passed through the center of our town, Matt gazed out at the small shops around the village green, taking his last look. His tanned, muscled back was to me. He had a scar on his left shoulder blade from a playground fight way back in second grade. After we crossed the covered bridge, he closed his eyes and tipped his face to the sun.

The whole way, I pressed my wet beach towel to my groin.

Jimmy skidded to a stop on the highway by our mailboxes, slamming me into the wheel well. I knocked the cab window with the back of my knuckles.

"Very funny, jerk." I wanted to pop him one in his smug, freckled face.

Normally, I didn't let him get to me, but everything about the place where I grew up pissed me off those last few weeks—the Victorian cottages with hollyhocks towering over their picture-perfect white picket fences, the folksy diners for the tourists, and especially the chimes that rang out from the tall church steeple every hour. Even the granite mountains surrounding our valley seemed to press down on me.

I needed to get out of there. Somewhere else, I'd be freer to be the real me. I had to breathe.

Like most summers, that one started out slow, but I never felt it pick up into a headlong rush for autumn the way it did every other year before school started. Time seemed to hang. I wished vacation would just end already.

Another day down, only two more to go, I reminded myself.

I hopped out of the back of Jimmy's truck and onto the highway. It was late afternoon, but the blacktop was still hot enough to sear my bare feet, so I hobbled over to the tall weeds growing on the shoulder of the road. Matt jumped down beside me and slapped his towel over his shoulder.

"Later!" Jimmy yelled as he pulled away.

The smell of cut grass hung sweet and thick in the air. Across the highway, Matt's dad rode the mower over the sprawling lawn of the bed and breakfast they owned. Matt said his parents didn't have many guests that week, but soon the foliage tour buses would roll through, and after that skiers would come to the resorts.

Matt poked his long fingers into the mailboxes gathered near the highway. They were empty, but he kept bending down to look inside, even the ones that weren't for his family.

His swim trunks plastered against his skin. Like most baseball pitchers, Matt had thick thighs. His shoulders were wide and built up from weight training, but he was real slim at the waist. All his ribs showed. He had a butt on him, a nice butt, all muscle, and I could see every inch of that perfect ass as he peered into a faded orange plastic newspaper tube.

Matt slammed a box closed. "Someone must have—"

"Picked it up already."

Matt blew a small gray bubble with his gum. It popped on his mouth. He rubbed off the film sticking to his thick bottom lip and wiped his finger on his beach towel.

"Hey, Kurt, remember that night we drove around smashing all those mailboxes?"

It wasn't that long back. Mostly, I remembered the sick pit of my stomach when Matt hit a black-and-white metal mailbox with his bat. What a glorious *BAM*! But someone jumped in their car and raced after us, bent on revenge. My fingers dug into the seat because I didn't want to look scared, but I was sure Jimmy would loose control on that dark, twisting road, or we'd get caught by the maniac in the car behind us, and Mom would get a phone call from the sheriff. Either way, I figured I was a goner.

"That was some crazy night." Pointless, stupid, and one of the thousands of reasons I was thankful that I had only two more days left before I went away to college.

"Yeah. You left one of your CDs in Jimmy's truck that night. I grabbed it for you. I've been meaning to give it back."

I almost said I'd get it later, but then I remembered that we didn't have later.

"I'll mail it to you at your dorm."

"You have—"

"Your new address? Yeah."

Matt's swim trunks slung low, showing his hip bones and the patch of hair curling in a wave over the waistband of his trunks. He was unmercifully easy to stare at.

Sweet Jesus, I had to stop doing that.

We were quiet a little too long. Matt blew another bubble.

A sign pockmarked by pellet holes warned that the dirt road behind us was a dead end. Two miles back into the dense woods, the road dissolved into weeds and gravel in front of the old farmhouse I shared with Mom and my three brothers.

Matt held a stone. Muscles bunched along his shoulders. Lifting his front foot, he got ready to step into the throw. He let the stone fly with that sidearm pitch that made him so deadly in games. The rock shattered against the Dead End sign, spraying me with stone shrapnel.

"Don't do that."

With a devil's grin, Matt reached down for another rock.

"I hope you listen when your drill sergeant tells you to knock it off, because if you flunk basic training, they're going to lock you away in a military jail," I warned him.

He snorted. I bumped him with my shoulder. He bumped me back. We grinned. He blew another mini-bubble with his gum.

To the east, the sky tinged indigo. We swam until they kicked us out of the county pool. Once they chained the gate behind us, the season was officially over.

"It'll be dark by the time I hike home. I should get going."

"I'll walk with you," Matt offered. "If I go home now, Dad will make me finish mowing the lawn."

It bothered me that Matt got to leave first, if only by a couple days. He had to report to basic training boot camp the following morning. A Marine. I bet he'd look good in that uniform. Fill it out real nice.

I had to stop thinking like that.

Impatience itched under my skin. I couldn't stand still another minute. When Matt picked up another rock, I turned for home, expecting that he'd follow.

Red maples, already crimson on their upper branches, crowded the edge of the lane. Dappled sunlight broke through the heavy leaf canopy. I couldn't hear the lawnmower anymore. The crisp edge in the coming night air felt like Friday-night football games and that sad sweetness that clung to fall.

When I got to the top of the rise, I realized that Matt wasn't with me. He was still out in the sun, absorbing the last of summer. I watched him wind up for another pitch and marveled at the way he moved. All that power, so controlled. Every muscle working in fluid grace. He was something to see.

Time broke free and flowed. It was a mistake to let go of summer, I realized in a rush. I wanted those weeks back, to do them differently.

I jogged back to Matt.

His swimsuit, still damp, clung to his butt. Earlier in the day, swimming underwater, I saw his trunks float above the tan line on his thighs. We pissed off the lifeguards by playing keep-away with Jimmy. Matt's ass bumped against my dick when I tried to climb his body to reach the ball in his up-stretched hand. He leaped out of the water with me clinging to his wet skin, twisted across my groin, and lobbed the ball into the grass where the girls worked on their tans. While the girls taunted Jimmy with the ball, I scurried to a stall in the men's locker room. Water dripped off my chin and nose as I quickly jerked off. It didn't take long. When I crept back to the pool, I glanced around to see if anyone stared or laughed, but no one seemed to notice.

Matt picked up another rock. He hefted it a few times and then hurled it into the woods. I heard it rustle leaves. The thick undergrowth in the woods to either side of the road was in deep shadow.

My throat got tight.

We stood for a while in silence. We could do that, not talk for hours, and usually it felt okay, but something was different between us. I wanted to say something, but I didn't know what to say to him.

A smile quirked at the corner of his mouth. He had nice lips. Girls at our high school used to talk about Matt's mouth, how they knew he had to be a great kisser because of how full his lips were. I always thought his eyes were his best feature.

There I went again.

Matt cocked his head to the side. Locks of hair swept across his face, so he brushed them back. He really had nice eyes. Bedroom eyes. I gulped.

"What's up, Kurt?"

Until then, I almost had it under control, but I blurted out, "I thought you were coming with me." I was all shaky inside. Nothing felt real.

"I forgot that Mom mentioned something about a going-away party tonight. You know how excited she is that I enlisted. Christ, they probably have cake and ice cream. Do you want—"

"To come over?" I looked down the lane. Lights glowed from every window of the two-story bed and breakfast. From that distance, I could still make out the gingerbread trim and the white wicker rockers on the long front porch. Tea lights marked the paths through the small herb garden and along the front of the inn.

"No. I'm going home." That was a shitty way to say good-bye, but there was no way I'd sit there eating cake while Matt's mom gave me sideways glances, as if she expected me to swipe her good silver.

"Wait a minute. I gotta show you something." Matt took his time looking up and down the road. "Come on." He shoved at me until I followed him up the rise and around a bend.

"What?"

He put his hands on my shoulders first, but moved them to my face. Somewhere between, the touch became a light kiss. Then he stopped. "You gonna hit me?"

I couldn't even breathe.

"Say something, Kurt." He looked worried.

Stunned, it took a couple seconds for me to react. I was so relieved that it wasn't just me. He felt it, too.

There was no way we were going to leave it at that little kiss. One kiss meant nothing. I lunged for his mouth. His lips were chapped, but the rough felt good. He turned his head and spit out his gum. That time, we parted lips and tasted tongues. Maybe it was just a kiss, but I felt it everywhere in my body. My heart tried to pound through my chest, and it felt as if every nerve tingled as my dick swelled.

"Sweet Jesus, Matt." I shook all over.

"Don't you dare get religion on me tonight."

Matt took my hand and pulled me after him into the woods. We only had moonlight and stars, but it was enough to see our way around the thin white trunks of a stand of beech trees. A firefly zoomed ahead of us, flickering, until I lost sight of it. We stopped at an oak.

I wasn't confused by that kiss. It made everything clear. But I wasn't sure what would follow it, so I leaned against the tree trunk and waited to see what he had in mind. So far, Matt had all the right ideas.

He pressed against me. His arm was over my head as he nuzzled my neck. Jolts zinged down my spine. I wanted more, so I mashed my mouth against his.

Matt's hand moved down my chest. He squeezed my dick through my swim trunks. I went hard for him. My brain skittered over a million thoughts but kept coming back to one: His hand was on my dick. It felt damn good. It felt like he wanted to and he liked kissing me and suddenly everything was perfect and right and good. His mouth tasted like mint gum. The tree trunk was rough against my bare back, and his chest hairs tickled my nipples.

"Is this how we're supposed to do it?" I whispered even though we were alone. Bugs buzzed, and a soft wind moved the upper branches of the trees, but everything else was quiet.

He still had a grip on me, but it seemed as if he was thinking. "Well, I want you to suck my dick, but if you only want to stroke me while I stroke you, that's fine." His voice was real quiet, too, but I could hear that he was excited and kind of happy.

"Over our clothes?"

He slid a hand inside my trunks and gripped my balls.

That felt a little too good. "Give me a minute." I paced a small circle and huffed deep breaths.

"What's wrong?"

"I'm gonna come if we don't stop."

Matt laughed at me. "Wanking at the swimming pool didn't do it for you?"

"You knew?" The back of my neck got hot.

"Jesus, Kurt. I probably have a bruise from your hard-on poking my ass." Matt slipped off his swim trunks without embarrassment. "I almost followed you when you ran to the bathroom."

I licked my bottom lip. "You want me to suck it?"

"Yeah."

"Yeah." I dropped my beach towel on the ground by his feet.

"But take off your trunks first."

Matt watched me pull them down while he stroked his cock. It felt weird to undress for him, and I was a little shy about it, but I liked the way he looked at me.

When I knelt in front of him, a faint chlorine whiff hit my nose. I'd seen his cock a thousand times, but I never really looked at it before. I wished we had more light. He was about the same length as me, a little slimmer, but curved up toward his belly. My hard-on stuck straight out. The skin over his head was smooth and soft. I licked around it. His scent was stronger the closer my nose got to the thick, dark pubes surrounding his cock. I liked the boy smell of him, earth and sweat.

Matt groaned. He leaned backed against the tree and put his hand lightly on my head.

Night had its own sound in the woods. An owl flew overhead,

nearly silent until it gripped its prey. Acorns dropped, branches creaked. Underfoot, the earth was dusty with decaying leaves and pine needles. For some reason, I was nervous about getting caught, even though I knew no one would ever see us.

Gathering my courage, I took him into my mouth.

"Fuck, Kurt."

Matt rocked forward into my mouth, pulled back, and then pushed hard down my throat with his hand holding my head in a tight grip.

I fell back. "Too much."

Matt held out a hand for me. "Sorry. It felt good, though."

I reached up for his hand, but yanked down hard. Taken by surprise, he toppled on me. Skin on skin, muscle against muscle, it was familiar and different at the same time. We kissed hard, grinding cocks against thighs while our tongues shoved back and forth.

I told Matt, "I don't want to come like this. Why don't you suck my cock while I suck yours?"

He propped up on an elbow. "That is one fucking inspired idea."

I never dreamed of kissing Matt, but I had jerked off to fantasies about him.

I got close to him, both of us on our sides, face to groin. My hand ran across his thigh, and then back over the curve of that great ass of his, and I lightly cupped it as I rubbed my face against his cock.

Matt exhaled warm breath close to my groin. My dick twitched in anticipation.

No wonder why he shoved into my mouth. Oh man. I never imagined it could feel so damn good. I was never going to jerk off again if I could get someone to blow me instead. His lips kept a tight ring around the head of my dick while he flicked the tip of his tongue across the head. It was awesome, but I wanted to feel that all the way down my shaft. Trying to give him ideas, I gripped the base of his cock while I took as much of him in my mouth as I could stand. It was hard paying attention to his cock as he spit on my dick and stroked me with his fist. I wanted to sit back and watch him go down on me.

My forehead bumped against his hairy thighs as I bobbed up and down his cock. The thick veins under his skin were like ridges to my tongue.

A jolt knocked through my body as Matt flicked his tongue across my balls. He did it again, sucking a little of my skin between his lips after the lick. He still pumped me with his hand, keeping his grip tight.

"Keep sucking me," he begged. "Yeah, like that. Like that. Fuck, Kurt." He hissed in a breath. I felt him tense up, and then my mouth filled with his warm come.

I coughed. "Could have warned me!"

"Sorry, man."

He spat on my dick again and jerked faster. "Tell me. Tell me you're gonna come. Tell me how you like it."

I felt stupid talking, but I told him, "It feels good like that. Lick my balls again." His warm mouth traced over my sac. Sweet Jesus. Everything in my groin felt tingly good. "Work your hand over the head. Not so tight. Faster."

"Are you going to come?"

I never heard his voice like that before. It sounded breathless, as if he were really turned on. "Not yet."

"Does it feel good?"

I closed my eyes. No wanking fantasy came close, though, so I opened them again and saw the top of his head. I groaned. Too hot for words. I thrust against his hand.

"Come on, Kurt. Tell me how it feels."

I could feel the come churning, bubbling up the shaft of my dick. Sweat slicked the nape of my neck and the backs of my knees. I spread my thighs, hoping he'd lick further down. "I want to shoot on your face, Matt."

He worked his hand in a blur. Always a bit of a slob, he made slurping noises as he tongued my taint. That was an incredible turn-on. I almost had my knees to my chin.

"Come on my face, Kurt," Matt begged.

That did it. Humping his fist furiously, I sprayed thick white jizz across his chin and lips.. He smiled the whole time as he milked my dick. The last shots flowed over his hand, covering his fingers. Then he licked away my entire load.

We kissed a little more, and ran our hands over our bodies. Mostly, we grinned like fools and broke out laughing at the best private joke ever. I felt stupid in some ways, but in others, I felt like my eyes were finally open. No more explanations needed.

"I think I got a pine needle sticking in my ass," Matt complained after a while. "Let's get up."

We searched through the clearing for our clothes. I found his and tossed them at him.

"Cake and ice cream offer still stands," he said as he dressed.

"No offense, Matt, but your Mom hates my guts."

Matt nodded. "I once heard her tell my Aunt Janie that we're like childhood sweethearts. Only Mom didn't mean it in a nice way."

"More like, 'That boy is corrupting my son?'"

"Yep."

I finally found my trunks. They were much further away than I remembered.

"You realize that we wasted the entire summer." I would have given anything for it to be July.

"We wasted high school."

"This sucks."

"In a way, you should thank Mom, because until I heard her say that, I never thought about us. When I did, I realized she was right. Then I started really thinking about you, how cute you are." He ran his hands down my stomach and squeezed my dick again. "Those MIT guys will be all over you."

"You're going to have to fight off horny Marines. Unless you want a gang bang." I was joking, but a wave of loneliness washed over me, and it didn't seem so funny anymore. "I guess I never really thought about it. After tonight, we'll be apart. First time since—"

"Since forever."

"Yeah." I felt a tear welling up in my eye.

"Aw, Kurt, we'll probably see each other at Thanksgiving. Christmas for sure. Gift exchange. You wrap the condoms; I'll tie a ribbon around the lube."

He could always make me laugh. "In your dreams, Matt. I'm the top."

Matt snorted. I bumped him with my shoulder. He bumped me back. We grinned. We were still old us.

We hiked through the trees toward the road in comfortable silence. For a long time, we held hands. We used to do that, until second grade, when Jimmy called us names for holding hands on the playground. Matt beat the crap out of him, but we stopped after that, so Jimmy won after all. That was a sweet victory to take back. I squeezed Matt's hand.

As Matt walked home with me, fireflies flickered across the road. I glanced up, watching them swarm overhead, until I lost track of which lights came from the fireflies, and which were the stars. A few times, we stopped to kiss. We were in no hurry to get anywhere. The end of summer was just down the lane.

Knots

Philip Clark

"Goddamnit!"

It was sudden, but not entirely unexpected. James thrust his legs over the side of the bed and shoved past me. His red dick stuck out from his body like a mast, as angry as the rest of him. As he continued to yell, though, it shrank and returned to its normal flesh color.

When he was pissed, James tended to lose any verbal finesse he might normally have. "What fucking kind of a fucking top are you!" he screamed at me. "A fucking lousy top, that's what kind! Sure, you can swing your dick around and stick it in whatever hole I show you, but ask you to do anything that takes a little imagination and you just flat-out suck!" James grabbed the coil of rope that I had only recently been fumbling with, trying to twist and tie it around his willing ankles and wrists. He wound up and slapped me across the chest with one end. "You can't even tie a decent fucking knot, you idiot!"

"James, I want to, it's just . . ."

"Forget it! Fucking forget it! All I ask for is a little imagination, a little skill, and what do I get?" He reared back once more, and the rope stung my stomach. "Just what kind of a fucking top are you?"

"The only fucking top who will put up with your third-grade temper tantrums!" I snapped, hurt by both the rope and his words.

I should have predicted what would happen if I yelled back at him—James's mood swings were legendary. His face crumpled as quickly as his erection had, and all the fight went out of him. "I'm so sorry, Ben!" he wailed.

Sigh. Our usual cycle: from fighting with the boyfriend to comforting the boyfriend. Big fat fucking surprise.

James dropped the rope and threw out his arms, and I let him grab me and sniffle into my chest. "I'm sorry, Ben," he said again. "You know how I get so frustrated. I'm horny and hard, and I just get to needing something more *interesting* than a regular fuck. If only you were more . . . creative, honey!" He looked up from our sloppy embrace and attempted a smile. "Don't get me wrong! I love how silent and strong you are, just . . ." His voice trailed off.

"But, James, what am I supposed to do? Everything seemed fine for so long, and now you're begging for midair acrobatics and double-headed dildos and being bound from head to toe. I'm a writer, for godsakes, what am I supposed to do? What do I know about tying knots?"

He pushed away from me, anger swirling again in his eyes. "You're smart, you figure it out. Hire a Boy Scout for all I care!"

And that was how it all began.

I first met James about three years ago through a mutual acquaintance. Despite what you hear about lesbians being the ones who break out the U-Haul on their second date, James and I were the ones who got hitched damned quick—six weeks of dating, and he asked me to move in with him. Our house was definitely his. You wouldn't think someone as flighty as James would make it as a lawyer, but his moodiness actually made him a great corporate attorney; all over D.C., lawyers were quickly learning not to mess with a pissed-off, cutthroat queen. It created a strange dynamic in our relationship: here I am, the stable, masculine top, and it's my short, slight, perverted bottom of a lover yanking down the big bucks. As good an author of porn and entertainment articles as I am, my freelance writing barely supplies enough money to buy the lube for James's fantasies.

Who knows why James decided to anoint me the love of his life? I suspect my dick has something to do with it. Last time I stretched out the ruler, back in high school, mine was 9 inches, its thick base tapering down to a nice heft around the middle and mushrooming slightly at the head. (Those of you who know me can learn why the heroes of my porn stories always sport "12-inch rods"—it's a little known fact that all porn authors add 3 inches to their own dicks when they fantasize. Porn characters tend to pack around 9 inches—you do the math.) James practically broke down in tears when he first saw it: it ended his lifelong Search for the Golden Cock.

And I have to say that I'm good with it. Even an experienced cocksucker like James was a little raw in the throat after the first time I put him on his knees and fucked his face. For the longest time, his favorite activity started with deep-throating my cock until it was hard and dripping wet. I'd follow by pushing him onto his back, driving his legs wide apart in the air, fingering the pink and sensitive skin around his shaved asshole. Once I'd worked him up into a whimpering frenzy, squirming against my grip, I took an ankle in each hand and forced him to stillness. Using my slick cock to pierce the soft ring of his hole, I pushed into the deep velvet heat beyond. No matter how deeply or quickly I thrust, James arched his back and seemed to pull my cock even further into him. For the longest time, this was all James wanted, and I was happy to oblige.

There was never a single point I could turn to and say, "That! That was when none of it satisfied him any longer!" Instead, it was a series of points on a slow curve. One day, he wanted to lick my feet, but I was too ticklish. Another, he brings home a plastic-and-metal cock ring; I got it on him, but something about his body looked unnatural while he wore it, and I couldn't get a really raging hard-on until he took it off. Dildos, handcuffs, a painful-looking set of tit clamps I didn't even want to think about. Every so often, James would trot home with a new implement. Without fail, something always went wrong. You can't imagine how embarrassing it was getting—me, the studly gay porn author, into nothing but vanilla sex!

James quickly lost patience with me, and my inability to tie anything but the simplest knot ("They call it a fucking slipknot because it fucking *slips*, you moron! How fucking useful is that when I'm heaving and straining at your feet?") seemed to be the last straw. God only knew I'd better find a way to make the man happy—to all appearances, even my Cock to Die For was losing its appeal, and in the equation of my life, unhappy James equals no James at all. Which equals nowhere to live. Which equals having to find a *real* job. To use James's favorite word, that's one big fucking problem.

Inspiration struck while I was mowing the front lawn. It often does. I insist on using one of the old-style push-mowers—no electricity, no gas, just whirling metal blades and a little bit of elbow grease—and something about the physical activity and the sweat gets my mind to working. Some of my best porn stories—"Hot Cop," "Frank Fucks Fred," "Initiation Night"—have come to me in a flash as I mowed.

While finishing the last strips of grass and thinking about the-problem-that-was-James, I noticed I wasn't the only guy on Stuart Street doing outdoor chores. Across the road and two houses down, the shirtless son of one of the middle-aged couples that dot our area was standing five rungs up on a ladder. He balanced a paint can, his arm swaying back and forth as he applied even strokes onto the porch's wooden frame. His back was to me, and never being one to pass up an uninterrupted look at a young male specimen, I watched him. It seemed to me that I had seen him before.

It took noticing his car for me to make a connection. Sitting in the driveway was an older model VW, and I realized that I had seen this kid tootling around the neighborhood in it. It wasn't too well maintained—a dent here, a little mud there. My eye landed on a bright bumper sticker attached to the rear window. In big block letters, it read: B.S.A. What the heck did B.S.A. stand for? My mind cranked up: Baptist Student Association? What a depressing thought. Black Scholars Association? If he were any whiter, he'd fade away. Then it hit me, the answer to my prayers:

Boy Scouts of America.

I tried, and likely failed, to look nonchalant as I sidled across the street. He grew bigger and more distinct the closer I got to him, thin but solid. There were muscles hidden in the bent shoulders and neck, and his left arm barely trembled from the weight of the paint can. He stood barefoot on the metal rung, and I noticed his top-to-toe tan. Was he a lifeguard? A beach bunny? Did he favor very few clothes? I had no time to arrive at a conclusion before he heard my not-so-subtle approach. Twisting on the ladder, he took me in from beneath a sweep of sandy hair, and said, "Hey." Turning back, he evened a daub of paint on the corner of the porch.

His attention caught in ensuring the smoothest possible application of paint-to-porch, I was a bit uncertain how to proceed. "Hey," I replied, casual.

"Hey," he returned, dipping the brush. He tossed his head to clear the wave of hair from his brow, but didn't seem inclined to say more.

The best I could muster was: "I'm Ben. I think I've seen you around before."

"Probably."

"You still in high school?"

"No, college. A sophomore."

He still hadn't turned around or looked me in the eye. The paint had to be smooth by then.

"Where do you go?"

"William and Mary."

I tried appealing to his vanity. "You must be smart. I could never have gotten in there."

This caused him to turn around, if not to get off the ladder. "I guess so. Smart enough to handle myself." I thought I detected a hint of a smirk, but there wasn't time to tell before the brush went back into the paint, and he turned away again.

I was running out of conversational options. What do you talk about with a kid other than school? I didn't know him, I didn't know his parents. What was I even doing here? I looked around me for more inspiration, and my eyes fell on the car. Retro must be in, because he wasn't the first young guy I'd seen driving a Bug. Worth a shot.

"Is the VW yours?"

He turned and smiled for the first time. His eyes stayed calm, though, big and pale blue. "Yeah, man, that's mine. Isn't it cool?"

Actually, to me it looked like junk. I got off the grass and took a few steps onto the gravel driveway, as if to get a closer view. The VW was light yellow, almost a cream color. The car's fenders were scratched, and there was a dent in the passenger door. But it *was* shiny, like someone had waxed it recently. "Yeah, it's cool," I lied. "Where did you get it?"

The ladder creaked as he climbed down and came over to join me. He put a protective hand on the front grille. "My parents wouldn't get me a new car. Something about teaching me responsibility by making me get my own. So I bought this one from Hornburger, that crazy old man up on Stafford Street. He only charged me a couple hundred bucks. It was almost totally junked, but I got a friend of mine to put in a replacement engine, and I did a little bodywork on it. Runs like new. Don't you love how it looks? It's not like those shitty looking neon ones they're making now."

After the monosyllabic greetings, this was a flood of information. Still, I wanted to stay on topic. "It looks great. Say, what's the bumper sticker for?"

"Boy Scouts."

"Were you a Boy Scout?"

"I'm an Eagle Scout. I got initiated when I was a junior in high school."

"Hey, that's great," I said. I nodded really big, like this was momentous news. "Actually, if you're an Eagle Scout, I bet you could help me out."

He looked at me curiously. "What with?"

"Don't all Boy Scouts learn how to tie knots? I need someone to teach me how."

"Sure! No problem," he said, flashing white teeth. "That's easy. You've gotta be able to do that really early in your scout training." He paused for a second, and the grin remained. "What do you need to learn to tie knots for?"

Shit. You'd think I would have expected this question, but it took me off guard. What was I going to tell him? If I don't learn how to put my sex-crazed male lover in basic bondage, my ass will be out on the street? Fortunately, this was just storytelling, and I'm good at that.

"I've got this friend with a really big boat," I said. "He and his wife want me to go on a cruise with them, but everyone's got to be able to pull his own weight with the sailing. If I could just learn some basic hitches . . ."

My Eagle Scout's name, as it turned out, was Chris. His parents were out of town for vacation, sipping piña coladas on some sandy beach in the Virgin Islands. They left him in charge of the house. We set up a time to meet the next day for my tutorial.

When I arrived, Chris greeted me at the door, shirtless and in flip-flops. The black plastic slapped against his heels as he led me into the house. It was possible that he hadn't changed clothes—what little he wore—since the previous day of painting. His all-over tan was even more pronounced under indoor lights.

"C'mon to the basement," he called over his shoulder. "We've got clothesline down there. Rope somewhere, too."

My sneakers squeaked on the rubber traction mats encasing the basement stairs. I ducked my head to avoid an exposed beam near the end of the stairs. Chris's basement was unfinished. Cement floors were covered with a scattering of throw rugs. In one corner stood a round poker table, packs of cards neatly arranged on it, and a set of low chairs. There were more exposed beams overhead with electrical wires racing along their edges. The only light was dim, provided by small windows half-set into the ground outside.

Chris was rooting around near a messy table. "My dad keeps his workbench down here," he said. From amid a clutter of bolts, tools, and cans, he came up holding a rough-looking length of rope and a long cotton clothesline. "These can get us started," he said, smiling.

"I'm in your capable hands," I replied.

"Yeah, sure," he said. The smirk I thought I saw the previous day had returned. "We'll start you off with something really simple: a square knot. Everyone should know how to make a square knot."

Using a pair of black-handled shears from the workbench, Chris sliced off a couple feet of the clothesline. "Curve one end over the other," he said, "like starting to tie a pair of shoelaces. Let me show you." He walked me over to a metal pole holding up one of the beams, threw the clothesline around it, and started the bow. "Then take the ends and cross them over each other again. Pull them through and you have your knot." He demonstrated the procedure as he talked, then handed me the ends. "Pull on them," he suggested. I did, and the knot tightened. "That's easy." I laughed.

"One warning," Chris said. "You've got a potential problem with a square knot." He yanked hard on one end, and the knot disappeared.

"Do you see what happened?" he asked. "You made yourself a slip-knot by mistake." He let the undone clothesline slide to the floor. "You've got to be careful about that."

"Oh," I blurted, "James wouldn't like that."

"Who's James?" Chris asked.

"A friend of mine," I answered weakly.

"The friend with the boat?"

"Yeah, the friend with the boat."

He grinned, and I wondered whether I had given the game away. It didn't seem so, though, because he shifted immediately into an explanation of another knot.

"You ever done karate?" he asked, cutting a longer length of clothesline.

"No."

"Then you've never heard of an *obi*. Here, I'll show you." Chris stepped forward, and his hands worked the clothesline three times around my hips. "The *obi* is the belt you see guys wearing in martial arts films," he explained. "There's a special knot for tying it. After you've wrapped the rope around a rail or a beam, you run one free end under the loops and tie it off."

The clothesline tightened around my waist as Chris fixed the knot. The faint odor of sweat clung to his hair. His hands were raw and wide, the palms lighter than the tanned skin on the backs, and I felt myself start to harden underneath my jeans. I hoped he didn't notice. The sensation intensified as he stepped back to observe the job he had done. His eyes on me, his physical presence, made me forget about the techniques I was supposed to be learning. "Pull on one end," he ordered. I did. The knot held.

"That's a pretty good knot," I muttered.

"Not good enough for what you need. It's useful for when you have to finish the rope off, but it's not strong enough." His hands returned to my waist, and he picked the knot out of the clothesline.

His bare chest, the nipples soft and pink, brushed against my clothed one as he pulled the cord from behind my back. I was almost fully hard, and hoped the lesson would end soon. I didn't know how much longer we could go without Chris seeing my erection. He'd probably be disgusted. Maybe he'd tell his parents. The basement was suddenly warm and close as I realized that I could get into deep shit.

Chris seemed oblivious to my thoughts. "For a beginner, you probably only need to know one more knot," he said. "It's a bit more complicated than the others."

"I bet those two you've already shown me would be good enough," I said. "I've taken up enough of your time. You've probably got better things to be doing than teaching me."

"Like what? Putting another coat of paint on the porch?" He laughed. "I've already worked like a slave around the house. I've done everything my dad wanted me to do while they're gone."

"Are you sure?" I wanted out of the basement, but couldn't come up with a graceful exit line.

"I'm sure. Before you leave, you need to know a lanyard hitch." Chris pulled a chair from the poker table and lowered himself into it. "It's better if you make this one for yourself. You need to get real-life practice. Here," he said, offering me the braided rope and kicking out of his flip-flops. "You can practice it on me."

I just about gagged. I looked at Chris's face for a clue, but he was as blank as when I first approached him on the ladder. "Why don't I practice it on the pole?" I asked quickly.

He shook his head. "No, a lanyard hitch is best for tying things together. C'mon, do my ankles."

Ever had that feeling that your body's making moves that your mind hasn't approved? That was me hunkering in front of Chris, but the action wasn't conscious. I followed his voice automatically. When he told me to put the clothesline aside and use the rope ("This is the kind of rope you'll use on the boat. It's best to get experience now."), I took it from his hands.

"Stretch the rope taut and double it up," he instructed. "Now stretch it taut again and put the midpoint behind my ankles." I slid the folded rope around his heels. "Pull my ankles together. Slip the loose ends through the loop you've made. Now tighten it."

Chris's calves were smooth under my hands. It looked all-natural, not like he had shaved. They were not highly muscled, but I could feel cords of strength tensed beneath the skin. He submitted to the rope, letting me move his legs as I had to. "Harder," he ordered when I failed to yank the loose ends securely enough through the loop.

"I don't want to give you rope burn," I protested weakly, not making eye contact.

"Don't worry about it. It feels fine."

I jerked the loose ends until there was no more slack. "Good," he said. "Now curl each loose end around the knot you're making, in opposite directions. You're done—just strap the ends together like you're starting a bow."

I did as he told me, then rocked back onto my heels. In front of me, Chris's ankles were neatly tied together. The soles of his feet faced me, and their pale skin matched the palms of his hands.

"Get more practice," he said. His voice was soft, but strong. "Tie my wrists to the chair."

What would have seemed an outrageous request five minutes before didn't stop me. Something about seeing Chris's ankles bound together made me want to follow wherever this was leading. Besides, he was right, wasn't he? I needed more practice.

I knelt at his left side and picked up his wrist. "Use an *obi*," he said. I felt his eyes as though he were the one touching me. Pressing the wrist against one metal strut, I wrapped the cord three times around, slipped a free end under the lines, and tied off the ends.

He nodded. "Now the other one. A square knot. Be sure it doesn't slip."

I crossed and tied the cotton cord once, twice around his right wrist. I tugged on the ends. The knot pushed into flesh, tightened, and held.

I stood and faced him, bound to the chair with his legs stretched to their full length. For the first time, I looked into his eyes. He flipped his head to clear the hair away, then held my gaze.

"There's no boat is there?"

I hesitated.

"There's no boat."

I nodded.

"Get naked," he said.

I was getting used to following orders carefully. Unlacing my sneakers, I removed them along with my socks. I pulled my shirt off, exposing the pelt of black hair that covered my chest. The jeans followed. Last, I eased my briefs over my erection. My cock dropped heavily from where it had been pressed against the ridges of my stomach.

Chris looked up at the nine inches hovering near him and sucked in air, surprised. The blue eyes, normally so empty, brightened and filled. The voice was eager for the first time. "Straddle me," he begged.

I felt my mind catch up to my body. This was more what I was used to. This was better. I know how to respond to naked need. "I'd better untie you," I told him.

Chris lost his composure, just slightly. "No!" he practically shouted. I picked up my jeans. "I mean, no," he said in a quieter voice. "Please straddle me."

"That's not all you want from me, is it?" I asked him.

His head shook from side to side. "Please."

I stepped forward and straddled his legs. I gave the side of his face a light slap. "Open up," I ordered. The jaw dropped, and I eased his lips onto my cock. With his hands tied to the chair, he couldn't control how I used his mouth. I let his tongue moisten the tip and his lips play with the head. Slight beads of sweat broke at his temples, and I pulled him off me. "This is what you want," I said. It wasn't a question.

"Please," he repeated. "Please."

I returned his mouth to its task, this time deeper, fuller. At the command of my touch, he slipped further onto the shaft, inhaling the odors from my crotch and balls. Fingers laced through his thick brown hair, I pressed him down. As his lips pulled and teased the skin of my shaft, his neck and shoulders forced forward, I looked at the knots I had tied to keep his wrists in place. They strained and held fast.

When one hand strayed to his nipple, Chris almost lost it. I rolled the pink flesh between my fingers, and he tried to pull away. With his mouth filled and his arms bound, he wasn't going anywhere. Something about the knots had me turned on, too: the way they held him steady, jerking into his wrists as I fucked his face. His struggling made me even hotter, and my cock bucked in his mouth, close to the edge. *I'm sure James will appreciate my new skills*, I thought as Chris's throat opened to the jets of hot cum blasting from my cock.

If he doesn't, I can always hope for more out-of-town vacations.

King of the Mat

Davem Verne

Dusty was King of the Mat.

His real name was Dustin McCanon, though everyone called him Dick-In-The-Canon. He acquired the jocular title in college due to the way his dick announced itself under his singlet during a wrestling match. I guess the hard cup at his groin was no match for his kingly hard-on. With hips pumping and hands grappling, his alert woody tore through its restraints and challenged the nylon seams.

I always felt that nylon was meant to provoke a guy's cock, be it on the long legs of a coed or the crotch of a jock. In Dusty's case, it was just the way his hormones reacted against the silky texture whenever he wrestled an opponent. Every inch of his firm body wanted to overpower the opposition, to break through his elastic singlet and get serious, including his upperweight dick. Somehow his full hips knew just how to leverage his weight on a guy, pinch the second layer of skin, and make his hard-on happy.

Dusty captured the state title in his freshman year and held on to it for three years in a row. During team trials he dominated every member on our team, including an undefeated sophomore like me. Off the mat, he dominated as well. He made me crazy competitive whenever I saw him. In the dining hall, he mowed through five chicken breasts at a time. I ate as much as he did *and more*. In the gym, he bench-pressed through the midnight hours. I worked out as long as he did *and then some*. Christ, I needed to place in his weight category somehow!

It all began during the state meet last fall. I was a freshman and named outstanding wrestler in the 149-pound class. Dusty was a defending champion at 174 pounds. During the finals, every athlete in college lined up just to see Dusty rule the mat. Those earthlings never felt so lucky; they were happy to get as near as the same tournament with him. I, however, had my eyes on someone else.

At the time I had a huge boy-crush on Dusty's best buddy, Gabe. Gabe was an upperweight, who had the thickest pair of thighs I'd ever seen. I was a virgin underclassman from Atlanta and sat in awe of the big Michigan boys. My idol was Brock Lesnar, of commercial wrestling fame, but Gabe was an attainable hero. On the afternoon of Dusty's match, Gabe was retired to the benches due to a mild concussion he incurred the previous day. During his last bout, Gabe's head got a good knocking between the colossal thighs of an Okie and he went down defeated.

"Crush him!" Gabe blasted from the stands.

Dusty circled his opponent. This was Dusty's crowning match. It was up to him to get in the best possible position. Coach Beasley couldn't help him now. He was all alone with the enemy, just as I was alone with Gabe.

Gabe's thighs spread wide, mimicking the moves of his best friend. The blond peach fuzz that covered his legs brushed against my knee. I got aroused at his touch and nearly swooned. I wanted to sink between his thighs and sniff his sweat and bite his oppressive jockstrap. I would worship him in public if he allowed it.

I'm not bad to look at, mind you: round in the chest, tight in the ass, with firm legs and an athlete's grin. But I missed the boat when it came to being mistaken for a gladiator. That was Gabe's territory.

Dusty's buddy was itching to get back in the meet. He squirmed beside me, wanting to help subdue the hairy-chested Oklahoman, the same wrestler who had made him faint. His ready muscles pulsed beneath his hide, remembering the raunchy scent of the victor's testosterone lapping against his cheek. Two hairy balls and out went the lights!

I glanced at Gabe through the corner of my eye and wondered what he looked like during sex. My imagination was very good and I fancied he had an eight-inch boner with two lime-sized balls bouncing in a fat, furry nutsac.

"Subdue him!" Gabe shouted. He glared at Dusty with intense eyes.

Above those blue eyes, a military buzz of blond hair crowned Gabe's head like golden fleece, recurring briefly across his eyebrows and chin. I admired the hard lump on his forehead that smoked of legend and the way his lips drew into his face. He had a square jaw that anchored his freckled chin, just like Lesnar. Only a Greek helmet made of bronze would suit him, a metal frame to guard his golden face against the Michigan sun.

My freshman roommates were anchored on my left. Josh and Cody tensed up as Dusty dropped the Okie. They were voracious Dick-In-The-Canon fans, greedily keeping score of Dusty's every takedown. They creamed in their shorts coveting his style: they wanted to wrestle on their feet like Dusty, apply his singular cradle, switch and roll just like the King of the Mat. Cody and Josh were so fixated that they even imitated Dusty's moves every night in their room. I could hear them through the dorm wall, panting and slapping and then, after a long bout on the floor, getting real quiet. I imagined they ended their dorm match with a double forfeit handjob.

That's what wrestling is all about. Ask Coach Beasley. Before practice, the coach would often say, "Find your best match, boys. Then get to know every inch of his body. Grapple with his gear.

Pump him dry. He's your mat mate, boys, not just for practice, but for life."

Well, I wanted to practice on Gabe.

Gabe's face reddened as Dusty applied a forward cradle. Gabe knew in his heart that he and Dusty, while best friends through college, were probably a mismatch on the floor. He watched his friend hook the opponent's leg and grew afraid of the day when Dusty would find his perfect match and discard his blond brother. I didn't know it then, as I grappled Gabe's clothes off with my mind, thinking how he must be the best partner for me, that the jock huffing and braying and earning the state title just a few feet away was fated to be *my* perfect match.

"He's reversing his attack!" Gabe howled.

The referee waited to hear Dusty's call.

Grapple with his gear.

"Has he ridden you?" I asked suddenly.

Gabe looked at me.

"I mean . . ."

I stammered, trying not to swoon.

"Dusty's a leg rider. If you've been under him, what's he going to do next?"

"He'll turn him twice in one period." Gabe spoke guardedly. Cody and Josh looked at me and nodded, having memorized Dusty's moves. "He'll keep going until the guy turns neutral. In the third period he'll top him. It'll be a tie at first. Then he'll choose bottom and in a matter of seconds escape, scoring."

"Wow," I muttered.

Casually, I dropped my eyes to a dumb stare. Gabe returned the dumb gaze and shut up.

I smirked. Both of us were playing dumb-to-get.

That's a jock's game. Most college athletes prefer not to act too smart, affecting a healthy stance of stupidity amidst their peers. We safely retreat from conversation, our eyes half-opened, not too wide and never seeing too much. Even in company, we talk jocular but leave clever declarations alone. The truth is, a young athlete is always wrestling with words, wondering what to say next, not wanting to give anyone the edge, the advantage, the opportunity to ultimately *know* him.

As Gabe turned his profile to the mat, my dumb stare glanced down to his lap and I saw his cock spring out from under his shorts. His dumb dick had heard my thoughts. Gabe's hungry woody pronounced itself with a pulsing dickhead that poked through the white trim of his jock!

"Stall! Stall!" Gabe begged.

The wrestling match was heating up and so was Gabe. My male fantasy sat inches away, aggressive, controlling, furious, and hard as a brick. His lap cradled a magnificent hard-on that glared at the tournament through one imperious dickeye. It grew larger with every whistle blown, incensed and demanding release. I turned to my classmates who were too involved with their note-taking to note anything unusual. And the crowd behind me clung to the bleachers watching Dusty's opponent dominate. With my own boner bouncing between my legs, I spit into my right palm and reached over.

Grapple!

Gabe's fleshy cock dove into my hungry palm. He didn't even notice—or maybe he did. I acted too dumb to find out. I watched Dusty struggle under the Okie as my hand pumped Gabe's shaft. My fingers rotated quickly, wetting the pink head and milking out a few drops of jackoff juice. The junior wrestler between Gabe's legs ballooned into a Cyclops.

Gabe squirmed nearer to me, leaning into my shoulder and solicitously knocking my knees. With a dumb groan, he warmly received my rapid fist-fuck and said nothing.

I closed my eyes and imagined swallowing his dick in my mouth. Gabe's meat was barbarous to the touch, and in my mind he pummeled my cheeks as he rode me. We were both on the mat, where else? He was on top, fucking my face, with golden sweat dripping off the mounds of fuzz that furrowed across his hips. He wrestled my jaw and roughened the inside of my throat. His dick was veiny and full of unfair amounts of cum, which he rigorously withheld. I grew anxious for my teeth to pop the cap! Easy does it, I warned. But in dreams, one rarely obeys warnings. I greedily drank his cum as it lunged out of his cock like Greek clay.

In a moment, barely a jock's breath later, the whistle blew a hole in everyone's nerves. Dusty scored and won the tournament.

I didn't notice. Gabe convulsed beside me, shooting a hot load out of his shorts and dousing the wood between our feet. More covetous cum gushed out of his dick, filling my fisthole. I choked his prick for more. His balls pumped the rest into my palm as his eyes beat a path across Dusty's ass.

The benches teemed with screaming fans. I pulled my hand from Gabe's shorts as my teammates pounced on me in celebration. Someone behind me hissed, but I didn't turn back to look, afraid that we'd been seen.

Josh and Cody dragged me onto the mat to congratulate their hero, leaving Gabe on the bench. Gabe's big blond body sank as our team surrounded Dusty and congratulated him royally. I don't think he was jealous; Gabe wasn't the type. I think he was horny—horny for that dick piercing through Dusty's singlet. The all-state pecker had broken another hard cup and once more protruded for all to see: big, hard, and bulging like championship pork.

"Dick-In-The-Canon! Dick-In-The-Canon!" Everyone laughed.

Victory over the Okie called for a healthy jackoff in the shower and I think Gabe wanted nothing more than to be there when Dusty came.

For weeks after the meet, my crush on Gabe grew to inexorable proportions. While everyone bowed down before Dusty, I found myself chasing Gabe into the shower or changing beside him in the locker room. There, Coach Beasley reminded us how proud we were of Dusty's accomplishments, but all I was proud of was the cum Gabe had left in my palm and the sweet hope of repeating our little performance in the bleachers.

Its funny how a bit of physical contact can make the body hunger for more. But Gabe cleverly kept me at bay. In the shower, at the lockers, during meals, he maneuvered so that Dusty stood or sat between us: a symbolic obstacle. It was unfair but predictable. That's the way straight men treat their male lovers in public. If I wanted more contact, I'd have to twist his arm to get it. Thus, I became even more disciplined, feasting and weight lifting, doing everything to increase my bulk just so I could be named Gabe's wrestling partner.

My determination to procure another handful of Gabe's wrestling glue took a significant turn the day I found out who was hissing at us that day at the meet. His name was Hollan Broshawsky. Hollan was a Polish junior with a round, perspiring face that ended at a pink point normally called a nose. His body was the maximum size for a junior wrestler, and his thighs were well known for their killer switch. He was Dusty's equal in build and, as I soon found out, in dick-size, too.

"How are you on your feet, Wolburn?" Coach Beasley asked one day at practice.

That's me, Carl Wolburn. I was a freshman wrestler with broad shoulders and a ripped cage and I had just bleached the tips of my hair so I would stand out at practice and get picked to freestyle with the dominant guys. That's an amateur tactic that often works.

"Are you dominant on your feet?" the coach asked.

"Most times," I answered.

"Then get on the mat with Broshawsky," he ordered. "Let's see your moves."

Everyone was present, including Gabe. I asked myself, Broshawsky *who?* My dorm mates, Cody and Josh, murmured on the sides. They seemed to know the big face that matched the big name, but I didn't. Quickly they made a bet against me and got Dusty in on it. *Et tu, dorm mates!*

Hollan Broshawsky glanced around as I climbed down the bleachers. He looked like a bottomless pit of male muscle. He was a Chicago native, the first generation son of a famous Polish wrestler, and he had no respect for Southern wrestlers unless they shared his own monumental scale. Word had it that commercial wrestling wanted to recruit his ass and call him Hollan, the Hole-In-Hell. He was *that* big.

Hollan wore a black singlet with a silver line streaking down each armpit. He turned to face me as I stepped out on the mat wearing my two-strap singlet: electric blue on top and bright crimson on bottom. My tight pecs showed to maximum advantage through the thin straps, and my aquamarine earguards matched rather handsomely. Hollan hissed. He had no patience for bravura amateurs like me. My mass was nothing compared to Hollan's bursting chest, hammered as it was six days a week.

I batted my eyelashes and looked to Gabe for help. But that dude was wrapping his attention around the sudden appearance of Dusty's dick.

"You have a good chance, Wolburn," Coach Beasley spoke, sizing me up. "Make it close, a tie or take the lead. Do the hard work now, and we'll see who else you can practice with."

Was that a promise?

The coach on any wrestling team is like a matchmaker. He decides which teammates have competing strategies and divides everyone into partners. Maybe if I were visibly crushed under Hollan's weight, the coach would assign me a more suitable partner to wrestle with: my estranged boyfriend, Gabe, for example. I didn't have to *beat* Broshawsky. How could I? All I had to do was act aggressive, leer once or twice, enough to show Coach Beasley that I was in good mental shape. If I was willing to prevent Hollan from upstaging me, while at the same time being utterly defeated by Hollan's massive weight, he would properly pair me according to my defenses and capabilities.

All that was going to be hard, however, since Hollan possessed an attribute I loved most in athletes: lumbering thighs.

"Top or bottom?" Hollan growled.

"Bottom," I squeaked.

Immediately, Hollan took charge of the match. I allowed him to choose his best position while I tensed my muscles, afraid he would rip me apart. He climbed on my back and pressed me facedown with a chinlock. My jaw strained against the hard cushion.

Suddenly, I felt Hollan's prick glide against my singlet. Hollan's wide hips thrust his crotch against my ass. He kept me down where I couldn't move and pretended to twist my arms over my head as he dry-humped me. His impertinent balls pushed his cock nearly out of his nylon and into my asshole!

"Wait," I whispered.

He gritted his teeth in my ear and muttered a few words that I dare not repeat here, but they went something to the effect that, if I was in his bed, he'd club my asshole and stretch it as wide as the Arkies.

At that moment I decided *not* to be defeated by Broshawsky. I maneuvered my pelvis out from under him. In response, he wrapped his massive hand between my legs and pinned me down, grabbing my balls and jerking them wildly. I gasped. I bit my lip as he pretended to roll me across the mat, gaining points while giving my balls a wringing.

Coach Beasley waited for me to make the call. I looked up at Cody and Josh for input, squinting under Hollan's illegal butt drill;

that is, his head intentionally banging against my ear. The coach and my dorm mates seemed to encourage my passivity.

So this is Broshawsky's style, huh? No wonder commercial wrestling sought him, the porn of all sports. I squirmed beneath Hollan's immense chest and swallowed my guts. His groin pressed deeper against my singlet and excited my hole. He dragged me about, another flagrant misconduct that the coach failed to stop, and I felt Hollan's swollen cock pierce our singlets and enter my bare ass.

His dick pulsed like the whistle around the coach's neck, wet and silent and all the more dangerous. Every motion of mine urged him to cum inside me. But I didn't want that. I was saving my virgin ass for Gabe. Only Gabe was qualified to fuck me. But for a heated moment, as Hollan's marvelous thighs made love to my lean hips, I lost my wits and fantasized that Hollan *was* Gabe.

"I'm going to give you my first child, fist-fucker," Hollan growled.

That's when the Chicago brute spanked my rump and made me cum in my cup. Instantly, the whore inside me emerged, and I humped his prick with delirious abandon, receiving and drilling his cock into my hole and welcoming a load of Polish cum against my crack. Hollan tossed me angrily as the ejaculation surged through his singlet.

Coach Beasley blew his whistle. The match was over. I fell back and felt the joy of male sex seep through my body. I was still intact, still a virgin, but I had enjoyed the tease of a pseudo-fuck, and I trembled with its illegal force.

Fortunately, sweat covered our cum tracks so that no one noticed the indiscretion. The coach in his wisdom threw us towels sensing that we had enjoyed ourselves a bit too much, and we hit the showers while another pair wrestled. Hollan kept me in his antagonistic glare, but I was the first one in and the first one out before Hollan could trap me and ask for a rematch.

That evening, back in my room, I lay in bed exhausted and angry. I recalled the fever of Hollan's hump and asked myself why had I betrayed my hole to the Broshawsky behemoth. I dreamed that Gabe was lovingly parting the cheeks of my ass and anointing my hole with oil.

"Yo, dude!"

Cody and Josh each grabbed a limb and shook me from bed. My eyes opened to their exhilarated faces. A glimmer in their eyes meant something was afoot.

"He's here!" they whispered in unison.

"He?" I asked groggily. "Gabe?!"

"No. The King of the Mat!"

"Who?"

"Dusty. Get up! He's waiting outside!"

"Is Gabe with him?" I asked.

"They broke up," Josh announced. "They're no longer partners. Coach Beasley picked Gabe as Broshawsky's practice mate!"

"Dude, you are *so* lucky," Cody rejoiced.

I sat up in shock. Gabe was to wrestle Hollan? That bastard!

"There's more. The coach has picked *you* to wrestle the King of the Mat! Dusty's in the common room waiting to get acquainted. Hurry up! It doesn't get better than this."

I slouched back on my pillow and stared at midair. All I could think of was Gabe. We were torn apart by the powers that be. I would never enjoy a period with Gabe riding me. I would never know the exhilaration of Gabe's famous single-leg takedown. I asked Fate why, why not Gabe? Who is better suited to wrestle my ass than Gabe? Who is the better match for my discreet affections than he? But Fate was unaccustomed to answering earthly questions.

"Send Dusty in," I said, defeated.

"Send Dusty in *here?*" Josh asked, his face curling in distress at the stale snacks and torn socks littering my space.

I didn't care. In fact, I was angry and wanted to show the world the new match meant nothing to me. Nothing!

"All right," they sang, exiting with alarm.

I remained on my back, tugging a loose thread from my shorts. I didn't feel like being civil to my new mat partner. I lifted onto my elbows just as Dustin McCanon paraded in. His muscles burst through his T-shirt to grand effect, and his shoulders separated the walls around him. I spied his dark goatee and was hopelessly disappointed. Dusty was no flaxen-haired wonder like my dearest Gabe. In fact, he was the antithesis to my happiness: a secondhand prize for staying in a bad match too long. I fell back on my pillow, worrying for my beloved who was now probably sparring with that butt-fucking, Chicago brute!

"This is your room?" Dusty asked, his voice a rich baritone.

"Yeah," I said, hostility in my voice. I reached out to shake his hand, which was only proper but hardly sincere. Dusty knew it. He nodded and stared back. I looked into his eyes, which were as guarded as mine. Maybe he was missing Gabe, too.

Dusty closed the door and turned on the radio.

"You tired?" he asked.

"No."

"Want to get into nylon? Wrestle?"

"No."

"You put Broshawsky to the test earlier. You handled him like a real upperweight. I think the coach knew you could. He was testing you. He probably had us in mind all along."

"Yippee. I got a sore ass, and you get me."

Dusty laughed out loud. He was smiling a nervous grin, one I hadn't seen before. In the state meet, during team trials, or even in class he was stony from cheek to cheek, demonstrating an iron man's stance that he had picked up from the pros. But here he was being himself, noncompetitive, at a disadvantage due to my indifference.

"Are you going to miss him?" I asked abruptly.

"Gabe?" Dusty shrugged. "I'll see him around."

We both felt awkward and the music helped.

What happened next was fantastically bizarre. Without pause or request, Dusty climbed into bed and collapsed beside me. The bed frame rattled. It could barely support one gladiator, let alone one and a half. I remained paralyzed, frightened by his gesture, afraid the bed would collapse and we would die.

Close contact is a wrestler's way of calming down and making new friends. Dusty butt my head playfully. The King of the Mat was looking to take things slow, start things on the right foot, initiate things on a small scale. But there was nothing small about Dusty McCanon.

Dusty's deep breathing betrayed his anxiety, and his hands prodded me hesitantly. His lips let loose a faint scent of bad breath.

Ahh, that was sexy; so he wasn't perfect after all.

I didn't make a sound. Dusty curled up on top of me, his chin nipping my neck. I felt his biceps wrap around my chest tenderly. They were huge and swept over me in waves of built flesh. And his thighs pinned me down, trapping my hips and gently rubbing my crotch for sensation. Dusty moaned and cooed, and closed his eyes like a baby bird waiting to be fed.

Was it my turn? I was losing circulation. I nudged him with my elbow, which was the only limb I could find that wasn't constrained. It so happened that I nudged him in his groin. He smuggled a naughty grin and mouthed a kiss between us. This is wrestler's foreplay? I get it. Grapple with his gear. I nudged his cock inside his jockstrap and turned my face to greet him. He was waiting to kiss me, so I kissed him. His breath was strong but tasted sweet, and his dark goatee felt gruff against my chin. I kissed him once more, and his tongue licked the inside of my mouth, wet and eager to please. Dusty was feeling adventurous and horny: a masculine guy who loved physical contact with other masculine men.

"Top or bottom?" Dusty asked.

"Neutral for now," I whispered.

He released my chest and exposed his cock.

Dusty's dick fell on my belly like a gigantic horn, pink, solid, and curved. It was the first time I'd seen it raw, at last freed from his singlet. Like a prehistoric instrument, it lay across my navel oversized and undermanned. Nature had cast his tool into a perfect musical shape, walloping to those who dared play it, and demanded that it be regularly tuned in a ripe hole.

Aroused and thrashing, he left it there for my eyes to digest and returned his arm around my chest, impressing me to the fact that with him nearby there would always be this extra mouth to feed.

Slowly, Dusty humped my side, rubbing his dick up and down my abs, exciting himself. His balls rolled against my hip and warmed his load. They were wildly hairy, making his boner even more in need of conquest. My hand reached and felt the hot head riding between us. His famous Dick-In-The-Canon, now in my hand, was moist with crotch sweat. I grabbed the width of him and made a tight grip like a pussy for his prick to screw in. He responded and pumped my fist slow and steady, filling the palm chamber with dick sweat.

The thick scent of him filled my bed. Dusty kissed my cheek and chin, tightening his grip on my chest. His heavy legs spread as his hips rocked.

Meanwhile, I was sweating under his lock and key. My own cock was bounded in my shorts, begging to participate in our first match. His friendly thigh rubbed me, welcoming my erection.

We were quiet lovers just then, with music playing behind us and cum loads jamming our nuts. No one could hear what we were doing, though I felt certain Cody and Josh were speculating to detailed accuracy.

Dusty kissed my lips and smeared my open face with his saliva. We wrestled tongues. My fingers tightened the hold on his privates, and he reached into my shorts for mine. I choked his male muscle in my hand until he began cumming in my grip, silently discharging semen into the cup of my hand. In mounting blasts he deposited his Michigan seed on my chest. He continued like that, with each thrust of his wrestler's hips pumping and cumming, until I coached a throttling climax that glued my palm to his dick.

From within my shorts, I ejaculated into his own fist where he could feel its sticky effect. I fantasized Dusty was pounding the wagon and scoring the next round inside me. My cock kept up his momentum and offered a blowable load for him to dream about.

Pump him dry.

There was no one around to count the cum shots between us that night, enough cum to father a nation of young wrestlers. Dusty wasn't satisfied until we did it all over again. He drained his balls some more, cum-caking the canvas of my chest, and I came in his other hand, stamping the deal.

Later, the King of the Mat stretched out beside me, wiping his palms on his thighs and mumbling with satisfaction before falling asleep. I coddled his cheek with kisses and with my hand nursed his pulsing pecker for future performances.

Wrestlers like Dusty are a primal breed. Most of them are distractingly silent, whether on the mat, in person, or in bed. It's in their training. They're bred to be physical observers, touching for knowledge and groping for power. But the fact remains that they make the best lovers because they throw themselves into the act, oblivious to injury, appreciating anyone who relished the chance to test their technique as well as taste their prize.

Dusty's sweat and odor crawled over me. He saturated my senses, compelling me to forget my previous affections. Gabe *who?* When Dusty snored, it was in the rich baritone by which he spoke. I laid my chin against his cheek and heard Coach Beasley's whistle lull me to sleep.

In the morning and for the rest of the year, Dusty was by my side. It was like we were married: we shared pudding in the dining hall, we took showers in the evening, we bench-pressed until dawn. We lost track of our studies and got reprimanded by the coach, but that was to be expected. There's always a honeymoon period between wrestlers that needed to be observed. And we usually spent the nights in my dorm room watching a taped tournament and studying every move, until we both grew horny and got busy. And in the end, when Dusty graduated and I had two years remaining, I was well suited to lead our team into the state finals, confident that where Dusty's memory lingered, we would win. And we did. Even Gabe returned to watch me roll an old rival, that Oklahoman who made it all possible, whose thighs turned off Gabe's lights and turned my life on.

Bonding

Thomas Fuchs

Bobby Lo was practicing his fighting forms under his favorite tree in the park when the guy came up and started watching him, a white guy with wavy brown hair and green eyes. Bobby had never done it with a guy with green eyes. Green eyes. *How exotic,* thought Bobby. And the guy seemed to have a good body.

When Bobby finished, the guy said, "Very cool."

"Thanks," said Bobby. "Are you interested in martial arts?"

"I took some karate," said the guy. Then he said, "I bet you could show me a few things."

Bobby had no interest in giving this guy lessons, but from the way those eyes were checking him out, Bobby suspected the guy wanted something else, which Bobby was quite happy to give him.

"My name's Terry," said the guy.

"I'm Bobby." They shook hands. Then Bobby said, "Let's see how strong you are."

Terry hesitated. "Do you want to spar?"

"Maybe you're too strong for me," said Bobby. "We better check."

"How?" said Terry. "You want to arm wrestle or something?"

"Choke me."

"Huh?"

"Grab my throat. Choke me."

Terry put his hands on Bobby's neck, lightly, tentatively.

"Go ahead," said Bobby, "hard as you can."

Terry began to squeeze.

"You can do better than that," said Bobby.

Terry squeezed harder.

"Are you a girl?" taunted Bobby. Actually, Bobby knew some girls who were very strong. He was just trying to make Terry mad. It worked. Terry squeezed so hard the veins popped up on his forearms but of course Bobby was using "iron neck" technique. He smiled at Terry. Then he brought his hands up and put his thumbs on either side of Terry's neck and pressed, not on his throat to cut off his air, but on the nerve points that made his blood pressure drop. Almost instantly, Terry's strength ebbed away and his knees buckled and he was out.

Bobby lowered him gently to the ground. To Bobby, he looked like an angel sleeping there . . . so peaceful. With his eyes closed. Bobby really wanted to look at those wonderful green eyes so he slid one of Terry's eyelids open with his thumb, but Terry's eyes were rolled back and up with mainly the white showing. Oh well. It was time to move on to the next step of his plan. He massaged Terry's abdomen, getting his energy stirring again, and in a few seconds Terry's eyes fluttered open. Bobby stared at those green eyes. Something about them . . .

"What happened?" asked Terry.

"You took a nap."

"That was a sleeper hold. You sleepered me," said Terry.

"Best way to end a fight without really hurting the other guy."

"No one ever did that to me before," said Terry.

"I can do lots of things no one's ever done to you before."

Terry, completely awake now, gave Bobby a sharp look but it wasn't anger or fear. Terry was excited.

"Want to do more?" Bobby asked.

"Here?" said Terry.

"Let's go to my place."

As soon as they were in Bobby's apartment, without a word, both of them pulled off their shirts, and then, both of them laughing about it, they pulled off their pants. Bobby was pleased to see he was right about Terry. The white boy was in good shape, well-defined muscles, and very nicely hung. Of course, Terry wasn't disappointed, either; in fact, he was a little surprised at just how much muscle his new friend was packing, and just how thick his dick was.

"You know what the key is to good martial arts?" said Bobby.

"Practice?" asked Terry. "Training?"

Bobby shook his head. "Chi. Energy."

"I've heard of that. That's Chinese."

"Everyone has chi. Every thing, really. Anyway, building your chi and focusing it, if you do that, then you've got it. And you know what? It's also really important for sex, too."

"Ah . . ." said Terry. He didn't really want a lecture on chi and was happy the conversation was turning to the subject he was interested in.

"I want you to help me summon up my chi. Will you do that?"

"Okay," said Terry but he didn't know what he was supposed to do until Bobby began stroking himself and pushed Terry to his knees.

Bobby spit into his hand and lubed himself and then took Terry's hand and guided it into position. Right away, Terry began a good rhythmic stroking. Bobby put his hands behind Terry's head, pushed him gently forward. Pretty soon, Terry was using his tongue. He took the tip of Bobby's cock in his mouth and began to suck, and then he took more, and more, and then he was at the base, and slowly pulled all the way back to the tip, letting his tongue slide into every fold and crevice.

Bobby felt his dick swelling, stiffening, felt the familiar but always thrilling power flooding him. He began pumping Terry, the two of them working together as Terry sucked and sucked. At one point, as Bobby was looking down, Terry looked up with those intriguing green eyes and Bobby almost shot. But he was saving himself for what was coming next, so he pushed Terry away and pulled out. His dick was swollen and dark red, pulsing with energy. "Look," he said. "You did a great job getting my chi flowing."

Terry didn't say anything but to Bobby it was clear that he was thinking something like, *Whatever. Let's not have a speech, okay?*

"If you had strong chi, it wouldn't have been so easy for me to knock you out in the park. So now I'm going to put some of my chi into you."

Bobby dropped to the floor behind Terry, and before the white boy could move, Bobby had his legs wrapped around his torso and his arms around his neck. He liked the feel of Terry's supple muscular body between his legs, against his cock, as the white boy struggled to get free, so he held off slapping on the pressure.

"Hey, Bobby, what you doing?"

"For my heat to get into you, I have to turn your flame down a little."

"My what?"

"Chi."

"Huh?" said Terry. Then Bobby flexed his arms, putting pressure on the same neck points as before along with a temple point. Terry resisted for barely more than a second, then slid into unconsciousness. A little saliva ran from the corner of his mouth.

Bobby let go, laying Terry flat, then went and got condoms and lube from a drawer. When he pushed Terry's legs up so he could lube his asshole, he was delighted to see how smooth he was. Naturally smooth, not shaved, even around the asshole. This was somewhat unusual for a white boy. Green eyes and a smooth ass. A fine specimen.

Bobby slipped on the rubber and began, gently but steadily, to push his cock into Terry's hole. Nice and tight. He pushed harder.

Terry began to stir. When Bobby started pumping him, he woke up all the way. What would he do now? He began to respond, working his hips and moaning. He cried out, "Oh ... Oh, God ... Oh, God ... Oh ... This is great. ... Oh ... Do it to me ..." He stroked himself as Bobby pumped him and pumped him, until Bobby saw that he was about to cum. Of course, Bobby knew all the secrets and tricks of cum and chi control, and he wanted to have a lot of fun now, so he pressed a point just under Terry's balls, stopping his cum, saying, "Try to hold it. Master this and you'll be on your way to controlling your chi. You'll shoot when I do. We'll do it together."

He worked Terry and worked him, watching the white boy's powerful chest surge and heave with the undulating effort and the beautifully defined abdominal ridges rippling, and feeling the waves of pleasure surging through his own body, the thrilling heat burning through him.

Finally he pulled out and tore off the rubber at the same moment he released the pressure on Terry, so that they shot together, their thick white cum running all over Terry's glistening chest and abdomen.

Afterwards, while they rested and had tea and took showers, Terry said nothing. Bobby wondered how he felt about this experience. Had he hurt him, been too rough with him? But then, just as Terry was preparing to leave, he said, "That was heavy. Chi, huh?"

Bobby nodded. Then Terry said, "Maybe we can do this again, huh?"

"Sure."

After he was gone, Bobby thought about Terry's green eyes, which had fascinated him so much at first. It had been a lot of fun, but of course, the eyes hadn't made any difference, after all. *Well,* he thought, *you have to try different things sometimes.* Of course, at this moment, Bobby had no idea how important a role Terry would soon play in his life and in the life of a young body builder named Mark Uchida.

Sometimes Bobby worked out in the park where he had met Terry, but he was using the gym the day he spotted the newcomer, the young Japanese body builder. Mark Uchida was magnificent—over six feet tall, beautifully proportioned and defined, massive thighs, slender waist, bubble butt, satin-smooth skin. And the face—high, chiseled cheekbones, eyes bright as a child's, lips that were full and sensual. His forehead was furrowed with the intense concentration of the serious athlete working out.

Bobby knew all the gym guys would want Mark, and he felt he had to protect him. Why? Maybe because Mark was so young and because he was Asian. They were both living in West Hollywood, where Asians were a minority, and so in a way, Mark was like a brother, a younger brother. But something else was also happening. Usually, Bobby didn't think that much about having sex with Asian guys, even when they were studly, maybe because of the brother thing. It was strange—to feel like brothers with the same guy he lusted to get sweaty with and fuck.

Mark pushed a lot of weight and kept to himself. Bobby said hello several times but Mark was only polite and nothing more. He didn't seem interested. This was not something that Bobby was used to. Usually when he went after a guy, he got him right away.

Maybe Mark wasn't gay? No . . . Bobby was never wrong about that, but—maybe Mark wasn't interested in Asians! That made Bobby angry in a way he didn't like to admit. Then he caught Mark looking at him. Well, he'd just have to make more of an effort. The boy was shy.

Bobby waited outside the gym, and when Mark appeared, walked right up to him and said, "Hi, guy!" And he did more than just say hello. He blocked Mark's way. He put on his friendliest face, but he wasn't going to let Mark pass without talking to him.

A long second passed, then Mark said hello.

"You're new here," Bobby said. "You like this gym?"

Another long moment went by. Suddenly, Mark blurted out, "Do you want to be friends?"

"Sure." Bobby smiled.

"Usually . . . it's funny, but usually I don't talk to people I don't know."

"If you want to meet people," said Bobby, "you have to talk to them. Do you want to come over for a beer?"

Mark said yes but when they got to Bobby's place he asked for just a glass of water. "My body building," he explained.

Bobby gave him tea instead and asked him if he'd won any contests. It took him a little while to find this out, but Mark confessed he had never actually entered a contest. Why? He didn't have the confidence.

"You're a very good-looking guy," said Bobby. "You have a great body. I can see you've worked very hard on it. You should have lots of confidence." Then he said, "Are you tight from your workout? Do you want a massage?"

Mark smiled and nodded. He wanted to be touched.

Bobby slipped behind him and began working his neck, then his shoulders.

Mark sighed and started to lie down. Bobby stopped him and began unbuttoning his shirt. Mark finished the job.

"It's better if you take off your pants, too," said Bobby.

In a moment, Mark was wearing nothing but a dark red bikini that set off the smooth, tanned sheen of his body. This boy had a lot of sweet, thick energy flowing through him.

Carefully, lovingly, Bobby leaned into the work of massaging Mark, giving him deep, graceful strokes he knew would penetrate the masses of muscle, relax him, make him ready . . . down from the broad, square shoulders along either side of the deep crevice of his back . . . pressing the key points, rubbing the surrounding flesh . . . down to that perfect bubble butt and the dark red bikini.

When he ran a light finger down the crack of Mark's ass, the big boy sighed and spread his legs slightly and Bobby knew for sure that exquisite joy would soon be his. He slid Mark's bikini off and pulled it down to his ankles. Mark kicked it away.

Once the massage was over, it was time to move on to the next phase. Bobby took off his own bikini . . . his cock had been rock hard ever since he'd first touched Mark. He slipped on a condom and asked, "Do you like to be on your back or your stomach?"

"This is fine," said Mark, drawing his knees up under him, pushing his magnificent hard brown ass high into the air.

Now Bobby began massaging Mark's asshole with a special cream made of herbs to increase the circulation, relaxing the muscles, making Mark open so that he could easily slide one finger in, then two. He reached in until he found the smooth, firm surface of Mark's prostate, which he pressed and rubbed lightly. The sweet young giant's whole body shivered with pleasure.

Now Bobby pulled his fingers out, slipped on a condom, and began pushing in his cock, slow and deep. Just how much could this hardbody boy take? Mark grunted once and gasped, but pushed back. He wanted more.

Bobby gave it to him—another deep stroke and another and another, pumping faster and faster, and Mark pumping back with that hard ass and those powerful thighs. He may have been young, but he was no virgin. All his earlier shyness was gone and the athlete's sense of rhythm and power took over. He and Bobby were one, each doing his part in the surging dynamic of male love, enormous strength and easy grace.

They pumped on and on, two perfectly conditioned guys with endless stamina. It was everything that fucking can be, building, building . . .

Finally, Mark began to shoot, great spurts of thick white cum . . . . Bobby kept pumping him and pumping . . . His own cum was ready . . . he held it, held it, held it . . . then pulled out and using the "hold back" technique—tensing the tendons and muscles of his dick and his prostate—he kept the semen inside him, sent it recirculating within him, shaking and bucking and groaning as the indescribable waves of pleasure rocked him.

Later, Mark said, "I've never seen that before. You were really getting off, but you didn't cum."

"I came all right. I just didn't shoot." Bobby explained about holding the semen in: "It keeps you strong, and it gives you a fantastic orgasm."

"I thought you were going to explode."

"And if you keep it in you, it's easier to go again, when you want to have more fun." Bobby was planning to do more with Mark. He wanted this fresh, innocent kid with those great legs and that iron cock to fuck him.

However . . . when he asked Mark if he'd like to do it, Mark said, "I'm bottom only."

"Well," said Bobby, "whatever suits you. But you should try it sometime. I can make it feel really good for you."

"I don't know if I can," said Mark. "To tell you the truth, I don't stay hard when I try it."

Bobby thought this over, then he said, "Well, some people are bottoms only and that's okay, but you're too young to be set in your ways. You could be a champion on both sides of the court. I'll bet you could do it."

The big guy's face clouded with uncertainty. "Maybe next time," he offered.

"Sure," said Bobby, "but I . . ." He wasn't giving up on getting what he wanted, what he felt Mark needed to do, right now, but before Bobby could say anything more, there was a knock at the door.

"I'm not expecting anyone," said Bobby, very irritated at the interruption. "Just ignore it."

The knock came again.

"I always have to answer the door or the phone when it rings," said Mark. "Don't you just have to know who it is?"

"No," said Bobby.

Then a shadow from outside fell across the blinds that covered a side window. Damn! They weren't completely closed. Someone was trying to look in.

"Hey, it's Terry. You home?"

Bobby was annoyed but not surprised. He often had this effect on guys he fucked. They got hungry for more. And when you've got that hunger . . . Bobby held a finger to his lips, to warn Mark to say nothing. The little conspiracy made the hunky boy smile broadly. He was trying not to laugh. He had a beautiful smile. He was so cute, so sweet. A big kid!

"Sshhh," said Bobby but then he began to laugh.

Terry was back at the door, knocking again, and suddenly Bobby realized this intrusion presented a great opportunity. He went to the door and opened it.

"Hey," said Terry again, then his eyes widened when he saw the hunky Japanese guy. "So, what are you guys doing?" he asked. Was he being a smart-ass?

"We're not doing anything much," said Bobby. "We were talking." He thought it was a pretty stupid question, since he and Mark had their clothes off, but Terry persisted.

"Yeah? What about?"

"White guys," said Bobby. "What else do you think Asian guys talk about?"

Terry suspected he was being put on, but in a few seconds he wasn't going to be thinking much at all.

"Hey, Mark," said Bobby. "Do you know about the sleeper?" And as he said this, he reached out for Terry, who tried to pull away, but Bobby caught him and locked his neck in just the right way, putting pressure on the sleeper points. "No, don't, please don't . . ." Terry managed to say as he clawed at Bobby's powerful arms for a second and then his hands dropped to his side.

Bobby was very precise in his martial arts. He didn't want Terry all the way under; he got him just to the point where he was goofed out but still able to stay on his feet. Then he turned to Mark and said, "After you do this to a guy, he'll always know who's boss." He handed the hold over to Mark.

Mark liked anything physical and he was curious about this so when Bobby let go, he wrapped his arms around Terry the way Bobby had. Bobby made a slight adjustment and then said, "Now put the pressure on."

Because Terry hadn't been completely knocked out, he was able to regain his strength and now he began trying to get away. Mark flexed, his thick arms bulged, and Terry went completely limp, his face flushed red and saliva bubbled from his lips. Bobby laughed. "Let him go," he said, "you'll give him a stroke. Let him down gently."

Mark did as he was told. Bobby was very pleased by something he'd been watching for. As soon as Mark triumphed by knocking Terry out, his dick had gotten hard again and popped up high.

"You have to remember how strong you are," said Bobby. "You're a very strong guy." Mark's dick rose even higher. It was throbbing visibly.

Mark smiled shyly, but then he looked at Terry with some concern. The white guy was lying very still except that one arm and one leg were twitching.

"He's probably having a dream," said Bobby. "You took him out real good. You're the boss man here. You know, it's kind of like being on top."

He bent over Terry and pressed a point that put him deeper and made sure he'd stay unconscious for a while longer. Bobby wanted some private time with Mark.

"Now, where were we?" said Bobby. "Oh yeah . . . " He pointed to Mark's dick, said, "Wow," then went down on his knees, opened his mouth, and folded his lips around the head of Mark's cock and made it wet with his saliva and then flicked his tongue back and forth across the head. Slowly, so slowly and gently, he began inching down Mark's cock. The big boy made the most wonderful sounds, gentle moans, a kind of whimpering joy.

After a while, Bobby stopped and stood up. He took Mark in his arms and said, "Now lie down, lie on your back."

Mark did and Bobby stroked his cock a few times before rolling on a condom. He lowered himself onto Mark's powerful rod slowly. It was really important that Mark not fail at this—not just for the pleasure Bobby was expecting but for the sake of Mark's confidence. He had to stay hard, so Bobby was very careful. He swallowed Mark's head with his pucker, squeezing and relaxing in intervals down the length of the big boy's shaft. Mark groaned with deep pleasure. Bobby was all the way down now, had all of Mark in him and he began to do squats, slowly up and down on Mark, then a little faster, and faster . . . Suddenly, Mark sat up, lifted Bobby up on to his knees, and plowed him from the back with great energy and perfect hardness. His technique was a little clumsy, but Bobby knew he would improve with practice, practice, practice. He would soon be a wonderfully satisfactory fucker.

Then Mark stopped and asked, "You okay?"

"Just fine down here," said Bobby.

"I'm gonna shoot."

Bobby gave him one more squeeze with his ass muscles, a powerful one, to keep the big guy from cumming in him, and when he relaxed the squeeze he said, "Pull out," and Mark did. Bobby grabbed the base of the big guy's cock.

"Hold it in, hold it in," said Bobby and Mark shook so hard that for a second Bobby thought he was joking but he wasn't. A little of his cum came out, but then the rest recirculated.

Mark sank to his knees. "Gosh," he said. "I never fucked anyone before. That was great. Thank you. Thanks so much." And then Mark did the most amazing thing. He kissed Bobby, deep but somehow more sweet than sexy, and Bobby kissed him back and they would have continued with this except that at this moment, in the corner, there was movement, and Terry sat up and moaned, "I've got a headache." Then as he came fully awake, he asked, "What are you guys doing?"

Bobby went over to him and rubbed his neck and his temples until Terry felt okay again. "I'll get you some tea," said Bobby. "Don't try to get up for a minute, you'll faint."

When Bobby went into the kitchen to get the tea, he signaled Mark to come along.

"What do you want to do about him?" asked Bobby.

Mark shrugged. "He's your friend."

"Not really," said Bobby, "But well . . . we can't be rude and just ignore him."

"What do you think he wants?"

"What do you think?" said Bobby. "He wants some Asian hard body to fuck him. Do you want to watch or do you want to do it?"

Mark smiled.

When they came back into the room, Bobby went over to Terry and without saying anything at all, began stroking the lower part of his back, then swept his hands down Terry's wonderful smooth round ass, down along the inside of his legs. The white boy began to shiver with waves of excitement.

Mark liked watching this, stroking his own cock, getting it ready but he also was studying Bobby's technique. He realized he could learn a few things from Bobby Lo.

Bobby was doing "vibrating palm" on Terry, front and back at the same time . . . one hand just above his cock, the other at the lower part of his back with the fingers pointed downward. This technique sent energy flaring around and up Terry's asshole, through his balls, out along his cock. His asshole began to open all on its own and his cock curled up high.

Now Bobby slid his fingers into Terry's hole, then slowly drew them back and forth. Terry's breathing became deep and heavy. Bobby gestured for Mark to come over and pulled his fingers out. Without missing a beat, Mark then pushed his cock in.

Terry grunted, Mark stopped pushing for a beat, then he pressed in, deeper and deeper.

"Yeah . . . yeah . . . yeah . . ." said Terry, taking it all as Mark rode him and pumped him, completely in control of this guy and having the time of his life. What Mark didn't know was that he was about to have even more fun.

Bobby slipped on a rubber and came over and touched Mark's ass to let him know what was going to happen next, and Mark said, "Oh, yes, yes . . . Please . . ." as Bobby rubbed his asshole with lube and loosened him up and then pushed into him.

Now Bobby led the rhythm. He was the most experienced, he was the strongest, he was on top. And even as the animal power surged through him, his brain was working. It was strange how clearly he could think sometimes, even as he was fucking. He realized that although he almost always tried to be a considerate lover, this was different. He was coordinating everything for Mark's sake, doing everything he could to put him in fuck Heaven. Was he beginning to really care for the hunky boy?

As for Mark, getting it up the ass from Bobby Lo at the same time he had his cock deep inside Terry, he had never, ever felt this good, in every way.

None of them, not even Bobby, could have told you how long this went on. They were three strong young guys giving it everything they had. It went on and on and on. Then, finally, Terry began to shoot . . . hot, thick cum on to the mat. Bobby stopped and pulled out of Mark and Mark pulled out of Terry, but they weren't finished yet.

Terry lay exhausted and watched Bobby and Mark strip off their rubbers and go at each other again. This time, each of them mouth to cock, each consuming and being consumed— their energies flowing together and growing with every pulse through the two-body cycle. More than anything, Bobby wanted to taste Mark, to have that young stud's sizzling cum in his mouth and down his throat and to give Mark what he had flowing in himself. He got even more excited with the first taste of Mark's slick precum . . . and Bobby stopped sucking and gently pushed the stud boy away. He had to protect Mark. Play safe. Nonetheless, they still shot at the very same instant, ecstasy surged through them and they were filled with the pure white light of complete fulfillment.

Watching all this, Terry saw something it would take Bobby and Mark a little longer to understand; there wouldn't be room for Terry or anyone else here again.

As for Bobby getting it on with an Asian guy . . . well he wanted to think about that, very seriously. Why had he not wanted it with an Asian until Mark? He went out to one of his favorite places for meditating, a tree-shaded point on the cliffs above the ocean. He was prepared to stay as long as it took for the answer to come to him.

Just as he was settling in, about to close his eyes and begin his breathing, he happened to glance down to the beach where a cute white surfer boy was just coming out of the water. Bobby smiled. If he weren't busy with his meditating, he'd probably go and get that boy and . . . and suddenly he had the answer! Usually he was very aggressive when it came to sex, and since he tended to see Asians as brothers, he couldn't be aggressive with them. It had been different with Mark. He cared about Mark and was excited by him and wanted to be with him. Mark was a kind of breakthrough for Bobby, a bridge between being brothers and well . . . there were many possibilities, weren't there, ready to be explored and experienced.

As for Mark, fucking two guys that afternoon when he'd never fucked anyone before, that had given him lots of confidence. A few weeks later, he entered his first body-building contest, a local event but with very strong competition. Bobby was in the audience and he really thought Mark was the hottest. In fact, Mark came in second in his division and was very happy. That night he and Bobby celebrated but not the way you might think. They went to the party held after the contest and then they went to Bobby's place. They got into bed and held each other and did what they were doing more and more often. They hugged and kissed and snuggled and fell asleep in each other's arms. They didn't fuck until morning.

Terry saw them around from time to time and they all always said hello. One thing about Terry was different. His eyes weren't green any more. They were violet. His green eyes had been contact lenses, and he'd decided to change them. He asked Bobby and Mark what they thought, and they agreed that yes, violet was very, well, exotic.

Here You Go, Nancy

David Christensen

In the early spring of 1981, my high-school choir—the Crestmont Madrigals—went on tour. Our final destination: Disneyland. The bus left Salt Lake at noon and pulled up in Cedar City a few hours later. We lodged in residents' homes, boys and girls under separate roofs as required by the school district. Three tenors and I stayed in an overheated bungalow filled with masculine bunk beds and plaid blankets. Our hostess had such a pallid personality I barely noticed her until she suggested we have dinner at Kentucky Fried Chicken. "It's pretty good if you don't mind the smell of the Negroes that come in. They're not really from here. They're athletes *up to the college*." Revolted by the prospect of spending more time with her, I opted instead for the seven o'clock showing of *Ordinary People*. Mary Tyler Moore was great in the role of the frosty mother, and it was titillating to hear Timothy Hutton ask his shrink, "So do you jack off, or jerk off, or whatever?"

After the movie I hit Rexall Drug for something to read, and that's when I first saw it: Nancy Friday's *Men in Love*. Its suggestive red-lettered title beckoned me from the pulp rack at the front of the store. I read the jacket blurb as far as the words "men's sexual fantasies" and knew I had to have it. I paid for it, slipped it inside my coat, and walked back to the bungalow with a hard-on, but I couldn't summon the courage to read a dirty book in front of the tenors. I packed it in my suitcase, hotly anticipating an occasion for privacy.

The next day we performed at Cedar High, then headed toward Southern California. There was nothing to do but stare out the bus's windows and watch the ugly desert become the ugly metropolis. After the Disneyland gig we got to ride the rides for free. I liked how the warning on the tickets read, "Snow White (Scary)."

Eighteen hours later we were back in a Utah blizzard. The bus dropped us off at school. Mom gave me the silent treatment all the way home. I never knew why. I went to my room, locked the door, and read.

Men in Love: The Triumph of Love Over Rage is a collection of men's erotic fantasies with commentary by amateur sexologist Nancy Friday. Each chapter features a different type of sex—oral, anal, bi, gay, groups, S/M, water sports, interracial, etc. My favorites are the straight men's fantasies about other men—surprising houseguests in the shower, discovering repairmen with their wives, and so on. Some stories are more exotic. Dr. Lewis Brown imagines being castrated by his wife's lover, a rival surgeon. When Jefferson describes sucking off his drunken father, Nancy Friday seeks input from three therapists, but stumps them all with this "new and rare idea."

I read *Men in Love* a dozen times. Stored in the bottom of my underwear drawer, it was my constant companion through the rest of high school and at college. When it wore out, I'd buy another copy. The first edition included instructions for contributing fantasies to a sequel. I wanted to send Nancy some of my fantasies, but it was too scary for me back then. So, Nance, if you're out there and you're still listening, let's try this again. Here you go.

Curly
I notice a new guy at work. He has a swarthy, leather-dude look, curly black hair, a bushy goatee, nice body, not thin. I decide he's straight. I get obsessed with the idea of rimming him, but he doesn't know I'm

alive. I overhear and memorize snippets of his conversations with others, gems like, "Back to the grind," and, "How 'bout those Giants?" There's something about his face; it's near-homely, and I have a hard time remembering what he looks like when I'm not looking at him. He reminds me of my dad, or a former boyfriend, both of whom had dark curly hair. I notice he seems awkward around women. He's probably lonely and horny, which means I have a chance.

I run into him in the men's room. He's standing at the mirror, pulling his whiskers, training them to lie in one direction. He catches me looking. His eyes are black and hostile. Undaunted, I push him into a stall, pull his pants down, and turn him around. His ass is as cute as I imagined, but not very clean. I try sucking his cock instead. It's skinny and I like fat ones, so I lose interest pretty damn quick. Then *he* kneels in front of *me* and starts sucking *my* cock. He's definitely sucked cock before. It's an outstanding performance. My cum splats against his perfectly straight whiskers, and I think: *Almond Joy.* He tries to wipe it off but only shampoos it in deeper.

On my way out I shrug. "Back to the grind!"

Experiment

This weekend I tell Scott I want to try something different: I want to play out a fantasy where one of us is a total top. The bottom has to do whatever the top says. I say we can switch roles if we end up doing this more than once. I'm in the mood to get fucked, so I'm glad when he says he wants to top.

I say we have to start out completely dressed so it will take longer. Scott has me stand facing him while he sits on my bed. He tells me to take off my shoes and socks, then my shirt, pants, underwear, one item at a time until I'm naked. Stripping doesn't take as long as I'd hoped, but being naked excites me and I get a huge hardon, which Scott kind of looks at but kind of ignores. He goes to my closet and takes out the belt I wear to work. He uses it to tie my hands behind my back, then just stands there staring at me. *What're ya gonna do?* Still staring at me. *Talk to me.* Now he looks mean. We haven't discussed safe words. I'm not even sure if he knows what a safe word is. *What're ya gonna do?*

He punches me in the gut. He punches me hard, again and again. I gasp for breath, doubled-up in pain.

Music (Ugly)
Manhattan, 1937. Intellectuals abound. I'm at an all-gay party where the young Leonard Bernstein fawns over Aaron Copland. Lenny knows Copland has connections, and he's willing to do just about anything to get connected. Lenny's hot, barely 19, with thick glossy black hair, broad shoulders, and a great smile. Copland's 37, has bad teeth, bad breath, and the biggest bird-beak nose in the world. He dares Lenny to play the notoriously difficult and dissonant *Piano Variations*.

Lenny: Won't it ruin the party?

Copland: Not *this* party, girlfriend.

I don't care what happens next, because Copland's ugly.

Music (Pretty)
I'm the little boy in Ravel's opera *L'Enfant et le sortilège*. I live with my mother in a cottage in the Normandy woods. It's incredibly quaint this afternoon—the pale winter sun is setting, cookies are baking in the oven, the fireplace is going. I'm supposed to be doing my homework. I get mad, throw things around, am sent to bed without dinner. I lie in my darkening room, not tired, still dressed in my short little jumpsuit, when suddenly, magically, the toys and furniture come to life. I pee my pants.

I'm not aware of any stream of piss, no golden shower, just a dark wet mass spreading from my crotch. I know it belongs to me, is mine only. Peeing my pants is more interesting than watching the dancing wallpaper, my pee's smell richer than the cookies. I get in bed, pull blankets over me until I'm hot and sweaty. I pee my pants again. Now I'm completely soaked, glued to the bed by rank, soggy sheets.

Songez, songez surtout au chagrin de Maman.

Night of a Thousand Waynes, or, Glitter and Be Gay

In college I have an affair with a married middle-aged professor—it's dumb. After he breaks up with me, he gets involved with Wayne, another student, who's cuter than me. I have a mini-breakdown and sleep through most of the summer. When the professor dumps Wayne a few months later, he picks up with *another* student named Wayne, and this one's even cuter than the first one.

Now the Waynes and I are in cahoots. Wayne Two makes a date at the professor's house while his wife's away. Wayne One and I plan to drop by and catch them playing around, then get into an abusive four-way: the professor on his knees, arms bound, surrounded by rigid boy-cock, forced to swallow piss and cum, to glitter, *to be gay*. We slap his pudgy body around. He's never let us fuck him, so now we fuck him, roughly, taking turns. We get shit on our dicks and make him lick it off. After a while we get bored and walk out. We go to Wayne One's and get stoned, then to Naugles for Macho Egg Burritos with extra sour cream.

Fast Track

I'm no longer a fag; I'm one of the boys. Everyone at work likes me. I wear Dockers, get raises, bonuses, promotions. First I'm in Sales, then Management, then Sales Management. On Saturdays I golf, I golf, I.

Daddy Bear for Hire

I move to San Francisco and read the *Bay Area Reporter* for the first time. I turn to the back section. It's full of ads for escorts, and I'm amazed that it's so easy to buy sex. I do a little shopping and find my ultimate fantasy type: a big, butch, salt-and-pepper daddy bear. I call him. My hands are shaking, my throat constricts, and I sound like the 12-year-old I want to role-play. The daddy bear answers, courteous and professional. I test the water with basic questions: top/bottom/oral/anal/safe/bareback/HIV? Then to the point: I ask if he'll help me reenact a scene from childhood. He will. I describe the scenario and offer a few stage directions.

Pacing through my flat, I nearly pass out from excitement. He arrives, growls at me, and heads straight for the bathroom, where he takes a quick shower as planned. Then he calls out to me gruffly. He tells me to come to the bathroom. He's just returned from a hike in the Rocky Mountains and I have to examine his body for wood ticks. I enter the bathroom and see him standing there, naked and dripping. I'm full of dread, embarrassed. I want to look; I want to look away. He growls again. Perfunctorily I scan his hairy chest and back, cock and balls, legs and feet, then glance up at his head. No ticks.

"You didn't look hard enough."

But Dad, I looked. There aren't any ticks.

"You didn't look hard enough."

But Dad . . .

"You didn't look hard enough."

I kneel. Drops of water from his curly hair sprinkle down on me. His cock, long and thick, warm and damp, dangles in front of my face like a horse's carrot. No ticks.

"You didn't look hard enough."

I can't put it off any longer. I do what I know he wants me to do. I heft his cock in my hand, trying to look medical. I twist it gently halfway to view the underside. I lift it to check his heavy balls. No ticks.

"You didn't look hard enough."

I slide the foreskin back. No ticks.

"You didn't look hard enough."

I take a deep breath and gather my courage. I crawl around until I'm facing my dad's butt, and it's beautiful: firm, well shaped, lightly dusted with brown hair. No ticks.

"You didn't look hard enough."

The last frontier. I part his ass cheeks to reveal his perfect, delicious-looking hole. I gaze for a moment at his spread-open crack, my heart pounding, unable to speak or breathe. His asshole is clean and pinkish, bigger than most, inviting. No ticks.

"You can go now," he orders curtly. I get up without speaking or making eye contact, walk back to my bedroom, and pick up Laura Ingalls Wilder where I left off. My eyes follow the lines mechanically, but my mind, numbed, registers nothing.

I've left three one-hundred-dollar bills near the bathroom sink. A few minutes later I hear steps down the hallway. The front door clicks shut.

Funky Little Shack (Sad)

I'm so depressed. Why? Because I just came out with a bang and still nobody loves me. This summer I'm house-sitting Solange's Upper West Side pied-à-terre, where one afternoon I entertain my friends by modeling her floral-print pajama-cut pants suit. I want to have sex but I'm afraid everyone has AIDS. I learn to masturbate with a dildo. I'm surprised how easy it is and how much I like getting fucked. I think about sex with butch types—leather dudes, daddies, bears.

Today is the twentieth anniversary of Stonewall. Daniel and I go to the parade, then dance at the party at the Queer Piers with tens of thousands of others. The event concludes with an "Over the Rainbow" sing-along. We take the subway back uptown, buy fruit at Fairway, and then I walk the last few blocks to Solange's alone. It's late and my neighbors are asleep, so I listen to *Cosmic Thing* through headphones and dance on the brick inlay near the kitchen sink. Later I put on Benjamin Britten's arrangement of "The Last Rose of Summer." Oh shit, now I'm gonna cry.

Claude Debussy, Superstar
I'm eight and I spend a lot of time listening to my dad's reel-to-reel tape collection. My dad's taste is eclectic: there's Carole King, the *2001* soundtrack, some incidental music from a magic show by Reveen, and something scary by Joan Baez, which I try not to hear when it's playing because it really does scare me. My favorite is Ernest Ansermet conducting Debussy. I memorize it. And *Jesus Christ Superstar*.

I'm the director of a children's production of *Jesus Christ Superstar*. I make cast lists from the names of my classmates. I get to play Judas, the most interesting part. I also coach the other singers. My best friend, Mickey Morris, learns all the parts because he's always at my house when my dad's playing the tape. One day we're riding bikes up and down the street, doing the confrontation scene between Judas and Jesus Christ Superstar. We both do both parts. The old man next door hears us. A few days later Mrs. Morris calls my dad and says Mickey can't play with me anymore because we're sacrilegious. I think sac- must be a prefix like un- or non-, that she means we're not religious, and it's true we don't go to church.

With Mickey Morris out of the picture there's nothing to do, so I enter a competition for young composers. It's the final round, only two of us left. The other is Barry Walters, another kid from school. The awards ceremony is held in the ultramodern Mountain Arts Center. It's packed. Barry and I sit next to each other while the orchestra plays our works. I'd like to hold hands but we're competing. My piece sounds exactly like Debussy's *Images pour orchestre*. Barry's is a dud, so I win. When I walk on stage to accept the award, I'm wearing a form-fitting crocheted sweater vest over a blousy dress shirt, a pair of dress slacks, and my best dress shoes—same as Barry Walters.

Jewish Porn Stars (Fun)
I get a part in an Adam Glaser (a.k.a. Seymore Butts) video, so I go down to LA for the weekend. I'm excited because I'm costarring with Herschel Savage, and I've been a fan of his since I saw *Night Nurses* in 1982. Herschel Savage's cock is perfectly shaped and proportioned, and always rock hard. He's starting to look a little like Burt Bachrach, but that's OK because I *love* Burt Bacharach.

Herschel Savage and I play delivery boys who stumble onto an all-girl dildo party at Seymore Butts's suburban home. There are five or six naked girls sprawled on the white modular living-room couch. They're eating each other's pussies, fingering asses, giggling, and squealing. I don't have as much patience even as Seymore Butts to develop this plot, so let's just say we're fucking the girls in the ass, or at least Herschel Savage is; I'm just watching. It's all bareback, of course. When he pulls out of one girl, her asshole retains an O shape. I immediately go down on him—in straight porn that's called ATM (ass-to-mouth)—then after a while he resumes fucking her. I wonder if fucking a girl in the ass feels the same as fucking a man in the ass, but I don't have the energy to find out.

Cops
Cops seem so hot until you really look at them. Here in San Francisco they are pretty dumpy. A group of six or seven are hanging out at my Starbucks—*Starbucks* for Christ's sake!—every morning when I stop on my way to work. They order the femmiest drinks on the menu—triple caramel cocoa-a-gogos, iced cherry macchiatos, hot banana frappuccinos—and discuss the freshness of the madeleines and scones. Whatever happened to day-old donut holes and pale 7-Eleven coffee in Styrofoam cups, I wonder.

I'm standing in line behind two cops wearing their summer outfits of navy-blue nylon shorts, even though it's in the fifties because of the fog. Their butts and legs look pretty good, but they're not very handsome. They have guts, too, although I don't mind that part. I kneel down and gently bite and lick one cop's calf, then move up his leg with more bites. He stops talking, relaxes, and goes, "Mmmm." I move to the other leg and do the same, but this time I go further, my face pressed against the blue nylon, my nose in his crinkly crack. I take a few more bites around his ass cheeks, then bring my hands around to his front so I can rub his hardening cock. He takes it out and starts jerking off. I push his hand away and take over. The cop standing next to him has his cock out and is jerking off. He kneels down in front of my cop and starts sucking him. We manage to pull my cop's shorts down. Now he's getting eaten front and back. I notice two or three cops at a corner table, watching us, rubbing their own crotches and then each other's. One by one their cocks come out. They start stroking, sucking each other.

Look, this just isn't working, so now it's Keith from *Six Feet Under*, Starsky, Baretta, and the cop from the Village People. I continue eating Keith's butt while Starsky lubes his own with the foam from his triple venti latte. Starsky bends over the counter and Keith shoves his cock up his non-fat ass. Baretta wants in on the action and bends over a table. The cop from the Village People pulls a 12-inch dildo out of his gun holster. Now it's working.

House Party at Wayne One's
Wayne One house-sits a mansion outside of the city. I go up now and then to visit. One weekend he throws a house party for five straight couples and me. His date is a slutty violinist. At night I walk into one of the bedrooms, looking for my things, and there's Wayne One sprawled naked on the bed and the violinist backed up against a wall with a sheet draped across her, startled or dazed, I can't tell which. I

wonder what they've been doing. The next morning she's already back in town before the rest of us get up. Now it's four straight couples and me and Wayne One.

There's an indoor swimming pool and sauna in this place. He invites me, just me, to get stoned and go skinny dipping after dinner. He's in really good shape and I'm not. I watch him dive in and swim a few laps. Then he suggests a sauna. We sit naked in the sauna, near each other but just out of reach, swapping sexual fantasies. We both have good cocks, they're hard and sticking straight up out of our laps. His is short and plump and cut. Mine's longer and uncut, but he doesn't notice. Sweat is pouring down our bodies. I want to sit down on his cock. We're so wet and relaxed, I bet it would slide right in. Just when I start to move over, Wayne One says he wishes he hadn't gotten stoned because now he's tired. He gets up and goes to bed.

Choir Concert with Negro Spirituals (Violent)
We head back to Cedar City to wrap this thing up. We find my hostess's plaid house and pound on the door. Keith from *Six Feet Under* carries a bag of chicken from KFC. The hostess is scared, doesn't want to let us in, so we elbow our way past her. Keith pulls his pants down, bends over, and spreads his ass. I kneel behind him and sniff and lick, then force the hostess to rim him. Her screams don't bother Keith; he's loving her tongue up his big black ass. The Madrigals sing Henry Mancini's "Sometimes (Not Often Enough)" and a few Negro spirituals, the entire cast of *Ordinary People* watch and jack off or jerk off or whatever, Keith's jerking off, too, and comes all over a masculine blanket.

We grab the KFC and walk out.

Manila Suites

R. Zamora Linmark

What Passes For Rain

Perhaps. An ambiguous word that should not have survived the sixteenth century. But it did. So best to begin this very short and simple story with an epigraph from the 1985 Pantheon paperback edition of Marguerite Duras's *The Lover*, since this is the book that Javier randomly pulls out from the two shelves of books that make up his personal library, mostly Self-Help and biographies of Marilyn Monroe, James Dean, and Montgomery Clift, while he waits for the monsoon rain to subside, hopefully by midnight, when the so-called overly fashion-and-grooming-conscious "Metrosexuals"—read: faggots with money—ramp into the Flintstones-inspired bar aptly called Government.

Perhaps unfold the story with a quote, something along the theme of waiting, like the waiting that takes place outside a closed door on page twenty-five of Duras's novel, or the Chinese man on page forty-nine who weeps from too much fear—fear of his father, fear of disinheritance, fear of love, which often accompanies fear. Or preface it with an epigraph; one that deals with memory, since *The Lover* is— or can be interpreted as—a pseudo-confessional text about the author-narrator-protagonist, Marguerite Duras, and her recollection of her almost-sixteenth year when she carried on an affair with a Chinese man nearly twice her age. If not that, then something to do with erasure, or the failure of forgetting. In other words, ambivalence toward resignation, or the clarity that comes with resignation, which is at the heart of our main character, Javier's, conflict. To move onward with—or without—Kingston, his Chinese-Filipino lover. To let go—or not—of the ten-and-a-half years spent with and for each other.

If Javier were a writer, as he sometimes fancies himself to be, possessor of that gift—or curse—that allows him to exist in two or more disparate worlds simultaneously, or, in the words of his undergraduate literature professor, "the ability to live in multiple levels of reality," he would find a thousand ways to hang on to the memories and another thousand to forget them. Writing has the power of achieving both. It is a transgressive act of remembering since it is, cannot, and will never be loyal to memory, as memory is never loyal to itself. And, as Duras points out in the story, regardless of what is preserved, something is always left out, forsaken, sacrificed. If not love, then hate. If not hate, then sadness. If not sadness, anger. If not anger, silence. All of which Javier is still having difficulty recognizing as emotions independent from each other because the breakup, which was long overdue (or so he thought), only occurred a little over a month ago.

If Javier had taken up writing in college instead of dentistry ("I numb gums for a living"), he would not have any trouble remembering then letting go of the fucks that followed the near-fistfights, usually caused by Kingston's wife, also a Chinese-Filipino, whom Javier dubs "the itchy cunt between our legs." He would be able to recall then dismiss the mutual apologies that followed the fights; the chain of Sorrys uttered with subtle signs of withdrawals; the annual itinerary to Europe, Continental U.S., Japan, and Hawaii; the joint bank account; the business partnership exporting hand-carved native furniture; the one-bedroom love-and-quarrel nest in Pasig that, during the day, served as their office. In a nutshell, the day-to-day expectations and uncertainties that, in the end, totaled ten-and-a-half years.

And had Javier traded the drill for a pen, Novocain for ink, he would be able to build passages from scratch just so he can lie, fake, grope his way in and out of the hurt. He would do as Duras did: Distance the past through the use of perfect past tense, eliminate the subject with third-person point of view. "He loved him just as much as rain," as opposed to: "I loved him just as much as rain," et cetera. Perfect past tense. "He," not "I." Until Javier is comfortable enough to relive the memory once more in the present tense and in the first-person point of view, as Duras eventually does on the night she and her Chinese lover soak the bed with blood and lust, while the city of Cholon and its assortment of sounds pass them by.

Had Javier the patience for putting, in word-order, his thoughts and feelings, conflicting as they are at the moment, he would know exactly what to do with the rain that, for the past ten-and-a-half years, he's come to associate with Kingston, for the mere—and laughably absurd—reason that whenever it rains, Kingston gets an instant hard-on that lasts way after the sky dries up. Javier would be able to invent a thousand metaphors to remember the rain and another thousand to destroy it. This rain drapes his window and continues to silence and strand this noise-magnet city of Manila, now and for the rest of tomorrow. Perhaps.

The Record Breaker

I like to think it was the one-thousand-peso bedhead look and the Armani cologne given to me by my sister Faye, who's been serving an American cultural attaché officer and his wife based in Hong Kong for seven years, that inspired him to follow me to the Men's room on the fourth floor of Megamall, so-called because it's the largest tomb-shaped mall south of Bangkok. I like to think it was my above-average wholesome looks and Jean Genet–borrowed glances in the mirrored walls that guided him right up to the urinal beside mine, where he flashed a semi-erect penis that would grow past seven inches in my mouth minutes later, inside his secondhand Toyota going fifty out of the mall's parking lot and onto EDSA, the highway that connects north and south of Metro Manila, and famous for staging snap revolutions and coup d'états. I like to think it was my glycerin-esque saliva savoring his sex that, like a Mapplethorpe lily, curved to the right. I like to think it was my Linda Lovelace throat that nearly caused the vehicle to sideswipe a bus crammed with so many passengers they were practically spilling out of it. I like to think it was my willingness to serve rather than be serviced ("I don't care if I come or not!" is my motto) that immediately put a smile to his night. I like to think he was doing me the honor when he invited me, the first stranger, according to him, into his Quezon City townhouse. I like to think he was telling me the truth when he repeated, "It's hard to believe, I know, but you're the first trick I'm letting into my pad." I like to think "trick" has a positive connotation, though I much prefer the comfort of the illusive word "stranger." I like to think I scored perfect tens in the categories of degree of difficulty, artistic impressions, and originality because when he ejaculated he shot for the moon then whimpered like a baby for a kiss. I like to think my kiss is worth a thousand jewels because, right before he excused himself to the bathroom, he asked for an encore. ("Don't worry, I'll drive you home.") I like to think that as he rinsed his belly he was wondering who this stranger was he'd allowed in the privacy of his bachelor's pad, this no-name guy who, at that very moment, was snooping at his things, memorizing titles of books on the shelves. *Learning to Love God. Disappointment with God. Harry Potter and the Goblet of Fire. God Are You There, Do You Care, Do You Know About Me. The Lion, The Witch, & The Wardrobe. The Trouble with Jesus. Dealing with Brokenness.* I like to think that he is now repaired or has found a way to negotiate Christianity, oral sex, and wizardry into his life. I like to think that, as he gave himself one last look in the medicine-cabinet mirror, he was telling himself that I was a one-of-a-kind twenty-year-old advocacy of behind-the-wheel pleasure whose impeccable English had an accent that teeters between a Merchant & Ivory–produced film and MTV. I like to think that he was thinking all these while I was telling myself: *Oh, shit, he's the third this week, seventh since September rolled in, and that was what, only five weeks ago, what's wrong with me, why am I attracting guys like him, is this an epidemic, am I its bull's-eye?* I like to think I was the poster boy just for the month, that he was just another coincidence, a seven-plus-inch déjà vu, a statistic to my rapidly-growing inventory of trysts with pent-up, hyper-sexual, guilt-ridden, straight or bi-identified, married-to-God, discreet-to-secrete-guys who have yet to reconcile Jesus with jism. I like to think that when he said, "Let me take you home," and I told him, "You don't have to... really... just take me back to Megamall... got tons of cabs there," he was only delivering his Good Samaritan scripted line. And when I asked him, "How many blow-jobs do you need to get through the day?" and he answered, "Depends. Four on a stress-free day, six if it's hectic," prompting me to say, "Then today must be a bad day because you're requesting for an encore," which prompted him to say, "Not really, I just love what you can do with your mouth"—that he was only affirming what I already know: I am the Megamall King of Fellatio, my mouth made of glory, my tongue, a muscle of miracles. And when I asked him, "What's the most blow-jobs you've had in a day?" and he answered, "Six," prompting me to ask, "What number am I?" to which he responded, "Six but seven with the encore"—his "encore" overlapping with my "Jesus"—I like to think that I was about to break his world record as much as he was going to break mine. I as his seventh, and he as my thirteenth-going-on-fourteenth trick.

The Importance of Being Er
The Source
Ramon, who goes by "Mon," believes his fixation with *ers*, as in

blue-coll*er* work*ers,* started one Sunday morning at the age of five. "And it's coll*er* with an E, not an A," Mon told his friends. "Old English spelling, according to *my* Websters."

Mon was in the front passenger seat of the family car, waiting with Carlo the family driver, for the bell to dismiss his parents and two brothers from Mass, when Carlo, who was behind the wheel and who could not be more than twenty at the time, asked Mon if he would like to see up-close, touch even, what Mon had been wanting to play with ever since a couple of dusks ago when Carlo, soap-covered and stroking himself inside the makeshift shower booth he had built from scraps of tin and wood bits, had caught Mon peeping through the holes while Carlo worked on exciting himself, his eye in Mon's eye, nothing disturbing the late-afternoon ritual, except the out-of-place crowing of a rooster and Mon's nanny beckoning him for supper.

"Go ahead, touch it," Carlo said, flashing a fully-erect penis with a mole on its head. Mon looked at the mole: He wanted to kiss it. Carlo reclined on his seat, his eyes half-shut. Heart pounding and head rushing, Mon placed a finger on the dot, circled the subtle bump with it, wondered if he, too, had a mole on his dick. Then he felt it throb. "Do it again," Mon said, giggling. Carlo obeyed. "Hold it," Carlo said, half-opening his eyes. "Go on. It's yours. Hold it like you're holding a Coca-Cola bottle." Mon complied. One hand first, then two.

Folding his right palm over Mon's hands, Carlo said, "Now, glide your palms up and down. Don't break the circle."

Carlo let go as Mon continued to slide his hands up and down the shaft. Carlo began to moan. Mon lifted his eyes to Carlo's mouth curving into a smile. Then Mon let go.

Carlo did not come in Mon's hands. Nor did he take advantage of the boy nor resume the lesson on how to conquer a lazy, Sunday morning while waiting for God to let worshippers out from His temple. But the brief moment ("It was shorter than a sigh," Mon would later recount to his friends) was more than enough to shape Mon's *er*-destiny.

Their first tryst did not take place until seven years later, right around Mon's twelfth birthday ("Talk about a seven-year itch!"). But how it happened was easier and quicker than thawing frozen leftovers in the microwave. All Mon did was ask Carlo, on a very ordinary Manila polluted day, if he could taste it. "And if I enjoy it," Mon told him, "I'll give you half of my allowance, which is a third of what my father is paying you a month."

Carlo, who was not the type to deprive or disappoint Hedonist-seeking teenagers like Mon, unzipped his pants to let the cat out of the bag. The afterschool taste-test stretched to two years—in the car, in the movie house of the neighboring town, in the family mausoleum late at night, behind the abandoned bowling alley that closed down after less than a year in business, on the bush-lined dirt road behind the church. And with each blow, Carlo received his share of Mon's weekly allowance. Their affair remained illicit ("Only cats, dogs, and the dead knew," Mon said. "No one suspected. Not even my sixth-sense-of-a-mother!"), until Carlo was dismissed from the De La Fuente household for impregnating two maids on the block. By then, Mon had already gotten addicted to servicing a man who was economically challenged and socially underprivileged. He had gotten hooked on bathing his tongue with underpaid sweat, especially in the groin area, burying his nose in bushy armpits, licking cigarette-stained breath, sniffing pee-stained briefs.

Ers became Mon's Viagra: Blowing and bottoming for them was his Marie Antoinette 2-for-1 way of feeding them cake and eating them, too.

Case History

After Carlo, an endless chain of blue-coll*er* blows and fucks followed, of which the most recent was a police officer, who had caught Mon blowing a construction worker in the parking lot of SM department store in the wee hours of the morning. The cop went home not only five hundred peso richer but also got a chance to experience Mon's canyon-sized mouth as it engulfed his and the construction worker's at the same time. The two ers came twice and would have gone through a third and fourth shoot-out if the construction worker did not remember he had a pregnant wife and two Montessori-aspiring kids, who, in an hour, would be whining over their Milo-chocolate-themed breakfast at the lack of desks, chairs, and teachers in their classrooms.

At one time, Mon had his weekly share of ushers in movie houses across Manila, especially the run-down theaters in the university belt, Baclaran, Pasay City, and, before it shut down, Delta. Most memorable was a suck-fest throughout the climactic escape scene in Pixar's *Finding Nemo*.

Waiters are a priori in Mon's *er*-list, since many do not receive any job benefits, like medical and dental insurance, sick leave, paid vacation ("How disturbing! They get charged for every plate and glass they break!"). He finds them slaving in Chow King, Jollibee, McDonald's, Aristocrat's, and other half-fine-dining restaurants, where the daily wage is equivalent to four dollars. There, he strikes a conversation, then asks them to stop over his place on their way home for a hundred-peso blow-job, which is the maximum that Mon will pay to service an *er* ("Otherwise, the guy is no longer an *er* but a high-priced whore!").

When Mon worked as a supervisor for a call center in Makati, a position that lasted for two years until he left the company to join the management crew of a five-star hotel, he sucked and paid just about every janitor (or custodian worker) who mopped the restrooms of the twenty-story building.

During the nineties, when he was living in Pasay City for exactly five-and-a-half years, he never ran out of carpenters, plumbers, and fumigators to re-enact scenes from Animal Planet's *Survival of the Fittest* special with, because the townhouse he was renting was poorly maintained—and managed—by the owner who, ironically, was an award-winning architect.

In his ancestral home in La Union, where Mon often goes to hide from the undesirable *ers* of Manila—sniper, murderer, robber, hijacker, and the butcher who, because he could not get enough of Mon's sap-like saliva, stalked him for five months ("It was so Anne Frank meets Freddy Kruger!")—Mon extends his services to the farmers who, when they are not available, send over their sons.

Because Mon is a reckless and restless driver, especially at night, which is the only time traffic is actually bearable in the land of diesel fumes, he often gets pulled over by traffic enforcers who readily accept his bribe with a complimentary express-window service.

Mon also has his share of substitute teachers and counselors, including the guidance counselor of his fifth-grade nephew Ton-Ton who is afflicted with hyperactive deficit disorder. They sixty-nined each other in his office, swallowed each other's load within fifteen minutes, while Ton-Ton fought urges to bang his head against the wall.

A weekly must are the taxi, jeepney, tricycle drivers, and construction workers referred to him by Chito, an engineer-friend who also has a chronic history of *ers*.

As for gardeners: Mon used to blow them quite often, until he ended up one rainy night with a three-inch dick shaped like a spatula. He still hasn't gotten over the shock.

That's about all the *ers* in Mon's life.

Unwanted Ers
Of course, there are many other *ers* grappling with the hyper-harsh realities of Manila, like writers, editors, and painters (of canvases, not homes). But Mon does not consider them *ers* because, although many

are—or refer to themselves as—starving artists, he argues that to be an artist in the Third World is already considered a privilege because it means he or she can afford to stay home, stare out into space all day, and may or may not produce something worth hammering a nail into the wall for. ("Besides, they're too high-maintenance, pretentious, and are afflicted with a never-ending list of case-study diagnosis.")

Epilogue
Whenever Mon is attacked for his *er*-tendencies, gets accused of doing nothing more than exploiting these below-minimum-wage earners and stripping them off of their dignity, and, in a bigger picture, the dignity of this never-ending-corrupt nation ("We are second in the world!"), he merely retorts by saying that what he has done for the near-bankrupt economy, alarming growth in unemployment, and beyond-hope poverty, is what the government has failed to resolve in the past three, four, five administrations. "I feed them, give them toothbrush and backrubs. I refer them to affordable dentists, and pediatricians if they have children. I introduce them to Chito and other *er*-addicts. If there's time, we sit in front of the TV and watch *Norma Rae* or the socio-politically overt films of Lino Brocka. If there's more time than time, we discuss the movie and its relevance to the now. And all I ask is for them to come to me reeking of sweat and heat and lie down or sit up or however way they prefer and stay hard in my mouth or inside me for as long as they can."

A Quiet Scratch

After I come in his mouth, Dick tells me he's never done it before. "I don't believe you," I say, "you suck better than a baby." "I mean, swallow," he says, then asks if I want to hook up with him again, maybe tomorrow night, dinner first, then head over to his house. "My wife is taking the kids to her province for the weekend."

I don't give it another thought, stick to my motto that bathhouse tricks and lets-get-acquainted dinner conversations should never mix. And although my friend, a bathhouse queen who goes by the drag name of Peter Pan de Leche, has known couples whose long-term relationship had blossomed from a bathhouse orgy ("So did gonorrhea!" I told him), I still cling to the belief that the function of a bathhouse is primarily to find a partner or two, get the party started, know your roles, transgress them. If it's an orgy, even better, jump in, shoot your load, towel-dry, then, like desire, vanish. If you're Catholic, go to confession, then return to the bathhouse the following night and repeat the sequence.

Besides, hooking up with Dick beyond the confines of snap-lust might ruin whatever necessary fiction I've already produced about him in my head. Bi-identified. Works out at Gold's Gym at least eight times a week, which explains for his to-lick-for smooth chest that the repressed, young, and old gym bunnies can jack off to in the sauna or steam room, solo or ensemble. And his last tryst? Probably a couple nights ago, with a gym buddy, who is probably married with another baby on the way.

The cubicle door opens, and I watch Dick disappear into the light-deprived passageway lined with booths comprised of ply board. I leave our booth shortly thereafter, where, for a good half hour, Dick worked hard on making his oral performance memorable. And it was. Still is. Otherwise, I wouldn't have surrendered my tongue for him to nearly tear. Afraid I would leave the bathhouse with a tongue shorter than Helen Keller's, I pushed him away, gestured for him to go down on me instead. He did, begged me to pump his mouth, and resisted when I tried to pull him up for an I-don't-want-to-come-yet kiss.

As he slowly worked his way up to my kiss, he licked every pore on my body, like a cat to a bowl of milk. "Oh, shit," he said, then called me, "*Pare!*" That machismo-loaded word often uttered during sexual trysts by straight-identified Filipino men. "I like your natural smell, *Pare*," he continued. The remark caught me off guard. I tried ignoring it but how could I? He had mistaken my natural scent for a bar of Safeguard soap. Then he said, "Fuck me." I didn't say anything, just pushed him hard against the wall, kissed him gently like the rapist he wanted me to be.

Dick wanted to be screwed like a man—simple as that. To be pummeled like a man while another man raged inside him, drowning him with every beat of his heart. A bona-fide Bottom to my Carte Blance-Top. In football lingua: He was my wide receiver, and I, his tight end.

I sensed it from the moment he and I exchanged glances, in the video room, where White Daddy was doing the missionary with Thai Baby in a pirated DVD copy where their moans were clearer than the screen. Dick stood there, a reproduction of a Michelangelo sculpture with arms, waiting for me to make the first move. I did, stepped so close to him I could taste his breath.

He asked again if I wanted to enter him. I answered by going down on him, spoke to him in tongues then pulled away only when he gave me the ten-second warning. He reciprocated by letting me come in his mouth.

You might be wondering why I didn't just comply with Dick's wish. He was so loose and ready I didn't need spit to open him up. My answer: I fuck strangers but not in the dark. Fucking is so much sexier, more intense, when it's done in broad daylight or in a well-lighted room. When it's not rushed or hushed. When time can wait because night is forced to wait. When you can see his face, oh, his face illuminated by the light expounding the dark-brown of his eyes and brows, the curve of his thick lips, the opening of his mouth as it releases a moan, a plea, a sigh that expresses a thousand and one desires, while the whole world listens to your bodies, envying your very raw and yet too-brief communion.

Most Perfect

If it weren't for his blow-job lips and the warmth of his saliva, I would not have treated him to a Happy Meal at McDonald's then taken the risk of bringing him, a complete stranger fifteen years my junior, over to my friend's three-story townhouse in the warehouse-dominated section of Project 7 in Quezon City, where I've been living for the past three monsoon-stricken months while I conduct research for my doctoral dissertation on the effects of the dengue outbreak on the thriving prostitution and human-trafficking industry in the second-most corrupt country in the world.

I was at Cravings in Shangri-La Mall, having my usual cup of cognac-spiked espresso with two Ateneo de Manila University professors, when I first saw John, leaning on the hustler-designated railing right beside the acrophobia-causing escalator that connects the fifth and first escalators. I continued to stare at him until he saw me. I smiled, he nodded, I shifted back my attention to the conversation with my underpaid-but-overworked friends who teach Literary Theory at the Jesuit-run school. One was a scholar of Semiotics, who earned his Ph.D. from—where else?—Harvard U; let's call him "Barthes," after his role model. The other was a Marxist-identified Post-Structuralist—let's call him "Derrida."

I thought John was a CB, a callboy, for he fit the gay-for-pay-hustle-in-the-Philippines stereotype: Straight-acting, wears chest-defining white shirts, blue jeans, imitation Diesel shoes, around-the-corner-beauty-salon-styled hairdo, solicits his customers in malls. And there was a diverse herd of cockshoppers that night, from drag-queens to beauticians a.k.a. "parloristas" to granddaddies to Metrosexuals to gym-bunnies to hypersexual Catholic priests and Seminarians. All cruising for an orchestra-seat blow inside the Antarctic-like Cineplex on the sixth floor, or a three-way inside one of the Disneyland-inspired drive-in love motels in Ortigas, ten minutes away from the mall without traffic.

Before the management discovered via blind-item columns in the tabloids *Hot Copy* and *Chika* that their mall was the oral sex mecca of Southeast Asia, staging daily suck-fests from ten to eight, Shangri-La was the hottest, air-conditioned, safest cruising spot in Manila. Not only because the restrooms were the tidiest of all malls and the toilets had seats (so nobody had to sit on piss), but because they also came with matching condom vending machines. But after a well-known gay-but-discreet politician was caught blowing one of the hustlers in the second-floor restroom, management beefed up its security by hiring undercover cops and installing hidden cameras; six, thus far, were apprehended, with one pending case for statutory rape. The arrests, however, did not scare off even the most closeted faggots; they merely switched venue from the Men's room (two on each floor) to the Sci-Fi and Classics sections of National Bookstore, located on the first floor.

"Look over there," I said, keeping my eyes fixed on John, who wasn't gym-defined but had anatomical flaws in the right places. In his right hand, he held a rolled-up paper. His high school diploma? I wondered.

"Not my type," Barthes said. "Too old."

"Too old? He can't be more than twenty," I said.

"They taste better when their voice is cracking," he said.

"He must be at least five inches, six-and-a-half at the most," said Derrida, who was devouring him with his eyes. "But he looks like he's got a fat one. The girth of a 555 can of sardines."

"He's in the C & D bracket," Barthes said.

"C & D?" I asked.

"Cash upon Delivery," Barthes explained. "Cock in my Dessert."

Sensing he was going nowhere with his metaphors, Barthes spelled it out. "Working class, unemployed, *masa*, borderline-*jolog*."

"How do you know?" I asked.

"His complexion," Derrida answered.

"That's what's so fucked up about our society," Barthes said. "It tolerates and perpetuates this type of class marker every day. Look at the billboard ads, watch the TV commercials, scan through the local fashion magazines. What is the overall message? Whiteness is better, and in the Philippines, it can be bought and sold."

"U.S. is no different," I said. "If you're black you get pigeonholed in the ghetto—"

"That's just blatant racism," Derrida said.

"So is this," Barthes argued. "In fact, this is worse. This is auto racism, the worst form of racism. Hating, oppressing, destroying yourself because you're brown."

"But, mind you, the side effects of these skin-whitening products are very frightening—and they're permanent," Derrida said. "My cousin is now more orange than an orangutan because of them."

"Besides, if your boytoy over there wasn't so economically strapped, he wouldn't be standing there, combating hunger pains by playing staring games with you," Barthes said.

To silence them both, I nodded, but kept my eyes fixed on John who gave me one last nod before disappearing from our view.

"He's got the most perfect blow-job lips I've ever seen," I said. "I'd pay a thousand to nibble on them all night."

Barthes looked at me as if I had committed an English grammar faux pas. I, too, was shocked, for I was not the type to pay for sex let alone entertain the thought. Too cautious. Too borderline-paranoid. Too Victorian. Too frugal with my wallet, as my friends often accused me of.

"I'd sell our house in Taguig to have those lips wrapped around my dick," Derrida said.

"You need to sell more than that," Barthes said. "Who the hell wants to live in Taguig. Every square inch of that place is crammed with squatters and butchered politicians."

Minutes later, I ran into John again, at the train station. He was standing on the southbound platform (I was on the northbound), preoccupied with his cell phone. I walked over and stood directly across from him, clearing my throat until he raised his head. He smiled; I nodded; he nodded back. I checked my watch, motioned him to go back up to the terminal for a quick chat, trade numbers, negotiate on a price, see if he and I were compatible, if he were willing to reciprocate—be the 6 to my 9.

"I'm not what you think I am, sir," John told me right away.

"Then why were you cruising me?" I asked, noticing the gold band around his finger.

"Honestly, sir, I thought you were the one cruising me," he said.

"You married?" I asked.

"Yes, sir."

"Any children?"

"Two. My wife just gave birth. Another boy."

"Why aren't you at the hospital?"

"She's in the province. In Iloilo. With her parents."

"How old are you?"

"Twenty."

Shit, he's young enough to be my nephew, I thought.

"And you?" he asked.

"I'm old. Very old."

"Don't look it to me, sir."

I was going to tell him to stop addressing me as "sir," but it sounded so sexy coming out of his mouth that I did not mind; it made me feel as if I were in a Merchant & Ivory period film.

"Where are you staying?" I asked.

"In Pasay City," he answered.

I nodded to indicate that I had heard of the notorious place. "You live with your family?" I asked.

"In a boarding house," he answered. "I am only here for a couple of days then I go back to the province."

"You want to join me for beer?"

"Sure," he answered. "But I need to eat something first."

* * *

We took my train and got off at the very last stop—North EDSA. We passed the toothpick-chewing armed security guard then climbed down a series of concrete steps riddled with the shadows of the city—beggars, vendors, malnourished children sleeping off their hunger. Alongside a dim-lit highway, we walked on a sidewalk riddled with holes, forcing us at times to either walk around—or hop over—them. In and out of darkness, I led John right up to the front door of McDonald's where I treated him to a cheeseburger Happy Meal because he wanted the free toy that came with it for his son.

"What were you doing in Shangri-La Mall?" I asked.

"I was supposed to meet my sister-in-law there," he answered. "But she never showed up." He paused to point at the rolled-up paper he'd placed on the table. "I was supposed to give her my résumé because she was going to help me get a job."

"Doing what?"

"To work at Burger King in Katar."

"Katar?"

"I think it's in East Arabia," John said.

"You're going all the way to the desert to char-broil Whoppers?" I said.

"I know it sounds ridiculous but at least I'll be earning more than what a nurse or an engineer makes here," he said.

I was not surprised for it is a fact that every day, an average of five thousand Filipinos were leaving the country for employment elsewhere.

"How about you? What do you do?" John asked.

"I'm a researcher," I answered.

"Researching what?"

"On the dengue outbreak and how it's affecting the prostitutes and human traffickers in Manila."

John became very quiet. "My mother died from dengue," he said. "Last year."

"I'm sorry to hear that," I said.
"Is it for a book?" he asked.
"Eventually," I said. "But right now, I need it for my Ph.D."
"You must be very smart."
"Not really. I'm just good at posturing, like many scholars."
"Posturing?" John asked. "As in imposturing?"
"Something like that," I said. Then, changing the subject, I told him that I lived nearby. "Only five minutes away," I said. "You want to come over for a beer?"

Ten minutes later, in my bedroom half assedly lit by the dim streetlights that managed to pass through the window: "Ouch," I said. I sat up from the bed and looked at him. "It's not your fault."

On the way over to my friend's townhouse where I was staying, John had confessed to me that he'd never had sex with a man, except for a blow-job he'd gotten in high school from his principal.

"I'm sorry," John said.

"You don't have to, you know," I said, remembering that the last time I had a tryst with a virgin was with a bi-curious Silicon Valley technocrat I had met on-line who went by the code name "BottomsUp"; his first name turned out to be Tom. Tom was you're All-American latent-fag next door who, in his midthirties, had finally come out to himself and had chosen me to initiate him into the world of crystal meth, circuit parties, body sculpting. So I fucked him until the moon got tired of us. It left a permanent scar of joy in him because he hounded me for months, had flowers and chocolates delivered to my apartment in San Francisco, with note cards professing his undying love. I let it drag (for who would be stupid enough to put an end to the bi-weekly gifts) until, one day, he logged on to Friendster and hooked up with a newly-arrived refugee from Cambodia.

"We can just jerk each other off," I said.

"But I want to," John persisted

"Careful," I said. "You might grow to like it."

I paused for a moment to explore my options. I could either end the night with coerced mutual masturbation or, with the patience of a Zen Buddhist monk, guide him, step-by-step, into the delicate art of fellatio.

I don't need to tell you how the rest of the night went. Except I'm still trying to find words to describe the sensation his thick lips, his pre-cum-coated tongue, his warm mouth had left me with, like a permanent bruise in my memory worth returning to again and again. As for payment, there was none, though I had to force him to accept the two hundred pesos to cover for the predawn cab ride back to his boarding house in Pasay City, known to everyone in Manila as the polluted version of Sodom and Gomorrah.

Fonts & Other Dilemmas

It is the kind of rain that will not give up until half of the city's rat population has drowned or migrated up north to seek refuge in the air-conditioned mausoleum of former deposed president Ferdinand Marcos, where his wax-suspect remains lie in a glass sarcophagus. Danilo is at the computer, living his other life in the zip code of in-between states or what his mentor calls "Still Life with White Noise." Senseless snow or not, he tunes in, listens to what's buried beneath the static, and types, pausing only to remind himself not to Page Up and fuss over grammar and logic until he's established some kind of notion, an almost-clarity. Anyway, it's a first draft, he tells himself, and first drafts are—what?— butcher scraps, muse stand-ins, illuminated madness, pure gold.

Right now, what matters most are that it's raining, the story is unraveling with Glenn Gould in the background, humming to the 1981 rendition of Bach's Goldberg Variations, and the muse is fueling Danilo's imagination for the fifth consecutive rainy day. Out the window, Danilo gazes at the darkness that holds the rain of his evening garden. Nice word—"gaze," he thinks. Subtle. Light. A

Monet canvas. Then he shifts his attention back to the screen, where Javier, his protagonist, is stranded by both the rain (he wants to go clubbing but it's also pouring on his side of the universe) and the memories coproduced with Kingston Lau, his Chinese-Filipino lover whom he has just broken up with after ten and a half semisolid years.

After three pages of Times New Roman, size 12, he arrives finally—a shaky word "finally"—at the period of all periods (for now). He scrolls to the first page and does what he loves least: Come up with a title—that necessary skin tag that sometimes consumes more time than the actual writing itself. But, like it or not, a title can make or break an audience. After all, it's the one with the largest font. "A title should come to the storyteller like a poem does to a poet—unannounced and, like a haiku, economical," his mentor said. "Otherwise, you're better off calling the story 'Untitled.'" Which is what Danilo ends up doing. The alternative is "Perhaps," after the story's opening word. But who wants to read a story with a one-word title that connotes the indecisiveness of the sixteenth century?

Craving for a drink, he goes to the kitchen still smelling of the dead rat that his maid, Melanie, discovered under the kitchen sink two-and-a-half months ago. He empties the rest of Shiraz into a coffee mug then returns to his desk with a half-filled box of Hawaiian Host chocolate-covered macadamia nuts that his mother included in a care package stuffed with Immodium ("Don't leave America without it!"), anti-fungal ointment (in case the fungus on his left inner thigh reappears), a one-year supply of Extra-Strength Tylenol PM and Ativan (for migraine due to Third World sales transaction, customer service, gridlock traffic, unruly commuters, et cetera), and a bottle of Astroglide lubricant (purchased at 80 & Straight, the one beside Sizzler's Steak House in Waikiki, and right below the apartment building where the elevator man was crushed to death a couple months ago because he forgot to put out the "Men at Work" sign).

Between sips of Shiraz (the one that keeps winning awards,

according to the gold-medal sticker on the bottle), he skims over the untitled story, asking himself why he has written another anti-relationship vignette when he and Rex, his current boyfriend of ten months, are happily together. It's his fifth fiction piece this week, sixth if he counts the soft-porn heartbreaking tale that went straight to the paper shredder about two steroid-pumped lovers—both married and with children and therefore bi-identified—who meet up at a sex club in Pasay City right across Manila Bay called "The Bungalow" (also the story's title) twice a week, every Tuesday and Thursday night, when the theme is "Undress 2 Impress." There, inside a room large enough to hold only a cot, they take turns bottoming for each other or for a third party, usually a steroid user with a body like theirs.

Danilo picks up the folder stacked in the MAYBE pile and pores through the fresh-off-the-printer vignettes, flash fiction with recurring themes of love, loss, sex, race, religion, class, and peppered with Manila's oversexed, repressed, romantic, and sexy men who, when they aren't grappling with religion and bisexuality, genuflecting in bathhouses and movie houses, or giving blows inside speeding Toyotas, are busily helping resolve the country's beyond-reparable economy and rat-level poverty by servicing the unemployed, blue-collar workers and teenage fathers for a hundred peso.

Where are these stories coming from? And why are they rolling in like dominos now that he is at peace with the world, himself, and the ongoing war in Iraq? Are he and Rex headed for the inevitable break-up sooner than he thinks? Questions he already has answers to: Don't Know, Will Never Know, Don't Care, Shouldn't Care. For the creative process is too mysterious, unfixed, complex, anti-uniformity, constantly mutating to spell out prophecies or point its genesis to a specific source—inspirational, influential, factual, experiential. Fiction, as Danilo has come to recognize and accept, is not a grocery list; it is not an annotation where the writer explains the sources for his text or defends his imagination.

As for he and Rex heading for Splitsville anytime soon, right now: highly unlikely. Unlike the couple in "Untitled," he and Rex, who is also an American scholar like himself, are as okay as that cool pre-rain evening when their paths crossed on the Manila Bayfront lawn of the U.S. Embassy on Roxas Boulevard, where they and other ex-pats and Filipino dignitaries were helping celebrate the annual Fourth of July celebration with hot dogs, bite-size burgers, pizzas, and fireworks.

When their one-night stand began to lengthen to sleepovers, they no longer could deny the fact that their compatibility would outlast their moans. So they agreed to commit only with the stipulation that there would be none. And since a great chunk of their relationship is based on intellectual, rather than semen exchange—Danilo is a Literature professor at University of Hawaii at Manoa while Rex is working on his doctorate dissertation at the U.C. Santa Cruz, Department of History of Consciousness—they would keep theirs simple and open, for previous experiences taught them that monogamy in a gay relationship is as near-extinct—if not mundane—as Ching Ching, Ling Ling, and the last dozen panda bears on earth.

Now and then, they have their casual argument, usually over pedagogical matters (e.g., Should Huck Finn be taught to black kids in urban ghettos?) and current events plaguing the Philippines (e.g., Should President Gloria "caught cheating on red tape" Arroyo resign? Rex: Yes; Danilo: Assassinate the bitch). Only once did they bicker over a trick—a sexually-repressed Chinese-Filipino professor of De La Salle University whom Rex had met in Gay Dot Com—but the fight was not because Rex had slept with him but because the professor, who turned out to be on psyche meds, had gotten obsessed with Rex; apparently Rex reminded him of his Scottish ex.

What Danilo has written this past week—and Danilo knows this—are merely wanna-be and could-be versions of himself, of Rex, and of their lives before, during, and after their initial week together. He simply made a mental list of memories then broke them apart, tinkered with them, falsified the evidence; exorcised anxieties (how to learn to sleep solo again after a ten-and-half year relationship); and stretched out his fantasies (suck-fest in a movie house, blowing the family driver and paying him for it, playing guinea pig to a young father of two after treating him to a cheeseburger Happy Meal). He manipulated his and Rex's age, turned the Rex-inspired character in "The Importance of Er," for example, into a fifty-something architect, when, in reality, Rex is an unassuming thirty-six-year-old, deep-blue-eyed scholar who is in the Philippines to research on the phenomenon of the endless-yet-gone-nowhere People Power peaceful revolutions. He also gave himself and Rex, who is Irish American and a nonpracticing Catholic, constant ethnic and religion makeovers. In "Untitled," which he later changes to "What Passes for Rain," he imagined himself as a woman married to a bisexual Chinese-Filipino carrying on a relationship with another man. In "The Record Breaker," "Rex" is a repress Born-Again seeking blow-jobs in the movie houses of Megamall. Where class is concerned, he placed himself in the double role as exploiter of, and financial provider for, blue-collar workers. In short, from the drop of truth serum, he magnified, exaggerated, dramatized, enhanced, and cancelled his and Rex's academic-driven lives, exchanging their world for other worlds. Like the garden outside his window covered with rain. Imagined and not.

Contributors

LOUIS ANTHES'S short stories have appeared in *Bear Lust, American Bear, 100% Beef,* and *Verisimilitude*. He is also the author of *Lawyers and Immigrants: A Cultural History* (LFB Scholarly). He currently lives in San Francisco and is involved with Guy Writers, a gay men's writing collective. Louis is currently working on *Let it Go*, a novel about gay soul-mating, betrayal, and enlightenment.

DALE CHASE has been writing gay erotica for eight years with over one hundred stories published in various magazines and anthologies including translation into German. His first literary effort was recently published in the *Harrington Gay Men's Fiction Quarterly*. *The Company He Keeps*, his collection of Victorian gentlemen's erotica, is due out in 2007. Chase lives near San Francisco, is at work on a novel, but erotica ultimately wins.

DAVID CHRISTENSEN lives in San Francisco. His work appears in *I Do / I Don't: Queers on Marriage, Gertrude,* and the forthcoming anthologies *Underground Voices* and *Sodom and Me: Queers on Fundamentalism*.

PHILIP CLARK is a Washington D.C.-area writer. He has been a contributing writer and editorial assistant for *Lambda Book Report* and *The James White Review*. Under the pen name "Clark Anthony," he appeared in the anthologies *Full Body Contact*, *Fratsex*, and *Dorm Porn*; "Knots" is the first porn story he has published under his own name. He is currently coediting an anthology of poetry by writers who died from AIDS. Anyone interested in publishing a collection of his erotic fiction should contact him via e-mail (philipclark@hotmail.com) or through the publisher.

LOU DELLAGUZZO'S stories have appeared in *Best Gay Love Stories 2006*, *Best Gay Love Stories 2005*, *Lodestar Quarterly*, *Harrington Gay Men's Fiction Quarterly*, *Velvet Mafia*, and *Blithe House Quarterly*. His work will be included in the forthcoming anthology *Bi Guys: Firsthand Fiction for Bisexual Men*. Lou has completed a short-story collection called *All of a Suddenly*. The sixteen stories focus mostly on first encounters and beginning friendships between men who are gay or bisexual. Presently, he's at work on a novel.

THOMAS FUCHS has spent much of his career writing television documentaries and some nonfiction. Over the past few years, he has discovered the joy of imagining and inventing afforded by the writing of fiction. He has had stories published in *Honcho*, *Locker Room Tales*, and the anthology *Ultimate Gay Erotica 2005*. He can be reached at Fuchsfoxxx@cs.com.

RIGOBERTO GONZÁLEZ is the author of the poetry book *So Often the Pitcher Goes to Water until It Breaks*, a National Poetry Series selection; two bilingual children's books: *Soledad Sigh-Sighs* and *Antonio's Card*; the novel *Crossing Vines*, winner of *ForeWord Magazine*'s Fiction Book of the Year Award; a memoir, *Butterfly Boy*, forthcoming in 2006; and a biography about Chicano writer Tomás Rivera forthcoming in 2007.

The recipient of a Guggenheim Fellowship and of various international artist residencies, he writes a monthly Latino book column, now in its fourth year, for the *El Paso Times* of Texas. He is contributing editor for *Poets and Writers Magazine*, a member of the National Book Critics Circle, and an Associate Professor of English and Latino Studies at the University of Illinois at Urbana-Champaign. Website: www.rigobertogonzalez.com.

PHILIP HUANG lives in Berkeley, CA. His poetry and fiction have appeared in numerous anthologies, including *Queer PAPI Porn*, *Charlie Chan is Dead II*, *Best Gay Asian Erotica*, *Take Out: Queer Writing From Asian Pacific America*, and *Fresh Men: New Voices in Gay Fiction*. He currently completed *American Widow*, a collection of short stories. "Pasadena" began as a meditation on the first sentence: "I'm doing a number on the husband's nipples when the wife pokes her head in waving a burrito." If you enjoyed the story, the author encourages you to contact him at philiphuang@aol.com.

Born in the Philippines and raised in Hawaii, **R. ZAMORA LINMARK** is the author of *Prime Time Apparitions* (poetry) and the novel *Rolling the R's*, which he's also adapted for the stage. His work has appeared in numerous journals and anthologies such as *Bamboo Ridge*, *Zyzzva*, *Charlie Chan is Dead 1 and 2*, and *Hanging Loose*. His honors include fellowships from the National Endowment for the Arts, the J. William Fulbridght Foundation, and the U.S.-Japan Friendship Commission. He currently divides his home between Manila, Honolulu, and San Francisco.

JAY LYGON is a military brat who lived all over the U.S. but considers Colorado home. If he could combine the Internet with camping, he'd be in heaven. He's into jazz and Zen philosophy, but admits he'd make a lousy Buddhist. Jay's stories can be found in *Myths* (Torquere

Press), and on Clean Sheets and Erotica Readers and Writers Association Web sites. Write to him at *JayLygon.blogspot.com.*

The erotic fiction of **CHRISTOPHER PIERCE** has been published most recently in the anthologies *Ultimate Gay Erotica 2006, Naughty Spanking Stories A to Z,* and *Men Amplified,* and the magazines *Mandate, Freshmen,* and *Honcho.* Write to him at chris@christopherpierceerotica.com and visit his world at www.ChristopherPierceErotica.com.

ANDY QUAN'S full-length collection of erotica and sex writing, *Six Positions,* was published in 2005 by Green Candy Press. A Canadian, living in Sydney, Australia, he is also the author of *Calendar Boy* and *Slant,* and his poetry, short fiction, and smut have appeared in many anthologies. He'd love you to visit him at: www.andyquan.com.

DARIECK SCOTT is the author of *Traitor to the Race* (1995) and the editor of *Best Black Gay Erotica* (2004). His fiction has appeared in the anthologies *Freedom in This Village, Black Like Us, Shade, Giant Steps, Flesh and the Word 4,* and *Ancestral House.* He has published nonfiction essays in *Callaloo, GLQ, The Americas Review,* and the collection *Gay Travels.* He is assistant professor of English at the University of California at Santa Barbara, where he teaches African American literature and creative writing.

TONY VALENZUELA lives in West Hollywood, California. He holds an MFA in writing from Cal Arts and has recently been published in *ZYZZYVA* and the *LA Weekly.* He is currently working on a collection of short stories.

DAVEM VERNE is one of the few erotica authors who believes the literary canon will eventually embrace the genre. And he wants to be there when it happens! Speaking sex and writing truth since 1995, he is devoted to erotic literature and the revelation of physical desire on paper. While his early stories lent themselves to fanciful journeys around the world, his latest work, including *King of the Mat*, focuses on the college campus and that sanctuary of sex, the dorm room. Revisiting the racy atmosphere of academia is top on his list! His stories have been printed in numerous anthologies, including *Best Gay Erotica 2005*, but Davem would like to express deepest thanks to the editor of *Inside Him* for allowing him to come inside.

About the Editor

JOËL BARRAQUIEL TAN is the author of two books of poetry, *Monster* (Noice Press) and *Type O Negative* (Red Hen Press, forthcoming). His latest limited edition chapbook, *El Canto de Animal,* is the first of a trilogy of verse, found text, and fictional autobiography. Joël is the editor of the anthologies *Best Gay Asian Erotica* and *Queer Pilipino, Asian, Pacific Islander (PAPI) Porn* (Cleis). His writings have been translated in various languages and appear in academic and commercial venues including: *Fresh Men: New Voices in Gay Fiction* (ed. Edmund White, Carroll & Graf), *Q & A: Queer and Asian in America* (ed. Alice Hom, Temple University), and *Porn!* (Haworth). Joël lives in San Francisco.